"Coomer is one of those rare newer writers who seems to have emerged fully formed. In Memorabilia, he uses the archetype of a modern American author to filter loneliness, fading dreams, mental illness, grief, bemusement, and an endless search for meaning that all but promises to remain elusive. The book evoked a feeling similar to reading John Williams' Stoner and Frederick Exley's A Fan's Notes. Smart, dark, and seductively compelling, it reads like a poetic autopsy of the creative process."

— Andersen Prunty, author of *Neon Dies At Dawn*

"A.S. Coomer's Memorabilia is a deeply unsettling monograph of psychological disturbance. The inscrutability of a friend's suicide, jostled with Professor Stephen Paul's lacunae nights and days of unmoored aimlessness, remind us that mental health is often nothing more than a polite veneer against an ever-degrading society."

— James Nulick, author of *Haunted Girlfriend* and *Valencia*

"Memorabilia doesn't remain in the unconscious. The often unforgiving livelihood of an adjunct professor, the harsh realities of loneliness, incarceration, and America's mental health system all make their presence known throughout the novel. The elastic nature of time and memory leave you questioning how much is the ranting of a madman, and what is stark, sad truth."

— Clifford Brooks, Pulitzer nominated poet & Editor-in-Chief of the *Blue Mountain Review*

"A.S. Coomer's Memorabilia is a fragmented journey through the structures of the mind. Navigating neural pathways in search of source traumas and psychogenic triggers. When the body is incapacitated, the mind wanders. Memories become unstable. Memorabilia reorients the position of the writer, rendering Coomer's Stephen Paul the subject of jarring and ever-changing narrative threads. Haunted by the poetry of a time he cannot remember. The images of Memorabilia linger long after the book's conclusion."

— Mike Corrao, author of *Gut Text*

MEMORABILIA

Memor-abilia

BY A.S. COOMER

MEMORABILIA

Requests for permission should be directed to 1111@1111press.com, or mailed to 11:11 Press LLC, 4757 15th Ave S., Minneapolis, MN 55407.

Cover by
J.N. Habiger & Jennifer Cralley

Interior Design and Formatting by
Jennifer Cralley & Ashley Bernhardt

LCCN:
2019944957

eBook:
978-1-948687-11-9

Paperback:
978-1-948687-10-2

FIRST AMERICAN EDITION

Printed in the United States of America

9 8 7 6 5 4 3 2 1

CONTENTS

Waning Gibbous

Stephen found the note. It was scrawled in tiny, exact blue letters on tracing paper. Something overlooked by the police, by Michelle, by Robert's brother and mother and sister, as just another fragment of something left incomplete. Something to be boxed up with the hoard of notebooks and digital files for some professor of American Letters to come back to once the grief and shock had worn off. Just another glimpse into a mind on fire, a heart lost at sea, all that.

But Stephen saw it immediately for what it was. He lifted it from the littered desk, and read:

> There are certain things you keep to yourself. Secrets, private musings, urges. Burdens, shames, acknowledged shortcomings. You carry them across your shoulders closely. You carry the weight as if it needs protecting, stopping every so often, if you're like me it's every thirty-sixth step, to make sure a zipper hasn't slipped, a stitch hasn't broken, not a flap of your flak has flurried the streets, peppering your insecurities under the noses of the unkind, the unaware, the unappreciative.

> You learn how to make the steps look normal. It's a dance. You don't dance but you can learn, and you can emulate and immolate in time with those not burning. You smile the smile of the unaffected. Holding your lopsided head, weighed down with worry and rot, hoping the shadows shield the lines, the taut skin working double to hold steady. You stifle the quaver in your words, the meaning barely concealed behind platitudes, rearing its ugly head like a hidden, burdensome child, the blighted fruit of a love gone wrong. The child wanting to cry out for light, for love, for acknowledgement, for a chance to be whatever everyone else gets a chance at.

> You don't write about them. Not really. You sidestep, you canter, you skip around, you allude, you delude, but never fully divulge. God knows you never talk about them. Not to a soul. Shrinks cost money, money you don't have (there's no money in the Arts).

You fill the confines of your limitations like cheap hotel curtains. You rub up against them constantly. You know the songs are there. You know the words are there. You know the stories lurk somewhere just inside the inky blackness of your heart.

But you can't.

You exist within your limitations. You spread your wings finding the enclosure more cramped than you remembered. You start to think that maybe there is a place without limitations. Maybe there is a place where you can exist freely. Maybe there is a place where you are complete, where you can make the things you see shining out into the dimness of everything that surrounds you, encases you in stagnant pools of disquiet and uncertainty. There is a place. There must be.

Then you see it. Right there. Outside you. You realize that if you just shed your skin, the thin layer of itch and flake covering your flimsy, spiderwebbed bones, if you get outside the blood, entrenched in chemicals, balanced and not, pumping in off-beats through you, you will be free.

Free.

Seeing and believing and making and trusting and alive.

I will be free.

Stephen didn't give it to the police. He didn't tell Michelle or Robert's family. What good would come of it? Everybody knew what happened, why muddy it with more words? Robert left plenty of those already, didn't he?

Stephen carefully folded the note longways three times and slid it into his breast pocket. He boxed the last of the books from his late friend's office and carried them out to the rented van.

A.S. COOMER

Another box of books, he thought. *Is this what your life becomes? Just another container of things you found useful? The things that helped you through for as long as you could manage?*

He set the latch but lingered at the back of the van. He turned twice towards the driver's side but did not move. Finally, Stephen sat down on the grated metal bumper. He felt his chest tightening, little knots bursting into existence like unexpected firecrackers. He clenched his fists, then relaxed them. Over and over again until the sting of the tears lessened, became just another smear he could wipe away without a breakdown.

Overhead, the magnolias brushed against each other in sibilant shudders. The burnt sienna of aged streetlight filtered through their dancing leaves and all around his feet in the driveway and small front yard Stephen watched skeletal fingers make shadow puppets.

§

He parked the van next to his battered Corolla in the lot outside the English Department but did not immediately get out. His hands seemed to be vibrating on the steering wheel. They hummed up to his wrists where his arms no longer felt like his own but something foreign, wooden and cumbersome.

Stephen sat there for some time, his hands clasped firmly in place, the static of the radio squelching out little snatches of melody in unpredictable bursts. The van idled roughly, a mechanical cough in the beginning stages of full-bore engine tuberculosis.

"Everything dies, baby," some inhuman Springsteen belched from the static plane.

That's a fact, Stephen finished in his head.

It broke the hum in his hands and he killed the engine.

Stephen made sure each door of the cab of the van was locked then doubled-checked the back latch. He fished his car keys from his pants pockets.

"Evening," a voice said from behind him.

Stephen spun and sent the keys to his Corolla skittering across the pavement. A bright, white light held him in place. He could make out nothing but the sound of booted steps approaching.

"Everything all right here, sir?" the voice asked.

"Uh, yes. Just heading home," Stephen said.

"You can't leave that van here."

The light was lowered, and Stephen blinked into the sudden darkness.

"This isn't a park and ride," the voice said.

"I'm well aware," Stephen said, feeling the hot, red curdle of anger taking shape. The taste of soured milk trickled across his dry mouth.

"You're gonna have to move—"

"That van was rented by Dr. Hagan, *Head* of the English Department, to bring the library of Professor Wilkins here," Stephen shouted.

His voice sounded louder than it was in the naked, empty night.

Through his steadily adjusting eyes, Stephen thought he saw the campus security guard take a step back.

"Oh," the man said.

"I'm not sure how much your superior would enjoy a phone call from Dr. Hagan at this time of night."

"Sorry, uh, sir," the man said. The flick of the flashlight found Stephen's dropped keys and a white hand retrieved them. "Here're your keys, sir. Have a good night. Sorry to bother you."

Stephen took the keys out of the man's proffered hand with a slap of his palm and didn't respond.

§

He let the screen door slam shut, a clatter in the night that sent something skittering away in the alley. Stephen walked straight to the cabinet and removed the Bulleit Rye and the little mason jar of marijuana. He took a long pull from the bottle then set about rolling himself a joint.

Everything dies, baby.

That's a fact.

It took him longer than it normally would. His fingers did not feel his own. A weight was settling about his body that seemed to numb him, slow each of his motions and thoughts pulling him down into a stupor.

He finished the joint, licked it once more for good measure, then lit it.

The clock above the dirty stove read: 1:35am.

Thirty-six hours and not a wink of sleep, he thought, holding the smoke in.

He closed his eyes as he let the smoke, very slowly, waft from his open mouth.

He coughed then wiped the corners of his lips.

He opened his eyes and saw that his small kitchen was dark, the only illumination coming in from the open blinds in slats.

No wonder rolling had been so difficult, he thought. *I didn't even turn on the goddamn lights.*

Stephen took another drag before crossing the room to the switch.

He flipped it and exhaled at the same time, a whiff and flick designed to snap him back to his senses. In the sudden brightness of the overhead lights, Stephen choked on the smoke. Standing there before him, not fully materialized, was his friend Robert, thick purple bags cloaking the dripping pools of his dark eyes.

Stephen lurched backwards, banging against the wall. His back flipped off the light switch cloaking everything in darkness again.

He sputtered trying to scream but his throat and nose and eyes were filled with dank, soured smoke. He coughed instead, leaning forward and holding his belly with the force of it. His wide eyes smeared with tears, an obscured impressionistic painting of a bachelor's empty kitchen.

When he could, Stephen turned the kitchen light back on only to find himself completely alone in the wisps of slowly rising smoke.

He held his aching head and let the weight of his tired body slide down the wall to the dirty linoleum. The lids of his eyes closed of their own accord and Stephen wept.

§

He arrived thirty-seven minutes late to the office the following morning. His clothes, the same he wore the night before, were crumpled and dusty from spending the night on the couch.

There were two students already sitting on the bench outside his office. He felt their accusatory eyes on his back as he unlocked the door.

"Give me a moment," he called over his shoulder before shutting the door.

He set his bag on one of the two ragged, university provided chairs and sighed heavily before setting about getting the pot of coffee started. He'd forgotten to set his alarm after the ghastly image of his recently deceased friend sent him scrambling to the couch and the finishing of the joint. Sleep came heavily and all-consuming.

The creak of his office door opening put his hair on end.

"Doesn't anybody knock?" he said, turning away from the steaming coffeepot.

"Sorry, Professor Paul, but I have to be in J-Quad in ten minutes," Sandra Somethingorother said, her head barely peaking around the partially opened door.

Stephen hated being called Professor Paul. It made him feel like a youth pastor.

"Come in, come in," he said, pouring himself a cup even though the brew cycle wasn't even half-completed yet.

The coffee sizzled on the warmer and filled the room with the sharp pang of burnt chicory as he returned the pot.

He took the cup to his desk and sat down heavily.

"Sandra," he said, "what can I do for you this morning?"

"I was hoping to have more time to discuss—"

Stephen, despite his best effort, felt his mind wandering. The shapes of branches in the street lamps dancing across Robert's lawn came back to him. The overgrown yard littered with the shifting outlines of people milling about made him think of waiting rooms. How many waiting rooms do we pass through over the course of our lives? It seems like you're always waiting. Waiting for life to begin. Waiting for life to get better. Waiting for life to mean something. Waiting for Beauty. Waiting for Fulfillment. Waiting for death.

"—that's why I scheduled this appointment for 8:15," Sandra said. "I feel like I really need to get my head around these next three pieces, so I can make that jump, you know?"

Stephen, completely unaware of what three pieces Sandra Herlastnam-estilleludedhim was trying to wrap her head around as well as what jump she referred to, nodded his head affirmatively automatically.

"Of course," he said.

An awkward, accusatory silence reared its ugly head.

"I'm sorry I'm late," Stephen said.

Sandra's eyes narrowed slightly.

For fuck's sake, Stephen thought. *Do I have to appease everyone?*

"The passing of Professor Wilkins has the Department in a bit of a… predicament at present," he said.

Sandra seemed unmoved.

Stephen took a sip from the stained mug to keep himself from biting his tongue.

Self-centered little cretin, he thought. *The world loses a shade of brilliance and all daddy's spoiled brat can think of is herself, herself, herself.*

"As I was saying," Sandra began but Stephen cut her off.

"Why don't we reschedule this for tomorrow morning," he said, rising from his chair. "Say same time?"

She opened her mouth to complain.

"Yes," he said with the air of finality even a lowly adjunct learns to wield eventually. "I'll see you tomorrow at…8:15. Good morning, Sandra."

He opened the door and held it wide for her to pass.

Before the other student waiting on the bench outside could rise, Stephen held out a placating hand.

"Give me ten minutes, if you please," he said, shutting the door on any response the student might've had.

§

Stephen walked into the classroom ten minutes late. The students were half-packed to leave, and a general sigh of disappointment spread across the room as he entered.

"Afternoon, afternoon," he said, setting his bag onto the desk at the front of the room.

He hastily removed his dogeared paperback copy of *Nausea* and let it plop onto the desk.

"Sorry I'm late," he shot over his shoulder.

Stephen steadied himself to turn and face the students, something that felt akin to a chore for him, when he saw another book sitting face down on the desk. He picked it up and turned it over.

"Sir," a shrill male voice called out.

Stephen turned, book in hand, and sought out the voice. He followed the turned heads to a small blonde student, boyish in all his features, in an aisle seat near the rear of the auditorium.

"Professor Wilkins had let me borrow that one, sir," the boy said.

Stephen turned his eyes down to the book in his hands.

Suttree by Cormac McCarthy.

A flood of images washed over Stephen, the way they often do for readers when confronted with a book they'd read several times. The sparse houseboat on the Tennessee River. The riff raff and misfits and misfirings of privilege of Knoxville. It was the only McCarthy novel that Stephen ever remembered laughing out loud at while reading.

"Ah," Stephen said.

Too much of time must have passed. Chairs squeaked and students fidgeted. Someone coughed drily.

"He said I was absorbing too much Oscar Wilde," the boy blurted.

Stephen looked up to see a splash of scarlet break out across the pale cheeks.

"No such thing," Stephen said, shaking his head and setting the book near his bag on the desk.

A wash of approving chuckles and one exaggerated groan came from the other students.

"Antoine in Mud town," he said, switching to autopilot.

§

Will it ever be enough to simply exist? The first thought of something more began this whole slippery sloped shit show. The stories could've just been daydreams—what story written is anything more than a daydream? —something fleeting, passing, not meant to stick around and torment. Just a simple midday reverie, slack-jawed and dull-eyed watching the boughs jostle in the wind, not an all-consuming, soul-crushing pursuit.

When did we decide that the American novel was worth the pursuit? Shit, before *that* even. Why did we ever decide to tell each other stories? Being the selfish creatures we are, we couldn't just let others be. No, we had to fill each other's minds with our own fantasies, had to script plots of intrigue, flowery images of drunks in bars having the deepest of conversations, somehow propping the thing up with a foil backing, something gaudy, shiny, and distracting enough to feign profundity.

We're liars really. That's all. We're liars and we just can't stand the thought of keeping all these lies to ourselves. We're liars really.

The vibration of the cell phone in his pocket made Stephen jump a little in his seat before the laptop.

How many times had he written this internal dialogue? Toying with the same sentiments through the same character's perspective in vastly varying syntax.

Stephen stared at the slowly flashing cursor, his brow knitted in wrinkles.

His phone vibrated again. He made a disgusted sound and retrieved it.

A.S. COOMER

```
Stephen,
I'd like to speak with you.
Dr. Hagan
```

"Great."

Another email had come in just after that one but also from the Head of the English Department.

```
Now would be great.
Thanks.
```

Stephen set the phone down on his desk and hit Save on the Word document.

How many times had he been interrupted while working on *Bondsman*. Two-hundred? A thousand? He was genuinely surprised the Word doc was even functional and not a corrupted mess after so many edits and overhauls and endless tinkering. He started writing the novel in Word 6 for Windows NT back in the late nineties.

He slammed the laptop shut and stood up, stretching his back, hearing more pops than there ever used to be.

Wonder what Hagan wants.

A subtle sense of dread took hold of him. Then he was slightly pissed off by the Head's consistent use of his first name in email and his last name in person. That faux familiarity that the electronic age ushered in.

He made to cross the office and make his way to the other side of the building, which housed the administration offices, but stopped himself and stood distracted for a moment. He picked up a pen and scribbled "a subtle sense of dread" on a Post-It note and set it on top of his closed laptop.

He had several bankers boxes of phrases or germs of scenes in the back of the duplex he rented on Main, probably to remain undisturbed until his death. The ideas always seemed like bright flashes from the void in the moment, though he knew better. They were the subconsciousness's, process of amalgamating his existence into something else.

Daydreams, daydreams, and more daydreams, he thought.

Stephen had a bitter taste in his mouth as he walked down the empty hallways.

He checked his watch: 7:45pm.

He always felt sick when he had to talk with Dr. Hagan or any of the other more seasoned professors. Despite the MFA, despite the well-received short story collection—mostly by the academic journals and one small column that read more like an ad in *Publishers Weekly*—despite the glowing recommendations from his former professors and Iowa Workshop cohorts, he felt like a fraud. The masses only seemed to buy soon-to-be-a-major-motion-picture YA novels.

He wondered why Dr. Hagan was still on campus this late on a Monday evening.

How'd he know I'm still here? he thought. This can't be good.

A.S. COOMER

He opened the door to the English Department, crossed the empty chairs and reception desk of the waiting area, and knocked on the thick oak door which stood mostly closed.

"Come in," the thick Irish-tinged voice of Dr. Hagan called.

Stephen steadied himself and pushed the door inward.

Dr. Hagan stood, his back to Stephen and the door of the office, before the floor-to-ceiling window overlooking the empty quad outside. He had both of his hands laced together behind him and did not turn to greet Stephen as he entered.

"Have a seat, Paul," he said.

Stephen hesitated then carefully perched himself on the edge of one of the shiny leather armchairs.

Dr. Hagan did not move. He studied the darkening scene outside. The setting sun was not visible from this side of the building. An eerie dusk, purple and gauze-like, gave the view a Stygian pallor. But Dr. Hagan's eastward facing office offered spectacular views of sunrises over scurrying students each morning.

Some time passed in silence.

"You wanted to see me, sir," Stephen said.

Dr. Hagan nodded but did not turn around immediately.

"I received an expense voucher bearing your signature from U-Haul this afternoon," he said.

"Yessir," Stephen said.

He waited for a response from Hagan and when one didn't arrive he continued, "I boxed up Robert's notebooks and manuscripts. There was also a lot of marginalia in the books in his library that might serve as illustrations of the mind of a working author—"

"I did not pre-approve any departmental expense for a U-Haul, Paul."

"Yessir," Stephen said, searching for what to say next. "I figured the University would want to house the papers and whatnot of one of its published—"

"I did not pre-approve any departmental expenses for that either, Paul."

Dr. Hagan turned slowly around, the scene outside the office window shrouded in darkness.

Stephen felt heat in his neck spreading up to his face. He was glad the office was dimly lit, the only light coming from a leaded Tiffany lamp on the corner of the gigantic desk.

"Paul, it's…" Dr. Hagan looked around the room as if the answer was in there waiting to be called on, "truly awful, what happened to—about Professor Wilkins—Robert's death. Awful. Truly."

Dr. Hagan glanced briefly at Stephen then turned back to the window, dusk fully settled in the quiet wing of the quad.

A.S. COOMER

"But things happen. People get sick. Make rash decisions."

Dr. Hagan's hands found each other, and the fingers interlaced behind his back. Stephen stared at them as the Department Head spoke.

"That doesn't mean things have to fall apart. One man's death can be a learning experience, Paul. One man's death, a colleague's death—"

"A friend," Stephen's voice worked against his will. He hadn't intended on speaking. His voice sounded husky and tired to his own ears.

Dr. Hagan seemed to flinch slightly, but his pause was momentary.

"A friend," he said. "Yes. Even a friend's death can be a learning experience, Paul. What in life isn't a learning experience. We must see things as they are and proceed."

Time waits for no man, Stephen told himself ironically, *especially not when the Departmental Budget is in question.*

"I'll sign off on the U-Haul, Paul," Dr. Hagan continued, "but I'm not sure if the Legacy Committee will take Wilkins' documents or not. I'll put it on the panel discussion for next quarter and we'll have to go from there."

"Not sure?" Stephen asked, his voice quavering despite his best efforts to keep it level and steady. "Not sure? The man wrote three of the best novels of the past twenty years. Robert was the best writer, hands down best *writer*, you had on faculty."

Stephen said the word "writer" as if the W was capitalized and stopped himself before any disparaging comments about the moth-eaten blazered fogies, the has-beens and never-was that made up the bulk of the staff, could spill out of his mouth.

Then his mouth opened, again, on its own accord.

"I mean, really, who has done more for the American novel in the past twenty years? He's your Faulkner with a side of Sartre and Vonnegut. He changed everything with *Burnt Sienna*. You know that. A lot of people say he even gives your precious Joyce a run for the money. If the blind crones of the *Committee* can't see that then what hope is there?"

Dr. Hagan sighed.

"That may be," he said, slowly. "But that doesn't guarantee the Committee will approve anything. You know how these things work, Paul."

Stephen barked a false laugh.

"Unfortunately, I do, Dr. Hagan. The Committee—"

Dr. Hagan cut him off.

"Have you returned the U-Haul truck, Paul?"

"Van. It's one of those vans with the sliding back door."

"Have you returned the U-Haul *van*, Paul?"

Stephen shook his head, more to clear away the disdain he felt towards his tenured colleagues than to answer.

Dr. Hagan must've known he hadn't because he didn't turn around but proceeded as if Stephen had replied in the negative.

"I need you to return it as soon as possible. I will not approve any more funds for this endeavor."

Endeavor? Preserving the work of an ill-treated genius?

"Sir—"

"And there is no room to store the documents on campus. We have no more storage available with the renovations of Storm Hall in full swing and the Fall Gala not three weeks out."

"What am I supposed to do with Robert's—"

"That is not the University's concern, Paul," Dr. Hagan snapped. "You took it upon yourself to retrieve the documents. Take it upon yourself to house them if you feel it necessary."

Stephen felt the blood roaring in his ears.

"As I said earlier, I'll put the housing of such…memorabilia before Legacy at the next panel. It shouldn't be but a couple of weeks and with a little luck, they'll approve, and we can even discuss display then."

Silence.

Stephen clenched and unclenched his fists to keep from speaking. He knew he was treading dangerous waters and didn't trust himself to speak.

"That is all, Paul," Dr. Hagan said, his back still to Stephen.

Stephen nearly leapt from the chair. He felt like each of his nerve endings was ablaze with a fire so hot he had to burst into flames. He saw himself shoving this pompous blowhard into the window and repeatedly bashing his head into the thick, immaculately clean glass.

He stalked across the spacious room to the door, but Dr. Hagan's voice stopped him halfway.

"Stephen, Robert's loss is felt by all of us," Dr. Hagan said, his voice slightly less entrenched in mechanical cool than before. "You remember I was on the committee that brought him aboard."

Stephen didn't move. He didn't reply.

"I swayed them. The initial reaction was not decisive," Dr. Hagan said. "I believed in his work, Paul. Just like you."

Stephen left the door standing wide open.

§

When you die your work becomes memorabilia.

He repeated this over and over again in his mind. Stephen was so flustered he took a wrong turn on the way back to his office, some synaptic misfiring that led him straight back to the small auditorium his early class occupied on Mondays, Wednesdays, and Fridays. He opened the door, flicked on the lights and stood there confused.

The empty chairs and naked desktop at the forefront of the room shone in the dull yellow light. How many classes had he taught? How many classes had he attended?

What about Robert? How many had he?

For what? To live and work and write and die. For the current of life, electric flashes of understanding and truth and beauty in neon blue, to get slapped with the *memorabilia* label and shuffled off to some musty university storage closet only to resurface, market depending, on some centennial birthday celebration.

If you're lucky.

Then, shuddering, he wept.

§

He left his car in the lot and walked home. It wasn't far and the night was cool. He carried the old thrift store sweater in his left hand and slung his bag over his right shoulder.

He thought about stopping at Froggy's for a drink but the thought of being in the presence of other people, oblivious sex-driven college-aged people at that, drove him by the open door and the smell of fried potatoes and stale beer.

How many nights had he spent in that little dive?

The accumulation of days and nights and moments seemed to be stacking themselves up on his back as he walked. He felt a gradual shift in the gravitational forces under his feet. The extra weight hurt his knees and back. His neck felt pinched and cramped. He could almost see the pulse of his tired blood at the corners of his eyes.

Somewhere just inside the conscious, he wished he'd driven himself home. The mile and a half was long. Longer than usual and Stephen felt so tired, so beaten down. When he rounded Front Street and saw his place, the thought of a little marijuana gave him a little dose of ease. He felt the weight slacken back a bit and he trudged up the paint-flaked steps with something like tired determination.

He found the faded red door unlocked but closed tight. He wracked his brain, trying to think back to that morning, searched for the image or sensation of his slightly bent key finding the scratched lock face but came back with a blank.

He'd been on autopilot. Shepherded through much of the day, one he'd, thankfully, never have to do over again, in an amnesiac shuffle, carried on some unseen stream of drudgery and obligation.

He stood there, key in hand, poised to sink into the lock and open the door to his cramped kitchen, for some time, lost in the discovery of a wasted day.

From a street over, a dog barked, a harsh cacophony of echoes off the larger brick houses in the alley beyond, and Stephen opened the door.

He missed the door-side key cling ring and the clatter of the small knuckle of keys slapping the linoleum made him jump. The light switch didn't seem to be where it was last. The sound of his palm spinning concentric circles on the cheap paint brought images of cats' tongues to the forefront of his mind.

He found the switch and the dull bulb flickered into life with an audible pinprick click.

Back in familiar surroundings, gravity seemed to find him with renewed interest again. He listened to his feet drag, a weary shuffle, the four steps to the second-hand circular table with mismatched chairs. He leaned over the table and let the weight of the bag carry it down onto the tabletop.

Memorabilia.

He set the sweater down next to his bag.

He opened the small cabinet above the sink and retrieved the little mason jar of weed and rolling papers.

He sat down at the little table and set about rolling a joint. He tore off a little more of the already shredded cardboard cover of the container of the rolling papers and used this as a filter. He let his fingers work unconsciously, going about a task they'd completed hundreds, probably thousands of times, massaging the clumps of the green in the paper into a smooth, fat tube. He twisted the paper into the cardboard filter and tucked one corner of the paper down, rolling the joint in a coddled, constant stroking. He licked just under the thin flap of the paper to close it then on the outside to seal it. He used the end of a spent incense stick to pack in the end and lit it.

The light above made a metallic tinkling noise. Once. Twice.

Stephen took a long drag. He held the smoke in until the tickle in the back of his throat became too much to stifle. He exhaled coughing, noting that it resembled a chuckle more than a direct cough.

The light tinkled again and then went out.

Stephen didn't move. He let the dark wash over him, keeping the smoldering tip of the joint in the center of his vision.

He took another hit.

Gradually, his eyes adjusted, his familiarity with the room helping to place himself in the world around him but for one fleeting moment he felt adrift, a collection of thoughts and ideas and memories in a shapeless void, anchored by a pinprick of heat held daintily between his thumb and index fingers. With each pull of the smoke from the joint, he felt more grounded in reality. He came back to his kitchen, leaving the void dripping wet and endlessly black somewhere just unseen.

He smoked the joint down to the cardboard filter then crushed it out on the table. When he stood, pushing himself up from the table with the palms of his hand on the cool, smooth surface, he jostled his bag. A book slid out onto the edge of the table, hung on the precipice then dropped to the dusty floor.

"Shit," he said, his tongue moving slowly in his mouth.

He heard the motion his dry lips made moving when he spoke and for the second time thought of cats' tongues.

Stephen leaned forward, steading himself with one hand still on the table, and picked up the book. The cover wasn't clear, but by its size and heft it had to be Robert's copy of *Suttree*. He went to set it down on the table and then something about its feel in his hand stopped him. Standing   in the dark of his kitchen, stoned and holding one of his friend's favorite novels for some time, he reflexively closed his eyes.

§

That night, Stephen dreamt he and Robert were in the Knoxville of old. Smears of memories and story welded themselves together until he couldn't tell what had happened and what was written. Robert and Stephen ran into Suttree just outside the small, slat shack houseboat on the Tennessee. Old friends. They laughed. Heads flicking back under a summer sun and their pink tongues lolled up screeches of mirth. They walked arm in arm to the dives and juke joints, drinking homemade whiskey, grains and screws jostling in the bottoms of refilled glass bottles. They barked catcalls up into the open windows of the whorehouses and hollered at the harvest moon.

Somewhere between the dredges of the blue-black night and the blossoming of the lemon rind sun, Stephen ended up stripped to the waist wading out into the swirling confluence of the Holston and French Broad, at the exact spot where they formed the Tennessee River. A bottle of homemade was passed back and forth as they sang in broken three-part harmony.

"You get a line, I'll get a pole, babe."

Stephen saw that Suttree was no longer with them.

"You get a line and I'll get a pole, honey."

The third man slowly turned in the muddy water.

"You get a line. I'll get a pole," Rivers Stanton sang, slapping the slick bottle into Stephen's outstretched palm, "and we'll both go on down to the fishing hole, honey sugarbaby mine."

Stephen tried to focus on the man's face but it was as muddy and swirling as the water lapping at his belly button.

Rivers. Robert.

When he woke, the sun was well up. Stephen didn't move right away. He watched the little dust motes dance under the unseen hands of some great puppeteer. The noise of traffic and the calls of birds filtered in through the open blinds.

He pulled his arm, numb and full of needles, out from under himself and checked the time on his watch.

11:17am.

Late, he thought. *Late, late, late.*

He didn't even brush his teeth. He still had on the same clothes he'd worn the day before. He shoved *Suttree* back into his pack, grabbed his sweater and slammed the red door shut, unlocked.

§

Several of the seats were empty when he arrived. The students remaining looked annoyed at having been made to wait.

Stephen didn't even bother with an apology. He launched straight into a lecture he'd given many times. The central focus of the author in side characters. The tale told through others. The minor characters combining into a chorus all their own and as sadly sweet as any sung in a minor key.

Not fifteen minutes in, he noticed the curdling of many an eyebrow.

He kept on.

In a sea of confusion painted gaudily on young, smooth faces, a hand rose.

Stephen tried to ignore it, but it remained upraised.

"Yes?" he barked.

"Sir," a timid voice said. "I don't recall seeing this lecture in the syllabus. Last week, we finished with 'A Clean, Well-Lighted Place' and 'The Ice Palace' so I thought today was supposed to focus on—"

Stephen's stomach dropped. He'd come back to the same auditorium by mistake again, this time mentally. How many times was this going to happen before he found a way to get his head screwed on right?

Fuck it, he thought.

"Do you wish to live a fully scripted life?" he asked, blandly. "Do you want to forever have your every moment scheduled? Do you want to know what you're having for dinner in twelve years, three months and six days?"

Silence.

Stephen crossed the room and stood behind the desk. He leaned forward and let the knuckles of both fists rest there, shifting the weight off his back onto his hands.

"Do you not have room in your existence for something off the cuff? Can you not sit there, comfortably, well-groomed and well-fed in that plush seat, and learn something new? Or has your experience, all nineteen, short years of it, blinded you already to The New?"

The silence was beginning to fill with the sounds of people shifting uncomfortably.

Easy does it, Stephen told himself.

He took a breath and held it for a five-count.

"Minor characters tell much about the author. Minor characters tell much more about the story than most people would have you believe. There is a lot happening on the fringes, people. We can talk 'Clean, Well-Lighted Place' and 'Ice Palace' in regard to minor characters too," he said.

He tried to steady his heart and keep his voice even. He wanted to scream at these over-privileged children in their name-brand clothes, cellphone illuminated faces, and BMW's, but he knew it wasn't their fault. He wanted to shake the whole damn room if only to wake himself from the nightmare he found himself unable to escape.

Ease it on back, he told himself. *Step back into the role of the teacher, the authoritarian such a comfort to the student. Let them do the work—the real secret of tutelage.*

"What do you think the drunk old gentleman at the café tells us about Hemingway's outlook on life?" he asked. "How about the younger waiter, impatient to escape the moment he found himself in?"

The shifting stopped. The silence ended. A hand was raised, and a question was answered.

§

Back in his office, Stephen sat staring empty-eyed at the document.

How many times have I rewritten this scene?

He couldn't answer himself.

He let the straight line of the cursor blink. It was there. It wasn't. There. Gone.

The time drained from the day, becoming just another soap scum line in a leaky tub.

He didn't bother to click Save—seeing it for the first time as the pagan ritual offering it was. How many times had he written a line, an entire scene if he were lucky and, on a heater, frantically made for the floppy disc icon? How many documents? How many stories? How many poems?

Memorabilia.

There weren't even floppy discs anymore. Everything was stored in digital clouds or flash drives the size of spare change. You could even get them in the shapes of your favorite sci-fi show characters. He'd seen students with Tardis flash drives. One overweight and pimple-speckled Creative Writing major had a Starship Enterprise that he perched on the corner of his desk like a trophy, the thin tether of a white USB chord plugged into the Mac his scholarship money or Daddy bought him.

Something about translating the creative into trinkets made Stephen lose hope for the future.

§

The cursor blinked. On. Off. There. Gone.

Stephen stared unmoving.

How long? How many times?

The knock at his office door made him jump. He knocked over the half-empty cup of coffee on his desk.

"Shit," he muttered, searching around for something to clean the mess up with.

The knock sounded again.

"Come in," Stephen called, taking a sweater down from the coatrack in the corner and using it as a towel.

The door eased open, but no one entered right away.

"Come in," Stephen repeated.

A.S. COOMER

The door squeaked to a stop halfway open.

"Jesuschrist," Stephen muttered. "Come in already."

No one entered.

Stephen mopped up the last of the spilt coffee and tossed the sweater in the back corner of the office.

"Who's there?"

Stephen came out from behind his desk and stood staring at the partially opened door. He'd begun to sweat.

"Hello?"

There was no reply.

Stephen put his hand on the door knob and pulled the door open. The hall outside his office was empty. The florescent lights shone dully on the faded tiles. There was a flier lying on the floor halfway down the hall. Not a person in sight. No sound of students or faculty this late in the evening.

Stephen looked both ways down the long, narrow hall then shook his head.

Was this some sort of childish prank? Some coed ding-dong-dash? He wondered if he'd really heard the knocking at all.

Stephen shook his head again. He checked his watch.

Shit. I need to go home. Get something to eat. Get some sleep.

He turned and stepped back into his office.

He nearly fell over his own feet when he saw Robert sitting behind his desk.

Stephen tried to scream but couldn't seem to get any air to move in or out of his lungs. His chest felt tight enough to burst. The blood squelched in his ears like a vise on a watermelon.

A shaking took hold of him and he couldn't steady himself.

"Robert?" he whispered.

Then he saw the floor rapidly approaching and everything went dark.

§

Stephen had no idea where he was when he came to. He had no clue as to how long he'd been out. He couldn't remember his own name for a time. He felt like some strange traveler waking up in a new world. A cryogenic experiment gone wrong. The frozen dethawed for the first time in ages waking up forgotten in a lost world.

Robert.

He remembered seeing Robert. His dead friend sitting at his desk in his office. Robert staring at him as he entered. No sense of shock or surprise on his friend's face. A blankness of the face funneling toward cold, unblinking eyes.

A.S. COOMER

Stephen pushed himself to a sitting position and peered over the edge of the desk.

No one was sitting there now. The coffee cup stood empty but righted where he'd set it after it'd overturned. The laptop was still open.

Stephen pulled himself to his feet using the desk as an anchor to steady himself. He felt weak, lightheaded. Something seemed to clang about in his chest unevenly.

"Hello?"

The quietness of the office was unnerving. It seemed charged, some great malignity poised on the point of attack.

"Hello?"

There was a fuzziness in his head that Stephen couldn't explain.

Must've hit my head in the fall, he thought.

Stephen checked his watch: 2:33am.

"Goddamn."

He crossed to the other side of the desk and sank down into the chair. He felt immensely tired, as if he'd just finished a marathon or emerged from lost wanderings in the desert.

He shivered, brought a hand to his forehead and found he was sweating.

The blinking of the cursor caught his attention.

"What the—"

The document, the novel, the work of hours, years, was still open but it'd been altered. In the lower left-hand corner of the computer screen, instead of reading "Page 247 of 247", it read "Page 1 of 1".

Stephen shivered and felt a wave of nausea sweep over him.

He leaned forward and scrolled up and down but there was only the one page.

"No, no, no, no."

He steadied his shaking hands and held the Control button then tapped the Z key. Nothing happened. The erasure of Rivers Stanton's story was not undone.

"Oh God," Stephen whispered.

A fear greater than any he'd ever known took hold of him. Stephen slowly sat back in his chair and shook.

His mouth opened but he could not speak. He could not cry out.

Where had it gone?

The cursor blinked. On. Off. There. Gone.

For the second time since he'd woke that morning, Stephen wept.

A.S. COOMER

§

He felt great, unseen eyes staring. Laughter dancing in the eaves. A relentless mirth unconnected to his own emotions crowding in.

He muttered to himself. Words empty of context or meaning. Just sounds jangling about in his head that erupted from his mouth with no conscious will of his own. The last gumball in the machine bouncing down the shaft after the quarter fell through the slot.

"The river runs."

Stephen didn't know where he was.

"In the shady pine, the fox sleeps."

In some dimly aware part of himself, Stephen understood that he was crying.

"Sundrenched and quaking, the rabbit scans for hawks."

§

His phone rang and Stephen answered it still half-asleep.

"Hello?"

"Stephen Paul?"

"Mm, yes," Stephen rubbed his sleep-crusted eyes with the hand not holding the phone to his ear. "Who is this?"

"My name is Miriam Shumaker," the voice was placid, a restrained cheerfulness. "I'm a grief counselor here at the University. I was asked to check in on you and see how you're doing."

Grief. Counselor.

"What?"

"I understand you and Robert Wilkins were quite close. I'm sure his passing has been rough for you."

Silence.

Stephen opened his eyes fully and sat up.

Muted sunlight, clouds hanging low and grey and pregnant, came in through his bedroom window.

Stephen did not remember coming home the previous evening.

He checked his watch and saw he was late. Again.

"Jesus, I'm late," he said.

"I'm sorry?"

"Oh, sorry. Right. Grief counselor," Stephen said, swinging his legs off the couch.

He saw that he was still fully dressed. His shoes were still on.

"I'm doing fine," he said, cradling the phone with his shoulder. "Fine."

He slapped some toothpaste on his toothbrush and set about brushing his teeth.

"Mr. Paul, grief is a complicated thing. It takes many forms," Miriam Shumaker said.

Stephen made a noncommittal noise through a mouth sudsy with minty foam.

"Sometimes it comes to completely shape our worldview. The world is recast and redefined by loss and absence."

"Uh huh."

Stephen leaned over the sink and spat. He wiped his mouth on the inside of his shirt as he searched the kitchen for his car keys. They weren't on the table or on the hook by the door.

"Mental health is something the University takes very seriously, Mr. Paul. There are people here that care about you and your well-being."

"Shit," Stephen whispered, scratching the stubble on his cheek.

Where did I put them?

"I'd like it if you'd come in and see me in the office this afternoon."

Stephen stopped and stood very still and erect.

"You want me to come in?"

"And see me, yes. How about 5:30 this evening, Mr. Paul?"

Stephen looked out the kitchen window down onto the little driveway at the side of the house. His car was not there.

"I've...I've got plans," Stephen lied.

"How about tomorrow evening then? Same time? 5:30?"

Stephen sighed.

The cheerfulness of the voice was grating.

"Sure. OK. You know what? This evening works fine. I'll see you then."

"We're in the Park Wing of the Health & Social Sciences Building. Room 345."

Stephen ended the call and stood staring at the space where his car should've been.

He couldn't recall anything after fainting in his office the previous evening. A void, a blankness, was planted firmly there.

Head doesn't hurt. No hangover. Can't be a blackout.

A gnawing fear was growing inside him. He felt it there, strange, foreign, impossible to ignore.

What happened last night?

His phone vibrated, and he heard the tone signifying a received email to his University account.

> Paul,
> I need to see you in my office.
> Dr. Hagan.

"Fucking great," Stephen said, slamming the door shut behind him.

His legs felt wooden and awkward. A colt's newfound legs. Unsure, off-kilter, unbalanced. With a pang of grief, he recalled the empty screen of the document, of the novel, of the story he'd been culling for years.

Gone.

He heard the slap of his feet on the sidewalk with each step.

Grief counselor. Hagan. Robert. Fainting. What's happening?

The walk was long and by the time he got to the auditorium he was sweating profusely. Just outside the door, he stopped and used the inside of his shirt to wipe the sweat off his brow. He took a deep breath then opened the door.

Dr. Hagan stood before the students, a copy of *Nausea* held before him. He'd been reading but stopped at the sound of the door opening.

All eyes turned to Stephen. He hesitated, felt heat rise up his neck and cheeks, then proceeded to the desk. He set his bag down and nodded at Dr. Hagan.

"Thanks for covering, Dr. Hagan," he said, briskly.

With shaking hands, he opened his bag and removed his copy of the novel.

"Sorry I'm late everyone," he said, turning to the watching eyes of the students.

"Yet again," a male voice said.

There were several snickers and a few grunts of approval.

"Professor Paul, we were just revisiting—" Dr. Hagan began.

"Let's discuss objects and their place in the novel," Stephen said, taking three steps away from Dr. Hagan towards the front row of seats. "Why is it that the—"

"Professor Paul," Dr. Hagan said, his voice not loud but carrying well in the open space.

Stephen straightened and turned slightly towards the Department Head.

Hot, red anger and the taste of bile filled him. He didn't trust his voice, so he raised his eyebrows in askance.

"Why don't you take this morning to collect yourself and meet me in my office in—" he checked the Rolex on his left wrist, "—forty-five minutes."

Stephen shook. He stood rigid, the paperback pinched between his fingers.

"Excuse me?"

Dr. Hagan's face darkened.

"Outside," Dr. Hagan said, walking across the room and out the door.

Stephen held his breath. He felt the eyes on him. The silence was heavy, bristling with a hostility that Stephen would've sworn was palpable.

"Scan for inanimate objects and Antoine's reactions to them. We'll discuss in a moment. Excuse me," Stephen walked over to the desk, forcing himself to take each step slowly, carefully, and set the book down on top of his bag.

He walked across the room to the door with legs bending and moving in a forced, rigid manner. He felt off-centered, like he could topple over at any second.

He opened the door and shut it quietly behind him.

Dr. Hagan stood waiting and glowering.

"Yes, sir?" Stephen asked.

Last Quarter

Dr. Hagan didn't answer straight away. He held the book, Stephen saw that it was from the library, in both of his hands. His knuckles were white with tension.

"Paul, you've been late every day this week."

Stephen nodded.

"You've missed appointments with your students."

Stephen's nodding slowed but continued.

"You're disheveled and unkempt."

Stephen seemed to feel the slept in rumples in his clothes squirm under Hagan's harsh gaze.

"I need you to pull it together, Paul."

Stephen continued nodding.

The anger was gone. He didn't acknowledge it until he felt its absence. Something more blue than black spreading across his insides, coating him, covering him.

"Take the rest of the day and collect yourself. I expect you to keep your appointment with Dr. Shumaker this evening. I mean it."

Dr. Hagan opened the door and entered the auditorium. The click of the door shutting hit Stephen like a slap. He flinched.

§

"Have a seat," Dr. Shumaker said, holding the door open.

Stephen walked into the large, well-lit space but did not sit. He walked to the middle of the room and stood looking around him.

There were several thick bookshelves lining most of the wall space that was not window and curtain. Scanning, he saw several of the books' titles: *Living with Grief, On Grief & Grieving, Silent Grief, Grief Recovery*, and on and on.

Stephen shook his head. He couldn't help but gravitate towards a bookshelf when he entered a room, but he got the gist of what this one offered and wanted nothing to do with it.

Grief. I'm not in grief. I'm not grieving. I mean, shit, I am grieving but not, like, clinically or anything.

Stephen turned to see she had shut the door noiselessly and crossed the room to sit in a birchwood armchair, notepad and pen already in hand, and motioned for him to take the matching armchair opposite her own.

Stephen sighed but complied.

The chair was cold yet comfortable. The leather felt worn, broken-in. It seemed to absorb some of his body heat and become even more comfortable.

Stephen resolved not to proffer any information.

A.S. COOMER

If she wants to talk to me—if Hagan thinks I need to talk to her so badly then she'll have to do all the work.

Dr. Shumaker's dark brown eyes looked into Stephen's. She smiled.

Stephen did not return the smile.

The silence stretched out for some time. Stephen fidgeted in the chair even though he was quite comfortable.

Say something already. Jesus Christ. Is she just going to sit and stare at me all afternoon?

Stephen's eyes wandered about the room.

On the wall behind a chic black desk were several framed pieces of art. From what Stephen could tell, they appeared to be oil paintings and oil pastels. Originals, not prints.

"Several of my patients find art healing," Dr. Shumaker said.

Stephen saw that she had followed his gaze and was looking at the framed works on the wall behind her desk.

"Even the most white-collared, business-minded have two sides to their brain."

"…"

"Grief can be a nearly crippling thing, but I've found that working with my patients to find an outlet of some sort can help lighten the load tremendously."

Dr. Shumaker returned her gaze to Stephen, who promptly looked back at the wall.

"People are highly individualistic. They need to deal with grief in their own way, but they do need to deal with it. That's imperative, paramount—"

"I know what imperative means. I don't need synonyms," Stephen said.

Stephen felt his face color. He wasn't used to snapping at people.

Dr. Shumaker didn't acknowledge the barb. She smiled and nodded her head slightly, beckoning him to elaborate. When he didn't, she continued.

"When we stifle emotions we don't want to or feel we can't deal with, we add baggage to our load. We make more work for ourselves in the long run. Sometimes we develop bad habits and practices that carry on for years, lifetimes. Dealing with grief, acknowledging its presence, its hidden hand in nearly all we do, all we say, all we think—"

Stephen couldn't stand it.

He bolted to his feet.

"We? There is no 'we'. There is only me. Quit with all this pronoun debauchery," Stephen said.

He felt sweaty and trapped in the large, mostly open space of the of-

A.S. COOMER

fice. He paced to one of the bookshelves, his back to Dr. Shumaker, and leaned forward, feigning a closer examination of the books there. He closed his eyes and focused on slowing his breathing.

Calm, he thought. *I need to calm it down.*

He felt riled up. Something hot and red just under the surface of his skin was trying to tear its way out of him.

The silence of the room was broken only by the faint hum of traffic outside and Stephen's heavy breathing. He heard the blood pounding in his ears and clenched then unclenched his fists.

"I'm sorry," he said, then quickly added, "but I've never been a fan of speaking in that manner."

He felt a strong urge to keep his back to Dr. Shumaker. An embarrassed child's dread of facing up to a parent.

Stephen stood up straight, relaxed his hands, then turned on his heels.

Her face remained placid and smiling. She motioned with the pen towards the birchwood chair. Stephen saw that she'd written several lines on the notepad.

Jesus Christ, he thought. She thinks I'm a basket case.

Stephen took his steps awkwardly back to the chair and sat down.

Dr. Shumaker did not break the silence.

"OK," Stephen said, finally. "I'm here because Dr. Hagan thinks I'm losing my shit, right?"

No response.

"Well, I'm not," he continued. "I'm just...well, I'm just a little upset."

It felt like he had to pull the words from the marrow of his bones. They did not want to come out of his mouth, like child unborn clinging to the womb.

Dr. Shumaker nodded.

"I mean, I think anybody would be upset if someone..."

Stephen struggled for the words. The same struggle he'd known all his life. That's why he felt so drawn to the writing life. He had the words, but they did not live or reside in a vocal capacity. Throughout his life, Stephen felt words were inky black pools one dipped in inside and brought screaming out into the world through writing. Words and ideas and stories were things you kept to yourself until you couldn't anymore and the only way to properly share them, without debasing them with awkward pauses and unfortunate stumblings, was to write them.

"Someone you admired, worked with—a friend," Stephen choked. All of a sudden, he felt his throat swell closed and his eyes and nose stinging something fierce.

Vaguely, he thought about allergies and Epi-Pens then he realized it for what it was. He was crying.

A.S. COOMER

Stephen tensed his entire body but was wracked with shaking. He saw a thin, threadbare sheet left out on the line, a supercell approaching. He covered his face with his tremulous hands.

Dr. Shumaker set a box of tissues on the arm of his chair.

Stephen took one and blew his nose. He took another and wiped his eyes and cheeks.

"Thank you," he said. "Sorry. I—I don't usually do this."

Stephen snuffled and hiccupped into another three or four tissues before Dr. Shumaker spoke.

"It's a natural reaction to a profound experience," she said.

Stephen blinked back what he hoped were the last of his tears.

§

Stephen stepped out into the dregs of the day. Thin shafts of the sun's angled orange light fell over the tops of the Park Wing of the Health & Social Sciences Building and the tall slender oaks surrounding it. There were a few students, heads down, long-toothed after a day of academia, trudging slowly along the clean sidewalks.

Stephen started walking with no destination in mind. Movement seemed key. One foot in front of the other then the other. He tried to keep his thoughts straight in his head, but they jangled about.

He'd cried in a stranger's office.

A car horn honked.

He'd fainted in his own office.

Somewhere overhead a bird cried out its dissonant song.

His friend was gone.

The sharp bark of an elderly woman's laughter.

His novel was gone.

The sound of glass breaking.

He'd seen the face of his dead friend.

An owl hooted.

Stephen stopped walking. He looked around. The sun had long since set. He had no clue where he was.

A great ball of suffocation welled up in his throat. He choked and choked, coughed then could fight it no longer. Stephen sat down on the cracked sidewalk, smashed beer cans and empty potato chip wrappers, and cried again.

He didn't try to fight it. He let go and the boat rocked with the great, heaving waves. He tried opening his eyes, but the world was a mix of blues and blacks and purples. He felt snot bubble and pop from his nostrils. His mouth and throat thickened with mucus.

"Shit," he whispered. "Shit."

Somewhere behind him, a man coughed. A throat clearing, announcing presence cough.

Stephen straightened. He lifted the neck of his shirt over his face and wiped.

The night was cool. Stephen seemed to feel it for the first time after letting his shirt sink back over his chest. The damp skin of his cheeks and the rawness of his nose felt the chilly wind as it fluttered the trash around.

"Uh. Are you OK, mister?" a voice asked.

Stephen nodded his head while searching for the sound of the voice.

The night slowly came into focus.

A rusted chain-link fence followed the busted-up sidewalk down a desolate side street. There were several hulking buildings, old factories or warehouses long since shuttered and abandoned, lining the street but great urban prairies filled the spaces between. Not twenty-five yards from where Stephen sat, straight as a flagpole on the sidewalk, was an oil drum, the thin wisps of a failing fire flickering out into the night.

"Yes," Stephen said.

He was forced to clear his throat before he could continue.

"I'm fine, thanks."

"OK."

There was no sound of movement.

Stephen's eyes adjusted more clearly to the dim lighting.

A man, hunched and bearded, was standing on the other side of the chain-link fence staring down at Stephen. He was dressed in rags. Grey stained black and greyer. Soot from the oily flames painted his thin, shallow face. His eyes looked bulbous and over-sized in the bad lighting.

"Want a drink?" the man asked, his arm reaching over the fence.

From the pale light of the fire, Stephen saw a thin pint bottle hovering just within his reach. The glass refracted orange and red through something wet and amber-hued.

His mouth felt dull, wooden.

Stephen took the bottle willingly and drank.

§

"The hen house shakes when the fox dances."

Bone fingers flittered in the branches. Something powerful was moving inside him.

"The hawk'll take the dive when the timing's right."

Boxed, heavy feet shuffled on uneven, unforgiving hardness. He stumbled. He fell, several times. Picked himself up without bothering to dust himself off.

Great commands were issued. Stephen couldn't find the issuers. He assumed they weren't meant for him and trudged on.

"The sun that shines at night is right for the mites that bite the backs of ye hands."

Great streaks of blue and white astonished and held him in place. Something cold and malicious bit into his face then his wrists. He couldn't seem to fill his lungs with air.

"Sleep deep in the bleak sheets of a valley low, a valley cold, a valley left, oh, so alone."

Stephen came to in a slate grey box of a room. He was laying on his side, his swollen face pressed against the cold stone of bare concrete floor. His eyes fluttered and stung. They felt like shriveled cherry tomatoes in decomposing sockets.

He moaned.

His head felt three times its normal size, with a tongue inside that hung awkwardly and foreign in his mouth. When he tried to use it to lick his cracked, sore lips, it moved without any lubricating properties.

He was also swimming in nausea, and with any attempted movement a rush of vomit filled his throat and spilled out of his mouth before he could even think about stopping it. A vile, nearly clear, steaming liquid surrounded his face. It burned from his jaw to his forehead and slipped between his clenched left eyelid.

"Fucking hell," a man's voice said nearby.

Stephen was roughly moved into a sitting position, the back of his head banging against more concrete.

He vomited again, this time into his own lap. He couldn't muster the strength to turn his head away. He couldn't lift his arms to shield himself. He puked again then again then retched three times before coming to a shaky conclusion. His body seemed to be vibrating with a pain and poison unlike any he'd ever known.

Stephen tried to keep his eyes open, see who was there with him but couldn't. He sank into a thin, hazy darkness.

§

"Wake the fuck up," a gruff voice was repeating. "Come on now. Wake the fuck up."

Stephen tried to open his eyes, but they seemed to be sealed shut. A sharp pang of pain erupted in the middle of his head.

"Wha—"

"There he is. Wake up, pukey," the voice said.

Stephen tried to open his eyes again and this time he felt the lids come unstuck slightly with a stinging dryness. Crust fell into his blinking eyes, scratching them.

"Fuck," he said, flinching at the sudden pain.

His body felt beaten, full of little and big aches, his stomach soured and cramping.

He was helped into a sitting position by rough hands.

"There we go," a different voice said.

"Fuck," Stephen said.

He moved his hands to his eyes and rubbed. Crust flaked off and sprinkled down onto his lap. His hands felt infinitely heavier than they'd ever felt. His arms strained under their weight.

"Where am I?" Stephen asked.

"Why you're in the pokey, pukey," the gruff voice said.

Stephen removed his hands and opened his eyes wide.

He was sitting in a small room on a doctor's examination bed. He saw the walls were slate grey with huge windows looking out onto more rooms of concrete and slate grey.

"Oh God," he whispered.

One hirsute man and one short-haired woman stood, both with their arms folded across their chests, before him, slight smirks on their faces. The woman wore a dark blue uniform; the man a pair of light blue hospital scrubs.

The woman, whose arms seemed to ripple with muscles on top of muscles, spoke and Stephen was surprised to find that the gruff voice repeatedly calling him "pukey" belonged to her.

"Think you're about sobered up now, pukey?" she asked.

Stephen didn't know what to say. His mind a mired haze of tangled images and emotions.

Loss. Suffering. Wandering. Confusion.

The man in the scrubs uncrossed his arms and turned to a countertop to Stephen's left, where he picked up a clipboard and pen.

"Blood pressure is high but not emergency high," the man said, clicking the pen with each word. "Went through two banana bags while you were out, you did. Electrolytes leveling off. Didn't have to send you to the charcoal room after all, buddy."

"Charcoal room?" Stephen asked.

His stomach swooned, and, for a split second, Stephen was sure he was going to vomit.

The woman took two steps backwards.

"Not again," she said. "How much more can you possibly puke, pukey?"

"Lie back," the man said, setting the clipboard down and helping Stephen ease back onto the hard bed. "Try to stay calm. I'll get you some Sprite or ginger ale."

Stephen closed his eyes and focused on the breath coming in and out of his lungs. There was a faint wheeze there and his chest felt tight and restricted. Sweat beaded on his upper lip and in the pits of his arms.

Stephen heard a buzzing noise then the opening and shutting of a heavy door.

What the fuck, he thought. *What the fuck is happening? What the fuck happened?*

He tried to arrange the tangled images in his head into coherent memories but couldn't.

"Hang on, pukey," the woman said from somewhere above but near. "Nurse Richards is working on getting something to settle that whittle tummy of yours."

The false baby-talk sickened Stephen further.

He retched but did not vomit.

"Jesus fucking Christ," the woman said.

§

Stephen slept. He slipped in and out of consciousness. He was sick again and again, shitting and vomiting on himself.

He lost all capability of tracking time. He gave up and slept.

§

In the fog, a pale light shone dully. An unseen but gentle wind moved the grey around in swirling rivulets. A man stood under the light, motionless and waiting. He was hunched forward slightly, his face shrouded in shadow. A thick lower lip protruded into the light. He was smiling.

"Rivers?" Stephen asked.

The man's smile stretched wider.

"Hello, chum," he said.

Stephen walked across the dew-covered grass, the wet blades sending shivers racing up from his bare feet.

"What are you doing?" Stephen asked. "Where are we?"

The smiling man, Rivers Stanton, did not answer, did not move or beckon.

Stephen picked up his pace until he was running towards Rivers but saw he was getting no closer.

"What?" he screamed. "What is this?"

§

Stephen jerked into wakefulness. He sat up, wide-eyed and gasping.

"Woah, there," a voice said. "Easy does it."

Stephen turned his head towards the voice. It was neither Nurse Richards or the gruff-voiced woman in uniform.

"Take a breath," a man said. "Take 'er easy."

He was in ragged clothing, an over-sized Toledo Rockets sweater, near-ly more stains visible than logo, and worn-thin grey sweatpants. His face was pocked and marked with angry red blisters.

"Who are you?" Stephen asked. "Where are we? Rivers?"

The man sat up on the small bunk he'd been reclined on.

"Welcome to Lucas County Corrections Center," he said. "As in, we've been deemed in need of correcting."

"What?"

"Jail, man. We're in fucking jail."

Stephen opened his mouth, but nothing came out.

Jail, he thought, horror and panic blossoming in his understanding like a stain. *I'm in jail.*

"But...but," Stephen stammered. "I didn't...I'm not a...I'm no criminal."

The man nodded his head.

"Innocent until proven guilty, yeah," he said. "Same."

Stephen took stock of the man's appearance again. How many homeless men had he seen in similar appearance? How many had he walked by and tossed his spare change at? How many times had he pretended not to hear their voices?

"You don't look so good your-own-damn-self," the man said.

The wry smile did nothing to beautify the man's face.

Stephen looked down and saw himself. He was stained and crusted. His clothes were in tatters. He smelled himself and nearly gagged. Dried vomit covered nearly his entirety. He shifted on the hard bunk and felt crusted shit break and move in the seat of his pants.

"Oh God," he whispered.

"I know," the man said. "He probably smells you too."

§

Stephen asked the man a myriad of questions.

"When do I get out of here?"

"What did they say I did?"

"Don't I get a phone call?"

"How long have I been asleep?"

"Do they have showers here?"

A.S. COOMER

"What time is it?"

The man answered the questions that struck his fancy.

"Sure, you get a shower. Once you're booked and housed and deloused. First though, you see the judge."

"You've been out for hours. Snoring like a honey-drunk badger."

"It's time for you to realize time don't matter here. They come when they come and you stay while they make you."

Stephen fell silent and continued failing at remembering what had happened.

"Why'd you ask about the river?" the man said.

Stephen had been so inside himself that the sudden sound of the man's voice made him jump, shifting more hardened shit around in his pants.

"What?"

"When you were asleep, you kept muttering about the river and when you finally came to, you asked for it. The river. What's your deal with the Maumee?"

"Oh," Stephen said, recalling the faintest wisp of the dream he'd had of Rivers and the fog. "I wasn't talking about the Maumee or a river. Rivers, is what I was saying."

"Rivers?"

"Yeah," Stephen said.

An overwhelming sense of loss hit him when he spoke the name of the character aloud. He saw the empty screen of the document that had housed Rivers' story, the novel he'd been slaving over every word of for years.

Gone.

He saw the blinking cursor flashing into existence on the white background.

There. Gone. There. Gone.

Tears filled his eyes.

"You some sort of environmental activist or something? Trying to save the rivers? That why you're covered in shit and smell like a port-o-john?"

Stephen wiped away the tears and blinked, hard, several times before responding.

"No," he said. "I'm no activist. Just a writer."

"A writer?"

"Yeah."

The man seemed to take new stock of Stephen. He nodded his head after a time, rubbing the stubble that had grown up through and around the sores on his face.

"Yeah," the man said. "I guess you are, aren't you?"

Stephen didn't know how to respond so he didn't.

§

Stephen slept.

He woke.

He slept some more.

He was too preoccupied with tracking down his misplaced time that he did not question or speak to his cellmate further.

§

"Paul," a man shouted.

Stephen sat up fully awake at once.

"Up and at 'em!"

Stephen saw a uniformed man standing just outside the open door of the cell.

The ragged, pock-marked man gave Stephen a wan smile.

"Good luck, Bukowski," he said.

Stephen was in the process of preparing a retort when the guard's assertive command for Stephen to "get the fuck up" cut him short.

Stephen stood and on shaky legs followed the man out into the corridor. He saw it was long and lined with thick doors like the one he'd just passed through.

No bars, he thought.

He'd expected thick metallic bars not heavy metal doors with thin slate peepholes.

"You've got a visitor and you're expected before Judge Tatum at three," the guard said.

Stephen nodded his head and tried to keep up with the man's hurried steps.

From all around, angry and loud voices reverberated off the concrete and metal. Stephen felt light-headed and hollow. His stomach turned over when, after several longer strides, a clump of shit broke off and fell into the left leg of his pants.

"God," the guard said, turning his head slightly as he strode. "You fucking reek."

Stephen didn't reply. His face felt afire.

He followed the man, head down, watching his puke-coated shoes slap the concrete.

§

He was taken to a small, wood paneled courtroom, empty save for one tired looking woman sitting high above him and three or four others a

A.S. COOMER

little below.

Stephen was set in a hard, molded plastic chair. His hands had been clasped together in the front by zip-tie.

Somehow, this felt more embarrassing than sitting before the judge in puke and shit coated clothes.

I don't even warrant real handcuffs, he thought.

The plastic was biting into his wrists. Every time he moved his hands, the plastic would pull some of his arm hairs out.

He sat there for some time. The woman Stephen assumed was the judge reading over several documents that were passed to her and speaking with the various members of her staff.

A bailiff stood just to his left. He shifted the weight from his left foot to his right. He looked at Stephen then at the judge then at the collection of flags on the wall.

Three other people were ushered in by uniformed officers and placed in the small seating area. Two had on what Stephen thought of as "jail scrubs", orange pajama-like clothes of rough, heavily starched cotton. The other prisoner was a small elderly man.

He's got to be seventy-five years old, Stephen thought. *I wonder what he did?*

"All rise," the bailiff shouted.

Stephen hadn't expected his voice to be so deep. It was sonorous, a herald of old announcing the coming of the king.

Stephen and the other prisoners shuffled to their feet and stood with their hands manacled together. He saw that the two men in orange had on real handcuffs. Like Stephen, the elderly man was restrained by zip-tie.

"The honorable Judge Tatum is presiding," the bailiff said.

The woman Stephen assumed was the judge quickly moved to a slightly lower perch, her air of superiority reduced to a low simmer. A door behind the bench opened noiselessly and a very small woman in a black gown emerged. She took in the crowd in the courtroom in a quick glance from behind slitted eyes before sitting down.

"You may be seated," the bailiff called.

"Thank you," Judge Tatum said.

The prisoners sat down with the sound of cheap plastic chairs bending.

It reminded Stephen of kindergarten. The plastic chairs. The threadbare carpet. The tired looking adults there for him and others with him, all doing their best not to look in their direction until they absolutely had to.

The judge called a name and asked a man to stand. The bailiff walked over to the man, one of the orange, and led him to the front of the court room. He stood, his head craned up, while the judge spoke.

"Mr. Crittenden," she said. "You've been accused of—"

Like the sound of thin paper catching fire, the elderly prisoner, sitting not two chairs down from Stephen, began to sing.

The judge didn't hear it, not at first. The bailiff must have registered something was off because he shifted the weight from his left foot to his right and cocked his head slightly to one side.

"Standin' on the corner," the old man sang. "I didn't mean no harm."

Stephen felt his body clenching in trepidation.

"Along came a police," the old man sang.

Stephen turned in his chair slightly. He could now see the old man and the judge and bailiff without having to move his head.

"He took me by the arm," the old man sang.

His voice wasn't loud per se, but it carried. There was a beauty to it; like a cracked violin, it could still be played but it wasn't ever going to be fully capable again.

Judge Tatum stopped talking.

Stephen saw that the heads of her staff were now pointed in the direction of the prisoners.

"Shut the fuck up, grandpa," the other orange clad prisoner whispered, his voice harsh and pleading. "You're gonna ruin her for the rest of us."

From the tone of his voice, Stephen had the uncomfortable impression the man had said lines similar to this before but in vastly different scenarios.

The judge lowered the glasses on her nose. Her eyes narrowed, and she squinted down at the prisoners.

"Is someone…singing?" she asked.

The old man sang another line.

The bailiff leapt into action. He crossed the small courtroom in three strides and towered over the elderly man.

"Shut up," the bailiff said. "Immediately."

The man sang, "He says, 'big boy you'll have to tell me your name.'"

"Sir, you need to stop singing," the bailiff said. "Immediately."

"Shut that man up," Judge Tatum called.

The elderly man was hunched over himself, his veiny hands clasped together between his legs. The long plaid sleeves of the man's shirt were rolled up and frayed at the ends. Stephen saw that the elderly man was wearing a child's plastic Batman watch on his left wrist.

His voice sang the lines as if he'd sung them a hundred times.

"I'm a Tennessee hustler," he sang. "I don't have to work."

He held the 'a' of 'have' then let it lilt on to the last two words of the line.

A.S. COOMER

The muscles in the bailiff's arms worked. His hands balled into thick fists.

Stephen found himself a ball of clenched muscles himself. He wanted to make the old man stop. He didn't want to see him beaten.

"Get that man out of here, Jimmie," Judge Tatum ordered.

The bailiff nodded and took the old man by the bicep of his thin left arm, jerking him to his feet. The bailiff shoved him towards the door Stephen had entered through. The old man stumbled but did not fall. He cradled his hands in front of himself in what looked like an act of supplication. He turned to face the judge.

The courtroom was quiet and tense.

"Move," the bailiff growled.

The elderly man began to yodel. It was a torrent of musical notes, rising and falling like a tempest of blues and blacks and purples.

Stephen found his mouth open, and quickly snapped it shut.

The bailiff hustled the man out of the room and everyone stirred uncomfortably in their seats.

§

Stephen didn't hear a thing that transpired between the remaining prisoners and the judge. He sat dumbfounded in the hard chair lost in thought.

"Stephen Paul," the bailiff called.

Stephen shook his head and rose to his feet. The room was empty now, save the judge, her staff, and himself. He couldn't help seeing the bailiff as some sort of trained dog. He even had the look of a controlled attacking machine.

The judge's dog, he thought. *Heel, boy. Heel.*

The bailiff brought him before the judge.

She had the face of a dragon. All her features were elongated, seemed to be on a slope down to her mouth. Her teeth were violently white. They were large and squared. Stephen saw wrinkles caked with makeup at the corners of her lips and eyes. There was a smidgen of lipstick on her left front tooth. It reminded Stephen of blood.

She stared down at him with an intense scrutiny. Stephen squirmed under the gaze and seemed to smell himself all over again.

"Stephen Paul," Judge Tatum began. "You're accused of being intoxicated in public, resisting arrest, disorderly conduct, failure to comply with the order or signal of a police officer, and present risk of harm to others or property."

Stephen didn't reply.

The judge set the paper down on the desk, picked up a pen and scribbled something.

In his head, Stephen saw great red, neon letters in an ornate cursive:

Guilty.

"This is a preliminary hearing. No findings of guilt or innocence will be made at this time. You're entitled to an attorney. If you can't afford one, one will be appointed for you."

The dragon is animatronic, Stephen thought. *Going through the motions. Another day. Another set of cases. More fire to breathe. More smoke to make.*

Stephen tried to still his mind and listen to the words the judge was saying but couldn't. His thoughts were buried under ice. His attempts at understanding just a stone skipping across the surface.

"Mr. Paul?" the judge asked.

Stephen shook his head then looked up.

"Do you need the court to appoint you an attorney?" she asked.

The dragon smolders in wait.

The eyes of the staff were watching him. Stephen felt the corners of their lips upturn in the beginnings of a collective smirk. Stephen smelled his stale vomit. He clasped and unclasped his bound hands.

The bailiff took a step closer.

"Do you need an attorney, Mr. Paul?" the judge asked, an edge in her voice.

Stephen nodded his head.

"Answer the judge," the bailiff said.

"Yes, ma'am," Stephen said. "Yes, your honor."

The judge stared down at him.

The dragon evaluates.

Then she turned to an older woman in a woolen blazer with towering shoulder pads and rapidly spoke.

"Take him," the judge said to the bailiff.

Stephen was led back through the door he'd entered. He was given over to a guard, ushered through several large metal doors, and taken back to the cell.

My cell, he thought.

The guard opened the door, told Stephen to step inside and turn around, then removed the zip tie.

"When do I get to talk with my attorney?" Stephen asked.

The guard shrugged his shoulders.

"Don't I get bail or something?"

The guard took one step backwards and closed the door. It clicked shut with a tiny clacking noise that felt like a clap of thunder to Stephen.

§

The scraggly man was still sprawled on the small bed. He watched Stephen enter the cell without a comment and, when the door shut, remained quiet.

Stephen tried not to look at him. He sat down awkwardly on his bed and rubbed his wrists.

What in the hell happened? he thought for what could've been the thousandth time.

Stephen scooted back on the bed until his back was pressed against the cold concrete wall. He felt his cellmate's eyes on him and avoided looking in his direction. He turned his attention to his clothes and set about picking off the dried vomit on his shirt.

"How'd it go?" the man asked.

Stephen didn't know how to respond. He picked off a chunk of puke the size of a nickel and dropped it into the open toilet next to the bed. It was so close he didn't even have to get up.

"I'm not sure," he said finally.

The man nodded as if he understood.

He probably does, Stephen thought. *He's probably been in here a time or two before. Knows the score.*

Stephen flinched at the phrase. Like everything that ran through his conscious thoughts, he imagined the words sitting in Times New Roman size 12 font on a printed sheet of computer paper.

"You got a lawyer?" the man asked.

Stephen shook his head.

"Never needed one."

The man snorted.

"They'll appoint you one," he said. Then after a moment, "Unless you can afford one of your own."

Stephen shook his head.

Not on an adjunct's salary.

"Just pray it ain't Corey Streeter," the man said. "Had him before and he couldn't pull his head out of his ass long enough to even read the charges against me. Never did listen to a word I told him."

Stephen didn't know what to say so he just nodded his head a little.

"This your first rodeo?" the man asked.

Stephen flinched at the cliché, seeing it as the title on the cover of a bad pulp detective novel.

"Thought so," the man said. "Man, you were really fucked up when they brought you in here. I thought for sure they'd've taken you to medical. Got your stomach pumped or something."

"I think they did," Stephen said, remembering the manly guard and nurse in scrubs.

"What'd you do anyway?"

"I don't know," Stephen said.

"PI?"

Stephen nodded.

"That was one of the charges the judge read to me."

The man laughed.

"What'd you take?" he asked.

Stephen shrugged his shoulders and continued picking puke off his clothing.

"You writers," he said.

§

The henhouse stirs.

The fox is on the prowl.

The farmer is asleep, a half-empty jug sitting between his bare feet.

The porch door bangs in the wind.

§

"You got a visitor," a guard shouted.

The pock-marked man in the stained Rockets hoodie made to get up.

"Not you," the guard said. "Paul. Let's go."

Stephen got up from the bunk and followed the guard—he couldn't tell if it was the same one or a new one—down the long hall. He was having trouble keeping his thoughts from wandering. He kept having flashes of animals or farm-life type scenes. He had no idea why this was the case.

The stress of being arrested, he kept telling himself.

"Think it's your attorney," the guard said.

Stephen nodded.

Maybe I'll get out of here. Finally.

The guard led Stephen through several doors, all locked and requiring the guard's ID badge or a guard on the other side to buzz them through. Before going through one of the doors, Stephen's hands were handcuffed. The guard didn't say anything. Just stopped before the door, retrieved the pair of metal cuffs from his belt, and clasped them around Stephen's wrists. He felt like a cow being led through the slaughterhouse. Everything was coldly efficient, concrete and easily cleaned, *just a hosing will do, thank you,* and there was the threat of violence looming just ahead (*or behind or to either side, shit, above and below too, for that matter*). Finally, he opened another slate grey door and there was a small room with a table and two chairs on opposite sides.

A rather large man in a shiny blue suit sat with his back turned to the door. At the sound of the door opening, he'd turned awkwardly in his chair to watch Stephen enter but did not stand. The room was lit by a single bulb in an industrial looking casing. It gave out a harsh, bright light. The man's face looked badly sculpted in this light. His features more putty than skin. Some over-eager sculptor's attempts at Claymation.

The guard's strong hand pressed the center of Stephen's back and shoved him into the room.

The attorney smiled and it did nothing to make him look more human. Stephen vaguely wondered if this is what a human face would look like if it were microwaved.

"Have a seat," the lawyer said.

Stephen was in the process of doing just that. He'd already pulled the chair out from underneath the table with both of his manacled hands and was poised, bent over, his ass searching for the chair as he clung to the table, when the man said this.

Stephen paused and looked at the putty-faced lawyer, then sat down.

"OK," the man said, opening a manila folder sitting before him. "Stephen Paul. Charged with…"

The lawyer, using the pointer finger of his right hand, skimmed several lines in a crisp, not-a-stain-on-it document, his mouth moving as his finger did.

Stephen pictured this guy in kindergarten reading in exactly the same way. His finger gliding on in front of his nose, his mouth working the words that were sounding in his head.

Jesus Christ, Stephen thought.

"What's your name?" Stephen asked, as the silence stretched on longer than he could stand.

"Huh?" the man asked, looking up from the document.

"Your name," Stephen said. "What is it?"

"Oh," the man said, straightening in his seat. "The preliminaries, yes. I am Corey Streeter of—"

Stephen didn't even try to mask the groan that escaped his lips.

§

When the door to his cell had clicked shut, Stephen stood with his head hanging, his eyes squeezed shut, a nearly unbearable pressure threatening to cave in his skull at each of his temples.

"You don't look so good," his cellmate said.

Stephen opened his eyes but didn't raise his head.

"Was that your girl?" the man asked.

Stephen grunted and sank down onto the hard bunk.

"Don't have one of those," he said, shutting his eyes again.

"Fag?"

Stephen opened his eyes and turned to face the man.

"If I were gay, you for damn sure would not be my type."

Stephen fell back onto the bed and shut his eyes again.

The man let loose one short bark of a laugh.

"Attorney then," he said.

Stephen groaned and turned to face the wall.

"You got 'im, didn't you?" the man was on the verge of laughing, Stephen could actually hear the corners of his dried, crusted lips upturning in a smile. "Corey Streeter?"

At the sound of the incompetent attorney's name, Stephen Paul began to cry.

§

"You're sprung, Paul," the guard said.

Stephen had been asleep.

Time was a strange thing when you had no windows. No way to gauge where the sun was or wasn't. No sense of night or day. Just cold, slate grey concrete. And the incessant need of his cellmate to chatter. What felt like hours would drift by like a sluggish, debris filled stream, filled only with the rush of blood in Stephen's ears, the sound of air wheezing in and out of his cellmate's lungs, the noise of their attempts to get comfortable on the hard, uncomfortable bunks, then the guy would just start talking. Stephen eventually tuned him out and did his best to treat the sound of the man's voice as some form of white noise in sun-browned skin.

Stephen rose to his feet, stretching as he moved, his back popping audibly and painfully. He followed the guard down the hallway, through the maze of locked, buzzing doors until he was given over to a man behind a tall counter.

"Name?" the uniformed man asked, not making eye contact.

"Stephen Paul."

The man nodded curtly and sank before the counter to click and stare at a computer screen. After a few moments, the man rose back up to his feet and walked a short ways down the counter. Stephen didn't know what to do, so he followed him.

The man looked up and, with a slight upturning of his eyebrows, expressed his amusement at this.

"You can just stay put, partner," he said. "It'll be just a few moments while you're signed out. Paper trails and all that."

Stephen couldn't help but smile. He was finally getting out.

He felt a strand of the rope wrapped around his chest bust loose, easing the tension he hadn't consciously acknowledged in some time. He felt good enough to scan the room around him. There were two more doors to his left, both with thick paned windows that stretched and contorted the image of the other side vaguely like a funhouse mirror, and through them, Stephen could see the outside.

The sun was shining through cloud cover on the concrete out there. He saw mulberry bushes and a bench and several uniformed people milling about smoking cigarettes and looking into cellphones.

His eyes stung with tears.

Stephen bit the inside of his lower lip, hard, to keep from weeping.

I've cried more in the last few days than I have in the past decade, he thought. *No more. Jesus please, no more crying.*

"All right, partner," the man said.

Stephen spun around too quickly on his unsteady feet and nearly fell over himself. He placed both palms down onto the counter and stared eagerly at the man, still not making eye contact with Stephen and shuffling around papers.

"Your lawyer has the specifics. Here's the charge list," the man said, sliding two sheets of stapled paper across the counter.

Stephen took the paperwork but did not look at it. He stared intently at the man behind the counter.

The man shuffled some papers into a folder, opened a filing cabinet and stuck the folder inside. Then he sat back down behind the computer and started clicking and typing away.

Stephen stood there.

The man went about his business for some time.

Stephen coughed softly.

The man looked up.

"Yeah?"

"Uh," Stephen said. "What happens now?"

"What do you mean?" the man asked.

"I mean…Umm, when do I get to leave?"

The man looked perplexed.

"You got the charge list right there," he said.

Stephen looked down at the papers in his hand then back at the man behind the counter.

"OK," he said.

The man nodded, as if this settled everything, and went back to his computer work.

Stephen skimmed the papers. It had some specifics: the date and time of his arrest, the county of the arrest, his booking time, his list of charges. It said nothing about his release from jail.

"I'm sorry," Stephen said.

The man twitched and stood up quickly.

"Yes," the man said, more statement than question.

He still did not make eye contact with Stephen.

"Am I free to go?" Stephen asked. "Like now?"

The man nodded vigorously, his face that of a parent losing patience with a stupid child.

"OK," Stephen said, not wanting to piss off what he assumed was the last person, the gatekeeper, standing between him and his freedom.

The man pointed towards the two doors leading outside.

"You're free to go, Mr. Paul."

The man was back in the seat, clicking and typing away, before Stephen turned back from where he'd pointed.

Stephen turned and approached the door with hesitation. If it refused to open for him, Stephen was sure he'd break down and cry like a baby. With the paperwork in his left hand, he carefully put the palm of his right hand on the handle and pushed down. It moved smoothly, and the door swung open. He stepped into a small alcove leading to the last door, the sunshine slipping back behind the clouds just outside.

Stephen opened the door and a rush of the guards' cigarette smoke greeted him. He closed his eyes against the sting and stepped out onto the sidewalk lining Spielbusch Avenue. The guards stopped their talking, several looked up from the tiny screens of their cellphones and watched him pass. Stephen kept his head down, afraid that doing or saying the wrong thing would be a sure-fire way to be forced back through all those heavy, locked doors.

The wind was cold despite the sun peeking back around the grey clouds. He wished for a sweater or jacket. He looked up, oriented himself, then started walking south towards Michigan Street. Stephen placed himself on a map in his head. He did his best to calculate how far from his crumby little apartment he was.

Six miles? Seven?

He kept his head down against the chill in the wind, fall was slipping steadily towards winter, and trudged on, one foot after the other. Despite the cold, it felt good to be able to move freely. He felt like running but didn't think his legs, still weak and unsteady under him, could manage it. He thought hungrily of the pack of frozen pot pies in the freezer. Then the thought of a blisteringly hot shower hit him like a truck. He nearly stopped walking to savor the imagining of removing the shit and puke stained clothes and dissolving back into a semblance of a human beneath the showerhead.

He picked up his pace. He had no cellphone. Didn't think payphones were even a thing anymore. No one to call to swoop in and save him from the long walk ahead.

Stephen tried to think of the recent past as a vivid, disturbing nightmare but couldn't. A quick gust of wind brought the scent of himself to his nose again. He nearly gagged. He refrained from looking at his reflection in the storefronts as he walked. He did not want to know what he looked like.

At a street crossing waiting for the crosswalk light to change, Stephen saw *The Blade* sitting behind the glass receptacle of the newspaper rack. With a shock, he saw that it had only been one full day since he'd been arrested. He was sure he'd been in that complex of grey and concrete for days. A week maybe.

One, single, solitary day, he thought.

The light changed and he crossed the street.

§

The walk home was a strange blur. He walked along boarded up houses, carry-out liquor stores, beater cars. He walked along front porches crowded with noisy people drinking cheap beer and smoking marijuana. He walked by small children bouncing flattening basketballs and laughing wildly. He walked by several houses seemingly guarded by elderly people staring stoically out of front windows like those owls placed on ledges to scare off pigeons.

The afternoon shifted slyly to dusk as Stephen walked. The cloud cover increased and the setting sun hitting the thin, flat cloud overhead casted a strange glow over everything. It felt dreamlike and surreal. He thought exhaustion had something to do with this perception.

When Stephen finally rounded the corner of his street and saw the rickety staircase leading up to his apartment, a flutter of joy erupted in his stomach like some birthed bird desperately trying to escape and flap its wings for the first time. He was able to quicken his pace despite his overwhelming sense of tiredness. He took the stairs two at a time, a broad smile breaking across his haggard face.

When he got to the door, he automatically slapped his pockets for his keys. They weren't there.

His stomach seemed to find its way to his knees.

He tried the door, but it was locked.

"Fuck," Stephen shouted. "Fucking shit. Fuck."

In a flustered burst of agitation, Stephen turned and yanked on the doorknob and, much to his surprise, there was a little click and the door inched open.

He stood there quiet and still for a second processing this.

Real secure, he thought finally.

He pushed the door inward and stepped inside. The sense of familiarity was welcome. After unlocking the bolt, Stephen shut and relocked the door. He crossed the kitchen to the little porcelain sink and poured himself a glass of water. He drank it all before setting it back in the sink and refilling it. He took the refilled glass, taking sips along the way, with him as he made his way to the bathroom, to turn the shower on. He cranked the hot knob nearly as far to the left as it would go. Great gouts of steam began filling the cramped bathroom but before the mirror was steamed over, Stephen caught sight of himself.

Twin sets of bloodshot eyes stared back at him. Great, pudgy purple bags hung under them. Little flecks of puke in various color speckled his face. His lips were cracked and split in several places.

It's the ghost of Stephen Paul.

The thought popped into the forefront of his mind before he could check it. Once there, it hung around like smoke, the smell still present, seeming to coat everything it had touched.

He turned away from the mirror abruptly and undressed.

The stinging shower felt like a baptism. It felt both freeing and condemning because with it came a semblance of normality.

Throughout the shower, Stephen kept returning to the otherworldliness of the previous day and a half's experience. The dreamlike quality of it all. The misplacement of time and memory. The snippets of horror. Everything spinning out of control.

It took him some time to realize he was crying again.

The hot water blanketed his naked body, but he was shaking.

Nothing is ever going to be the same again, he thought, squeezing his eyes shut.

He tried his best to clear everything from his mind. He focused on the patter of the water on the thin metal tub he was standing in. He placed the palms of both of his hands against the bulging tiling and tried to slow his breathing.

In, he thought. *Out. In. Out. Breathe.*

Then, under the steam and hot water and new stance, a berg of crusted, dried shit dislodged from the crack of his ass and hit the tub between his feet with a heavy splat and he was laughing, laughing like he hadn't laughed since he was kid. Wild, crazy trills of it pouring out of his mouth. He kept his eyes shut, head under the showerhead and let it happen.

§

When he was out of the shower and toweled off, Stephen looked for his phone, his wallet, and his bag. None of these items were in his apartment. His car was not out in the front drive either.

The shower and the crying had exhausted him. He'd wished desperately for his things to be in the apartment. All he wanted, the most he could wish for in the entire world, was to find his things neatly sitting on the kitchen table and his warm bed waiting.

"Fuck it," he said.

He sat on the bed, feeling the springs give under his weight, the familiar scent of the room, the softness of the quilt. He let himself slowly sink into the bed. Felt the tiredness wash over him and closed his eyes.

A.S. COOMER

But his brain wouldn't turn off.

Images of his keys and wallet and cell phone and bag and car on infinite repeat, mixed with snippets from the previous day. The cell. The puke. The weird, hallucination-like images of stumbling around in the night that he wasn't sure was real or imagined.

"Fuck," he said, opening his eyes.

He sat up and threw his legs over the side the bed.

Not gonna be able to sleep until...

The thought trailed off.

Until what? Until I find my wallet? My cell phone? he thought. *What about all that lost time? Am I going to be able to find that? Find out what happened? What happened to me? What I did?*

Stephen stood up and slid his legs into a clean pair of jeans. He found a shirt then a sweater and made his way back into the living room. He slipped his bare feet into a pair of shoes and tied the laces slowly. Every motion seemed to take all the effort he could muster.

I'll walk to the office, he told himself. *If my shit isn't there, I'll walk back and sleep. I'll deal with this mess tomorrow.*

He unlocked the door, opened it and stepped out. Out of habit, he turned to lock the door.

He cringed and shut it with something just less than a slam.

The stairs squeaked and groaned under his weight.

"Ditto," he breathed out.

He put his hands in his pockets and walked to campus. He hadn't even made it off his block when his stomach growled.

They didn't even feed me, he thought. *I was in there for an entire day and the fuckers didn't even feed me.*

He shook his head and balled his hands into fists in his pants pockets.

That's something I'll be sure to tell the judge, he thought.

Then he realized he didn't know when the hearing or trial or whatever it was to be was. He slowed as a new sense of panic swept over him.

What if I miss it? What if they lock me up again for missing it and I didn't even know the date. That idiot attorney didn't tell me anything.

His brain, frazzled and tired, now seemed to squeeze his skull like some emerging black hole.

What is happening?

He picked up his pace. Movement felt vital. As long as he was moving, he could keep the panic just below the surface.

First things first, he thought, using his calmest internal voice. *Find the phone and wallet. Make sure some hobo doesn't have my debit and credit cards. Then I can call that asshat, Streeter, and figure out how to make this absurdity disappear.*

He was breathing heavily. His stomach reminding him with every other step that it was empty. The slight hill rising to the building housing the English Department, looking like a great brick and stone fortress overly lit in the deepening night, loomed ahead.

What if Hagan finds out?

The thought hit him like an icy slap, and before he knew what he was doing, Stephen was running up the hill towards his office.

§

The door to his office was ajar. Stephen was wheezing badly and sweating freely as he pushed the door open.

He flipped the switch just inside the door and a harsh white light flooded everything. He blinked several times. He never used the overhead lights because of their harshness, the lights tended to give him headaches if he worked under them for too long; he much preferred the easy yellow softness of his corner and desk lamps.

He quickly scanned the room. His bag, which he desperately hoped contained his cellphone and wallet, was not on his desktop nor hanging on the coatrack in the corner.

Then he saw a portion of his bag's strap peeking out from under the desk.

He heaved a sigh of relief and crossed the office. Plopping down onto the chair and leaning forward to pick up the bag, Stephen caught the presence of something on his desk out of the corner of his eye. He picked up the bag and turned to the desk.

A yellow Post-It note was stuck to the open screen of his laptop.

```
We need to talk. ASAP.
- Hagan
```

Stephen stared at the note for a long moment.

Great.

He tore himself away from the note and sunk his hands in his bag. His cellphone was there. He pulled it out and unlocked the screen. It was bombarded with emails and texts. He had several missed phone calls from the English Department office line. He turned to his office phone and saw the red blinking light of voice messages and missed calls.

Great, he thought. *Just great.*

He started scrolling through the notification screen then stopped himself remembering his wallet. He put the phone down on the desk and sank his hands back into the bag.

It wasn't there.

"Shit," he said.

He checked again, turning on the desk and corner lamps and holding the bag under the light, examining each pocket quickly, then slowly, then quickly again.

"Shit!"

He let the bag fall onto the floor.

He had no clue where his wallet could be. His identification, debit and credit cards, health and auto insurance cards, a little bit of cash, everything was in there.

He picked the bag up again and searched for his keys. They weren't in there either.

"Goddamn it," he said, throwing the bag across the room. It struck the half-open door and sent it slamming shut.

Stephen plopped his elbows onto the desk and covered his face with his hands.

He felt on the verge of an exhausted, tearful breakdown. He sighed heavily and clenched his eyes shut against the stinging of fresh tears.

Will I ever run out of the damn things? he thought. *I didn't think anybody had this many tears in them. I'm going to shrivel up and die from dehydration if I cry any damn more.*

There was a quick succession of raps at his door.

He snapped his head up and caught his breath.

No, he thought. *Not now. Please. Not now.*

He didn't answer. He continued holding his breath.

The knocks sounded again, this time in triplets.

Knockknockknock. Pause. *Knockknockknock.*

"Yes?" Stephen asked, his voice sounding hoarse and nearly breaking.

The door swung open and Dr. Hagan, stony faced and impending, stepped inside.

"Professor Paul," he said.

"It's not a good time, Dr. Hagan," Stephen said.

The Head of the English Department stood in the middle of Stephen's office looking down at him.

"Where have you been?" he asked. "You haven't returned any of the phone calls or emails I've left. You missed your class this afternoon."

Stephen nodded his head and looked away.

"You've got some serious explaining to do, Paul," he said.

Stephen didn't reply.

A silence, charged and brimming, filled the room.

"Well?" Dr. Hagan demanded.

"I need a little time," Stephen said.

"A little time?"

Stephen nodded.

"You also missed your appointment with Dr. Shumaker this afternoon."

Stephen must've looked confused.

"For your grief counseling."

"Oh," Stephen said.

Another long, pregnant silence.

Dr. Hagan took a step closer, leaned over the desk, his face remaining unreadable to Stephen.

"Professor Paul, I'm doing my best to keep you on this faculty," he said, "but you're not doing yourself any favors."

Stephen looked up, made brief eye contact, then looked down and away.

"Go home, Paul," Dr. Hagan said. "Get some rest. You look terrible. Reschedule your appointment with Dr. Shumaker for tomorrow, do not miss it, and see me in my office first thing in the morning."

He stared down at Stephen for a several more uncomfortable moments then turned and left Stephen's office, pulling the door closed behind him.

§

Stephen sat for some time staring at the grain of the closed door. It was late; Stephen heard no passing footsteps in the hall outside. The place was quiet, the sound of a phone ringing on unanswered from several offices down, and Stephen's own breathing the only sounds.

Tears fell from his eyes, splashing down onto his pants. He didn't bother to wipe them away.

Stephen turned to the computer and set about checking the thirty-four emails in his University inbox, sixteen of which were marked "urgent" in the various shades of red the University's email client used. There were emails from all the people you never wanted to receive emails from: the Provost, the Dean of Academic Affairs, the Dean of Student Relations, the Office of Legal Affairs, the Office of Talent Development, Chancellor of Advancement, the list went on.

It seemed all of the emails used similar catchphrases: troubled, assistance, leave, professionalism.

Stephen read what he assumed would be the most important of the emails first: three from Dr. Hagan, one from the President's Office, one from Dr. Miriam Shumaker, and one from the Provost. Stephen was being placed on unpaid leave for a period of two weeks beginning the next day. He was required, according to some obscure clause of his adjunct contract, to meet with the grief counselor twice weekly, which was to be "closely monitored" by the English Department, the Office of Legal Affairs, Talent Development, and the Provost.

Stephen felt his face brightening in a mixture of embarrassment and rage.

He quickly skimmed the rest of the emails, relieved that his arrest had not been mentioned once. He thought about emailing Legal Affairs back and asking if there was any protection in his contract against being canned for being arrested if he beat the charges, but stayed his nervous hands.

No use opening that can of worms, he thought. *They'll find out or they won't. I'm not gonna be the one to tell them.*

He closed the emails and looked at the blue screen.

Rivers. The light.

Images of the dream he'd had in jail. He opened the file named "Bondsman" and felt his body tensing. He hoped against everything that the file would contain all the work he'd put in. All the lines he rewrote over the years. The internal dialogue honed to a shining blade of honesty and truth. The mired haze of otherworldly description and allusions to inner planes of existence.

The cursor blinked, on and off, aligned left, in a sea of blank whiteness.

A great rushing sob escaped his lips. His hands shot up unconsciously to stifle it.

Gone. It's all gone.

It felt like a gigantic fist of ice sucker punched him in the guts. The air rushed out of his lungs and Stephen could only gasp at trying to get them refilled.

No! his mind screamed. *No, no, no, no no no!*

§

The henhouse is an abattoir painted red, red, red.

The hens and the rooster are all dead, dead, dead.

The fox is sly, keeps a watchful eye.

Patience pays a pretty penny and the hawk still gets fed.

§

Stephen came to in his apartment. He was standing at the kitchen sink, both hands clasped around the basin, the bones creaking audibly with the pressure of his squeezing. The water was turned as hot as it would go. He was hovering over the steam as it rose from the dish-filled sink. His face coated in sweat and condensation.

He shut the water off abruptly and stepped backwards away from the intense heat of the steam. The front of his clothes was soaked. Sweat coated his body.

What the fuck.

All the lights were off in the kitchen. He crossed the room, bemused to find he was barefoot, and flipped the light switch. A metallic tinkle, then the overhead light flashed on much too brightly, then petered out, then came back on slowly.

What?

Stephen looked down from the light to see his feet were filthy. They were covered in mud, his toenails grimy and cracked, and, by following the little trail he'd made across the living room, Stephen could tell they were bleeding. He leaned back against the door and brought his right leg into his hands, twisted over and examined the bottom of his foot. It was scratched to all hell, several of the cuts still bleeding but most coated

A.S. COOMER

with dried blood or in various stages of clotting.

Stephen let go of his foot and slid down to the dirty linoleum.

His body was shaking. The beginning of a migraine, blinding tornados of pain he'd endured on a monthly basis since childhood, was blossoming between his eyes at the place where the bridge of his nose met his forehead.

Stephen pressed hard at his temples. He couldn't remember leaving his office or the University. Didn't know how he got home. Didn't know where his shoes were. Didn't know why he'd been hovering over the steaming sink.

Something is very wrong with me, he thought and resolved to keep the appointments with Dr. Miriam Shumaker.

§

He woke to the sound of his cellphone alarm. He shut it off and sat up in bed. It was raining outside, little splashes all over the inside of the window-pane. He stood up, shut the window, and dressed. He made himself a pot of coffee, something he hadn't done at home for some time, and sat at the kitchen table with a steaming cup of black coffee watching the light, hazy rain fall through the dirty, cracked window.

He tried his best not to move. His entire body hurt, felt like he'd been hit by something large and moving fast. A truck or bus maybe. It felt like the beginnings of the flu or the day after the most intense workout of his life.

He lifted the cup with both slightly shaking hands and sipped. He felt the heat trickle down his throat into his stomach and waited. He had four hours before his appointment with Dr. Shumaker and he was on leave. No classes to teach. Nowhere to be. Nothing to do. He sat and watched the rain and drank the coffee doing his best to think of absolutely nothing.

§

The hens.
The fox.
The hawk.

§

"Did you have some transportation trouble this afternoon, Stephen?" Dr. Shumaker asked.

Stephen was sweating. He'd run nearly all the way to the Park Wing of the Health and Social Sciences Building.

"I know I'm late," he said, sitting down in the same chair. "I'm sorry."

Stephen had lost all track of time. He'd been staring out the kitchen window all afternoon, a great blankness filling him like rough cotton stuffing. The pitter patter of the falling drops hypnotizing him into a torpid stupor. The screeching of locked tires on wet pavement brought him to consciousness and, with a panicked horror, he saw the time.

Dr. Shumaker didn't say anything. This was something Stephen was learning. She liked to let Stephen do the talking. She wanted to see where he'd take things, what topics or thoughts or feelings would bubble to the forefront of his mind. It was a bit unnerving to Stephen, who always hated silence in small groups. He'd read, in hundreds of books, of a "comfortable silence" but had never in his life experienced this.

He fidgeted in the chair.

"I…" he began. "I'm sorry I'm late."

He didn't know what else to say.

Help me, he thought. *I'm losing my mind. I've got vast tracks of time I can't place. I don't know what's happening to me.*

"How are you feeling today, Stephen?" Dr. Shumaker asked after several minutes of uncomfortable silence.

"Fine," he said.

He cringed at the lie.

At the far edges of my consciousness, I keep having little nursery rhymes or something pop up. I don't know what it means.

"Fine?" she asked. "Are you fine with being placed on leave?"

He flinched before he could stop himself.

Everybody knows. They're all talking about me, he realized. *The whole hierarchy of them. All talking about little ol', grief-stricken Stephen Paul, adjunct.*

"I guess not," he said.

"Why do you think you've been placed on leave, Stephen?"

"I was late to some classes."

"What do you think the underlying causes of your tardiness might be?"

Stephen moved around in the chair. He wanted to tell this person, this healthcare professional, that he needed her professional help. He didn't know what to do but he couldn't open his mouth and let the words out.

"Alarm didn't go off," he muttered.

"Uh hm."

Silence. Awkward, fidgety silence.

Is everything boxed up, categorized, labeled "Memorabilia" when we're done? Does Rivers mean anything to anybody but me? His story a blank screen and flashing cursor. My story something sad and pathetic and skippable. Adjunct professor loses his mind after colleague's death. Goes on to produce absolutely nothing of lasting value.

"Stephen, there are people here concerned about you," Dr. Shumaker said finally.

There it is. The dreaded sentence.

People. Concerned. About you.

It didn't feel so much as concern as it did accusation.

Why can't you fulfill your contractual obligations to the University and your students? Why couldn't you produce something worth reading? Why? Why? Why? How come, huh?

The tears were stinging his eyes and nasal cavities again.

The tears, he thought bitterly. *I've never cried so much in my life. Something is wrong with me.*

"Talking helps, Stephen," Dr. Shumaker said. "We can work through this. Together."

The tears mounted the rims of his eyelids and spilled down onto his cheeks. He wiped them away briskly and rose to his feet. With short, uneven steps, he crossed the room to the window and looked out on the gentle rain and manicured lawn.

Dr. Shumaker did not speak. She was giving Stephen some leash again. Waiting to see what he'd say or do, gauging his mental processes like an auto mechanic starting a troubled engine and listening to the sputtering, broken sounds it makes.

Stephen closed his eyes and tried to control himself. He felt on the verge of an implosion. Something wildly destructive but only visible on the inside of himself. He was going to implode and disappear. He was going to be outside his own realm of control and culpability. He was terrified.

"Stephen," Dr. Shumaker said.

It was something in the voice. A slight edge, a tiredness, a mother approaching the end of the tether of her patience.

Stephen turned around and he found he was suddenly, frighteningly calm. His hands were relaxed. The weight that had been sitting and increasing on his chest released. He hadn't known how much it was affecting him until its absence.

"Yes, ma'am," Stephen said, sitting back in the chair. "I'm sorry."

He felt in control again.

"Sorry, Dr. Shumaker," he said. "I was a bit out of sorts but I'm OK now."

Dr. Shumaker's eyebrows made twin humps across her forehead.

§

Stephen walked home from his appointment slowly. He stopped several times when, just barely audible, he heard a childlike voice whispering or singing. He saw no children or person around. He watched the branches dance in the wind, shedding raindrops like glassy pearls of tears.

§

Stephen remembered Archie late that night. Archie Remington, who'd Stephen played countless hours of video games and *Dungeons & Dragons* with in middle school, had also returned to Toledo after several years to teach at the University.

Archie taught Master's level courses dealing in the Computer Sciences, all with titles that Stephen heard and then, immediately, forgot: Algorithm Analysis, Network Architecture, and the like. Stephen had never been too web-savvy and had turned to Archie on several occasions in the past year and a half that Archie had been on faculty for tech assistance. The University Helpdesk was atrociously hard to contact and work with.

Archie can retrieve the story, he knew. *He can do whatever it is that they do to mine the hard drive for deleted data and restore it, right as rain.*

Stephen smiled. He felt better. He emailed Archie from his phone as soon as he pushed in the unlocked door of his apartment.

§

They met in Archie's office, in the post-modern Franklin Building, all shining glass and a strange mixture of sharp, jangled angles and round, sweeping curves, the next evening. Archie had suggested that Stephen bring his laptop in during the workday, but Stephen cited some imaginary entanglement and pushed the meeting until late, when most students and faculty would be gone. Stephen did not want to run into any of his English Department colleagues or students on his way to pick up the laptop or his way across campus to the Franklin Building.

"How's it going?" Archie asked, through a mouthful of pizza.

"Hi, Archie," Stephen said, pulling the office door shut.

Archie motioned for Stephen to take one of the two black metallic mesh chairs beside his desk.

"Want some pizza?" he asked.

Stephen shook his head though he couldn't remember the last time he'd eaten. He hadn't felt hungry in some time.

"Why'd you close the door?"

Stephen turned back to the door as if it held some answer.

"I don't know, I just—"

"It's cool, man, it's just that this is an Overlapping Zone."

"A what?"

"An Overlapping Zone. You've read that University of Michigan paper about it, right?"

Archie did not wait for Stephen's response.

"These researchers studying a laboratory saw that scientists were more likely to collaborate in these little areas where their workspaces intersected," Archie made twin circles, arching the four fingers of each hand until they met his thumbs, and overlapped his hands until a fleshy Venn diagram was formed.

"So, you all don't have individual offices?" Stephen asked, noticing a gig poster for the English band, Muse, on the wall behind Archie.

Stephen shook his head. He couldn't imagine the old, cranky, cat-like English professors ever getting on board with an office setup like that. Stephen knew he'd hate it.

"No, man, we do it's just that we don't like to think of them as *our* offices, you know? We like to think of ourselves as a *collective*."

"I see."

Archie finished the last of the crust.

"So, you've got some hard drive problems?" he asked, wiping his mouth and thick but tidy beard with a napkin.

"I don't know if it's that," Stephen said.

He unzipped his bag and pulled out his university-issued laptop.

"I had this document..." Stephen said, handing the laptop over the desk to Archie.

Archie nodded his head, but a look of disdain came across his face when he saw the laptop.

"What?" Stephen asked.

"I can't believe they still got you all using Inspirons."

Stephen shrugged his shoulders. He knew it was a Dell but that was as much as he really knew about the thing.

"Jesus Christ! An 11 3000?" Archie let loose one sharp bark of laughter. "I can't believe it. At least it's the two-in-one model."

"The what?"

"Two-in-one. It's touchscreen."

Stephen watched Archie open the laptop screen and fold it backwards. He kept expecting to hear the sound of plastic straining and shattering but, to his surprise, the screen moved smoothly backwards and the start-up screen loaded.

"See," Archie said, using his finger to tap the screen and open the computer's settings screen. "You can even fine tune it based on your finger sensitivity."

Stephen watched him carefully tap several times on the screen then move the cursor about on the screen with varying speeds.

"I had no clue," Stephen said.

Archie looked at his friend incredulously, then laughed.

"You English profs."

Stephen did his best impression of an ingratiating smile and said, "Guess that's why we keep you all around."

"So, where's this file?" Archie said, tapping away on the screen. He'd folded the computer like some sort of technological origami until it was standing like a capital A, the screen facing him.

"If you go to My Documents, then the folder named Stories. It'll be the fourth—"

"How about just the name of the file doc? It'll be easier just to search for it."

"Oh, OK. It's called *Bondsman*."

A.S. COOMER

"Bondsman? Like James Bond? You writing spy stories, man? I can get behind that. They always have the best tech. Even the old ones, you know with Roger Moore and the pimps."

"It's nothing quite..." Stephen searched for the word but came up blank, "like that. I'm using bondsman as a metaphor for artists."

Archie raised his eyebrows and continued tapping away at the up-turned laptop.

"We're all born with innate gifts or aptitudes: for some it's technological acuity," Stephen motioned towards the computer, "some can intuit or comprehend the inner workings of molecular biology, for others it's the ability to create works of art."

Archie nodded but did not look up from the computer.

"The premise of the novel is that we're all our own bondsman. We've been released on bail, set loose on the world with these innate traits or skillsets and if we don't fulfill our artistic obligations then we'll have to pay in the long run. Everybody has a deeper purpose and finding that purpose then maximizing it to the nth degree is the goal, but what happens when you purposefully ignore that purpose? What if there's a psychological ghost or, at least, a mental deterioration due to the pains of ignoring what you're hardwired to do that drives one crazy enough to imagine seeing a ghost or ghosts, that haunts you if you don't meet your obligation to yourself and the world, in general? What happens if you jump bail?"

Archie made a noise that sounded like "ah".

"The protagonist is a failed writer who no longer wants to write. He feels every urge and pull and prod to write but he hasn't been successful in his career thus far. Been rejected by all the major literary magazines and journals, even by most of the smaller ones too. He's started several novels but never finished them. He feels the pressure too acutely. He decides one day that it's not worth it, despite everything in him screaming otherwise. He ignores the urge, his calling, the writing, and becomes haunted."

Another noncommittal noise from Archie, who still hadn't looked up from the screen.

"Rivers, that's the protagonist, goes off on a wander. Walks, hitchhikes, camps, flees his duty, his creative responsibility, in a myriad of ways and is, all the while, depending on your reading of the thing, either steadily and increasingly haunted by his bondsman or loses his mind and goes mad."

"I see the file here," Archie said, still staring down at the upturned computer. "Bondsman. The logs show it's been opened and closed consistently for a while. Created. Modified. Accessed. Revision count is…" Archie looks astonished, "4,789. Jesus, you've tinkered with this thing quite a bit, huh?"

Stephen felt a momentary embarrassment that his pride quickly extinguished.

"Of course, writing requires great revision."

He revised the line in his head: *great writing requires revision.*

"But the thing is, indeed, blank," Archie said.

"I know," Stephen said. "That's why I came to you. Everything in there is gone. The whole thing. Gone."

Archie nodded but did not look up. His face showed a concentration Stephen often saw on mechanics when he was getting his oil changed or work done on his aging Corolla. He'd seen the face on musicians in open jams too, which he used to attend often in undergrad. Standing up on the stage, listening to what was being played around them, that look would flutter across their faces as they pieced together the song as a whole and their part in it. It was a careful weighing and scrutiny that went beyond the immediate sense of being watched or putting on a face matched specifically to the place or time. It was the look of total mental commitment.

"I see," Archie said.

He tapped the screen several more times then fell silent, his eyes still locked on the computer.

"You're sure it was this document?" he asked, finally. "This one titled *Bondsman?*"

"Yes," Stephen said.

Archie pushed himself back from the desk, the wheels on his computer chair gliding silently, and looked at Stephen.

"That document has always been empty."

"What?"

"It seems there was a title on there at one point," Archie looked back at the screen, tapped a few times then continued, "and your name but there was never anything else in there. You're sure you're not mistaking this one for another file?"

"What? No. There must be some mistake."

"You've got Word set to automatically Save even if you don't click it. I've been through all the .WBK files and they're all the same. Blank. Or blank but with the title. Or blank but with the title and your name. There's nothing else here," Archie said.

Stephen sat back in the chair and didn't speak.

Archie looked uncomfortable. He glanced from the screen to Stephen then back to the screen. He scooted forward in the chair and started tapping again, not looking up at Stephen.

"I'll search for other Word docs. Maybe it got misnamed or something."

Stephen knew this was not the case. He felt lightheaded and tired. He wanted to feel angry and shocked that his work had vanished.

Hours. Days. Months. Years, he thought. *All that time pounding away at what I knew was going to be a damn fine novel. Something with meaning. Not just another airplane paperback, Janet Evanovich or James Patterson or Nora Roberts, to pass the time with but something of value, something lasting. Gone.*

"Man, I'm not seeing anything on here," Archie said. "You grab the wrong laptop or something?"

A.S. COOMER

Stephen shook his head.

Hours. Days. Months. Years.

Gone.

§

The henhouse is empty.
The farmer's passed out.
The corn hangs plump, unpicked and drooping.
Old Betsy's got the gout.

§

Stephen was sitting at his kitchen table. He'd been asleep, or thought he had been, but there was a cup of black coffee on the table before him. The rain was trickling down the overfilled gutters and running in little rivulets down the cracked window. Some of it was slipping through the crack and pooling up on the inside of the windowsill.

Stephen picked up the coffee and sipped. It was cold.

He hadn't remembered making it.

He set the mug down.

He didn't remember leaving Archie's office.

He checked his watch and saw twelve hours had passed. It was morning. To find himself sitting at his kitchen table with a mug of coffee shouldn't feel abnormal, but it did.

He began to shake.

What is happening to me?

The needle of a record was stuck on a slipped groove of vinyl. Infinite repeat. Skip. Skip. Skipping.

Where was Rivers? Did I imagine him? he thought. *I mean, of course, I imagined him, but did I imagine* writing *him?*

Stephen saw himself from above, hunched over the laptop, stoned or dazed, sober or crazed, the vistas of his various apartments, student computer labs, faculty offices, staring at a blinking cursor on a blank screen. *Nothing and nothing and more nothing.*

The breaking of Rivers' ties to his family. The sinking of the cargo ship his brother worked on. The rapid rise and fall of his short-lived fame as a short story writer. The marriage. The miscarriage. The divorce. The life Stephen felt fell from the ether into his fingers then onto the screen. The life of a person real to him. Rivers Stanton. Rivers. Stanton. Bondsman. Gone.

Stephen shattered the kitchen window with the coffee mug. It wasn't as loud as he expected it would've been. The thin pane of glass exploded outward and fell into the rose bushes below. Stephen had no recollection of a plan to shatter the window. No rise of fury to blame. He had just picked up the mug of cold coffee and flung it at the crack slowly dripping water.

Stephen heard exclamations of surprise from below. The opening and slamming of his downstairs neighbor's, and landlord's, door then the sound of stomping steps on the staircase. The full-fisted beating at his apartment door.

Stephen did not move. He sat, mute, watching the droplets fall into the kitchen.

Waning Crescent

T he police cruiser pulled up to the house, siren off but lights flashing. The rain had petered into a light mist. Two police officers emerged and were immediately enveloped by Wren Risner, Stephen's landlord. Through the shattered window, Stephen could hear her near hysteric voice spitting out invectives and laments in rapid succession.

He hadn't answered the door when she pounded. He knew she had a key and could open it if she wished but she hadn't so he hadn't bothered getting up from his place at the table. He'd never liked Wren Risner but hadn't ever had an actual problem with her before. When he first moved in, soon after taking the adjunct position he still held, his first paycheck had been delayed by some Accounts Payable screw-up, probably some stoned student's blundering work-study, and he'd had to ask for an extra two weeks to pay his first month's rent. Ms. Risner hadn't thrown him in the streets, but she didn't shy away from showing her disgust at Stephen's financial situation.

Both officers stared at Stephen through the broken window for several moments while Wren Risner's incessant voice ran on. Stephen did not shy away from their gaze but held it and remained seated. The officers shared a look, then the male, pudgy and bald-headed, led Wren Risner to her first-floor apartment and the female, short but muscled, walked around the house to the stairs that ascended to Stephen's kitchen.

The officer knocked on the door. Stephen got up, slowly, and answered it.

"Hello," he said.

"Hi, there," she said. "What's going on today, Mr. Paul?"

"Nothing much," Stephen said. "Come on in."

He stepped aside allowing the police officer inside.

"There seems to be a large hole in your window there," she said, the corners of her lips hinting at a droll smile.

Stephen shut the kitchen door and turned slowly, first to the officer then to the window. He raised his eyebrows in mock surprise.

"There does, indeed, seem to be a large hole in my window there."

"Care to elaborate on how that there large hole occurred in said window?"

Stephen looked back at the window.

"It was an accident," he said.

"An accident?"

"Yes, ma'am."

"I see."

They both looked from each other to the window and back again.

"And why wouldn't you let Mrs. Risner in when she came knocking after hearing that there window break?"

"She was yelling a lot."

"I see."

"Well."

"Well."

"I'm going to get the window replaced."

"Yes. You are."

"Would you care for a cup of coffee?"

"Was that your only mug?"

Stephen couldn't help it. He laughed. He laughed and laughed and laughed.

As he laughed, Stephen saw the moment when the police officer's amusement ended. He saw this very clearly. Her posture changed. She stood more fully erect. The hands, crossed at her chest, fell to her sides, closer to her holster. She did not take a step backwards, but Stephen sensed that she was a bit further away.

This did absolutely nothing to stymie his laughter.

"Mr. Paul?" the officer asked. "Are you OK?"

Stephen wiped tears from his eyes.

"I've got another," he said, knowing it was no answer at all.

§

The other officer, perspiration and raindrops slipping off his bare, shining crown, came up the stairs panting and entered without knocking.

Stephen had finished laughing but felt his entire body vibrating with another fit of it threatening to break out at any moment. The muscles in his face and stomach hurt.

"What'd we got?" the male officer asked his partner.

"Accident," she said.

"Accident?"

She nodded.

The man looked at Stephen. It was a scrutinizing, sizing-up look that made Stephen shake with nearly bubbling over laughter.

"You're paying for a replacement window, then," the man said.

It was not a question.

Stephen nodded, not trusting himself to speak.

"OK. Write it up on an Incident for HQ. We'll have to—"

He thought about offering the man a cup of coffee too and a squeak leapt from his closed mouth.

"What was that?" the man asked.

"Nothing. Sorry," Stephen said. "Throat is itchy. Allergies, I think."

The man hesitated, eyeing Stephen with a growing suspicion, then turned back to his partner and discussed paperwork.

Stephen walked over to the window and set about picking up some of the glass shards that remained upturned and jagged in the frame like an anglerfish's teeth. He set them carefully on the table while the officers finished up.

He signed a report including a short two-sentence paragraph as to his description of what transpired.

The cup slipped and broke the window. It was an accident.

He nearly erupted in fresh waves of laughter at the words. His stomach was beginning to hurt with the tension of keeping himself from laughing.

Stephen hadn't even hesitated when handed the pen and form. He wrote those two sentences immediately, signed it, and returned it to the female officer, who was watching him carefully, all traces of a smile gone from her face.

"Get this fixed ASAP," the male officer said over his shoulder as he exited the kitchen.

"Yes, sir," Stephen said. He had to stop his arm from rising in a military salute.

The female officer stood for a moment longer, watching Stephen.

"You sure you're OK, Mr. Paul?"

Stephen felt his lips trembling.

He nodded his head.

She turned and left the kitchen, shutting the door softly behind her.

Stephen sank back into the chair at his table and covered his mouth. The little peals of laughter were muffled but he was afraid the police would still hear him.

He heard the downstairs apartment door bang shut and watched Wren Risner race across the damp yard barefooted in pursuit of the officers. Her voice carried easily through the glassless window, but Stephen only caught bits and pieces of what she said. His focus was on laughter containment.

"Always smells like pot up there."

"Not going to arrest him? He damaged my property willfully!"

"I just can't believe this!"

"I'm going to talk to my councilman about this!"

And so on.

The officers got into their cruiser despite the protestations of the frazzled landlady. Stephen saw both of them, harried faces of the overworked and underpaid and often abused, look up from inside the vehicle one last time at him before they pulled away.

§

Stephen quivered. He'd laughed until he was tired. His nose was dripping snot and his cheeks felt bruised. He still sat at the kitchen table.

The knock at his kitchen door made him jump. He hadn't heard anyone ascend the stairs. He turned in the chair but did not get up.

Wren Risner stood peering in through the kitchen door window. Her face was stern, the crow's-feet at the corners of her eyes made bold stretched lines nearly to her ears. She stared at him with hard, angry eyes and knocked three times on the door without blinking.

Stephen rose and smiled. He opened the door a crack and spoke with his landlord through it.

"Hi," Stephen said.

"What's wrong with you?"

"I'm fine, thanks."

"You're fixing that goddamn window," she said. "I don't care what the cops say."

"Yes."

"You're also moving out."

"Moving out?"

She nodded and smiled. It was not a pleasant smile. It was more a baring of nicotine-stained teeth than anything else.

"Yes, sirreebob," Ms. Wren said. "You're moving the hell out of here by the end of the month."

Stephen said nothing.

Where will I go? he thought.

"I think the lease calls for a notice of—"

"Fuck that lease. You voided the lease when you willfully destroyed my property. Private property. Something the founding fathers would hold as sacrilege. Hippy potheads like you and your college degrees think you can jus—"

Stephen softly closed the door on the diatribe.

He watched Wren Risner's face blossom red and pink. Her voice rose and curses were issued. Stephen smiled, his face crooked with the cramped, over-used muscles, as most of what his landlady yelled was heard through the gaping hole in the kitchen window.

§

Horses run.
Sparrows sing.
The harvest moon's sad smile sidles

As the fox slips between corn row aisles.

§

"How have you spent the past few days, Stephen?" Dr. Shumaker asked.

Stephen crossed his legs.

"Oh, I've kept busy," he said.

At something in Stephen's voice, Dr. Shumaker cocked her head slightly to the left.

"Oh?" she asked.

Stephen smiled.

"I've drank a lot of coffee."

The grief counselor's face showed genuine concern when Stephen's laughter stretched longer than a minute.

"Are you OK," she asked when Stephen finally got control of himself.

"I don't know."

"What's going on?" she asked.

"I don't know."

"What are you thinking?"

"I'm wondering if our talks have doctor-patient confidentiality coverage."

"You're afraid to speak candidly to me?"

"I'm afraid of what you might tell Dr. Hagan."

Stephen was astonished with himself. He hadn't intended on saying any of these things. He'd planned on keeping his appointment then strolling through the student center to check out the fliers advertising cheap, student-friendly apartments for rent.

I'm no longer in control, he thought. Stephen saw the sentence in black, inky letters on a pristine white sheet of paper. He saw it like that and read it to himself. Then he read it out loud.

"I'm no longer in control," he said.

Dr. Shumaker waited for Stephen to elaborate but when he didn't she said, "I see."

Stephen found he could not make eye contact with the grief counselor.

"I can't stop laughing," he said. "I can't stop crying."

Out of the corner of his eye, Stephen saw Dr. Shumaker nod and make some notes on the legal pad. The pen moved smoothly and made no noise.

"I have tracks of time I can't recall."

"What do you mean?"

"I have these little jingles in my head," Stephen said, straining to remember. "Like nursery rhymes or something. That's all I can remember."

"Stephen," Dr. Shumaker said, "you're not making a lot of sense."

"No," he said. "I'm not."

"What do you mean when you say you have tracks of time you can't recall?"

Stephen uncrossed his legs, fidgeted in the chair, then crossed them again.

"Well…" he began, "I'm not sure. I'm there one moment, then there's some sort of jingle or song or something and then I'm somewhere else and can't recall where I've been or what I've done or anything."

"That sounds frightening."

Stephen turned to her. The brimming of tears made her face a smirch of white and glasses and lipstick.

"Yes," he said. "It is."

"You said you've been crying and laughing a lot," she said. "Have you been experiencing any other sort of emotions or feelings that you feel you can't control?"

Stephen saw the coffee mug hit the window in slow-motion. He saw the glass flex then shatter, exploding out into the rainy morning.

"Yes."

A pause.

"Stephen, I'd like to refer you to a colleague of mine," Dr. Shumaker said. "A good friend and psychiatrist that might be able to help us get a fuller understanding of things."

A fuller understanding of things, he thought. He saw that sentence appear on the pristine paper.

I am not in control.

A fuller understanding of things.

The two sentences formed a circle of sorts in his mind. He now knew that he was not in control. That lead him, eventually, to want a fuller understanding of things. He processed these two points in the circle, feeling each as profound and frightening. A perfectly smooth sphere, unblemished by pock or ending.

How do I regain some sense of control in my life? How do I achieve a fuller understanding of things?

Stephen felt numb taking the card from Dr. Shumaker. He waited as an appointment with the psychiatrist was scheduled for him by Dr. Shumaker's assistant for the following day. He waited, unseeing, unhearing, as another appointment with Dr. Shumaker was scheduled for the day after that.

Stephen walked home in a foggy silence. *I am not in control.* He saw the hard eyes of Wren Risner from behind the curtains of the first-floor apartment but paid her no mind. *A fuller understanding of things.* He

A.S. COOMER

took the stairs slowly, his head panging with the first signs of another migraine. He stopped and stood staring uncomprehendingly at his door. Something was amiss. It took him nearly a minute to figure out what was a wrong.

A yellow sheet of paper was taped to the door's window.

It read: *Notice of Eviction.*

§

Stephen took the yellow paper off the glass and entered the kitchen, leaving the door unlocked since he still hadn't found his keys.

Can't ask for a new key now, he thought.

He set the paper on the table, but it was promptly blown onto the linoleum. A stiff wind buffeted the little kitchen then died away. The curtains were all pushed to either side of the broken window. They ruffled in the breeze looking like wallflower ghosts at a high school dance.

Stephen didn't pick the Notice of Eviction up. He left it on the floor and walked to his bathroom. He stripped naked and stood under the hottest shower he'd ever taken.

He thought of his bank account: a pitifully small amount of money in there. He didn't think he'd have enough to scrape together a security deposit for a new apartment. He had some friends he could crash with, but he didn't know how long it'd take to get off his Hagan-imposed leave. *Tenured professors at least got paid leave when they lost their minds.* Without any money coming in and a $50 co-pay for each of his twice-a-week sessions with Dr. Shumaker—not to mention his appointment with the psychiatrist the next day, who knows how much that'd set him back— Stephen was afraid he'd hit the Big Zero soon. He'd been hovering there for some time.

Not to mention medicine, he thought. *Lord knows, the shrink'll want me on some medicine.*

He toweled himself off and stepped out of the rust-rimmed bathtub, the cheap plastic shower head still leaking water. He watched a slowly thinning river of water run down the bulging tiles on the wall, briefly picturing the amount of water-logged wood behind it. He pictured thick curds of white and dark green mold sprouting like some poisonous garden just on the other side of those stained, soap-scummed tiles.

Rot and decay just below the surface. Now, that's a metaphor.

Stephen wiped the steam from the bathroom mirror. He leaned forward, the cold ceramic sink pressed against his bare stomach, the towel wrapped around his waist, and stared at the fuzzy image of himself. A small, disheveled beard was growing on his cheeks and chin. The mustache coming in shades darker than the rest of his facial hair. There were thick, purple bags that seemed to hang like over-ripened fruit, plums maybe, nearly to the middle of his cheeks.

Jesus, I look awful.

There was something about his eyes that he couldn't look away from. Stephen leaned forward for a closer look.

Was one of his pupils slightly smaller than the other?

A.S. COOMER

Or is it that one of them was slightly larger than the other?

Little pinholes of light began a soft dance, a sugar plum fairy's measured jerk, sway and flit, starting at his peripheries then slowly cascaded inward until his field of vision was flooded with them. Stephen saw all of them with increasing horror but always from his periphery. He couldn't tear his gaze from his own two, slightly differential sized pupils.

He watched one until he felt as black as the pupil, then watched the other. An inky wasteland stretched out across the blank horizon. There seemed to be nothing there. No sense of identity. No sense of Stephen Paul, the struggling novelist and adjunct professor. No sense of humanity. Just a wasteland. Just desolation.

On some level of his inner workings, Stephen realized he'd been holding his breath the entire time he stared at himself in the mirror. He couldn't seem to break the tension of his muscles to let the stale air in his lungs out. He couldn't reengage the autopilot function of breathing.

Stephen gripped the edges of the vanity top swimming in an increasing dizziness. The sugar plum fairies fluttered and danced. The last thing Stephen saw before everything went black was the change in his facial expression: he was smiling.

§

Farmers come and farmers go.
The sun it sets and the moon it glows.
The fox is hungry. The owl is too.
Night comes in sweeping, looking for you.

§

"Mr. Paul?" the receptionist called.

Stephen looked up from the *Men's Health* magazine he'd been absently flipping through. He'd already been through three *National Geographic*'s and a three-month-old issue of *Time*. He realized as he dropped the magazine onto the table beside the chair, that he'd been picturing long, hanging, tubular breasts, those of some out-of-contact tribe in some far-off jungle region, on the photos of a young male, shirtless action-movie actor.

Stephen shook his head and followed the receptionist across the small waiting room to a closed door, which she opened and held for him to pass through.

"Stephen Paul?" a voice from within called.

"Yes."

"Have a seat," the psychiatrist said.

He was much older than Dr. Shumaker, probably in his late sixties or early seventies. He wore a small Van Dyke beard and rimless, oval-shaped glasses.

Stephen nearly laughed at how stereotypically shrink-ish the man looked.

"I'm Dr. Theo Trenton," he said.

Then he noticed Stephen's face.

"Oh dear," he said. "What's happened to your face, Mr. Paul?"

Stephen almost didn't stop himself from replying: *Repercussions of the sugar plum fairies dancing in the Wasteland.*

That'd be a perfect way to start a relationship with my psychiatrist, he thought.

"Slipped in the bathroom," he said, sitting on the thickly cushioned loveseat.

The office was an interesting mix of visual aesthetics. A large, expensively-framed print of Kandinsky's *Blue Segment* seemed to be the room's main focal point. There were three distinct bookshelves on three of the office's walls. The fourth wall was a heavily curtained window; thick mauve and green curtains of a somewhat paisley design kept most of the sunlight out.

From the vantage point of the loveseat where Stephen sat, the Kandinsky print hung just above and to the left of Dr. Theo Trenton. He found he could not focus on the psychiatrist but instead stared ceaselessly at the print.

"I see," Dr. Trenton said.

There it was again. That waiting, patient silence.

Stephen found it easier to accept the silence with the abstract painting to stare at.

"Mr. Paul, Dr. Shumaker said you were concerned about yourself."

Stephen nodded, not looking at Dr. Trenton. Stephen remembered the painting from an art history class he'd taken during the summer of his sophomore year. He'd initially thought the thing child's play, something anybody could throw together, just shapes and primary colors and no real sense of mastery about it, but the more he studied it, the more he came to gravitate to it. He finally *saw* the painting. He processed it through himself and found similarities. He saw the reaching hand of questing perfection. The crescent moon of a blue truth hidden somewhere in there.

Maybe not really hidden, he thought. *Maybe more like hidden in plain sight.*

"What do you find concerning, Mr. Paul?"

Where do I even begin?

Too much time must have passed for a reply.

"We can start elsewhere if, perhaps, it is easier?"

"Sure."

"Let's try starting with the University and your employment there?" Dr. Trenton asked. "I also heard that a friend and colleague of yours recently passed away."

"Robert," Stephen said. He hadn't intended on speaking out loud.

"Yes. Robert Wilkins. I've read one of his novels and a few of his short stories," Dr. Trenton said. "Very talented gentleman. A shame about his passing."

His passing, Stephen repeated. *Robert killed himself.*

"Yes," he said, a sour, metallic taste filling his mouth. Rusted pennies in turned milk.

"That must have been hard for you to deal with."

Farmers come and farmers go.

"Yes."

Stephen saw the beginnings of more sugar plum fairies and realized he was holding his breath again.

Dr. Trenton's gaze seemed to intensify.

Stephen followed the black lines of what he came to think of as claws. They hung suspended in the lower right side of the piece. One set of fingers seemed to be reaching for several brightly colored splotches of color. The other seemed to be reaching for the most complex portion of the painting: a collection of shapes vaguely urban, a piano-esk shape suspended amongst clouds and skyscrapers.

Stephen heard a faint humming and turned to locate the source.

Dr. Trenton's voice was audible, but he couldn't dissociate its sound from its meaning. There weren't any words there. Just the sound of his voice like the babble of a rising creek. The humming wasn't Dr. Trenton's, it sounded like it was coming from behind him, towards the door to the reception area.

"What's that sound?" he asked.

He didn't turn to receive Dr. Trenton's reply.

Stephen stood up, the sugar plum fairies spiraling and blanketing his peripheries, and made his way on unsteady feet towards the door.

"Where's it coming from?" he asked.

It was hard to speak.

Dr. Trenton's voice was alarmed now. The creek rising from a downpour somewhere upstream.

It took several fumbled attempts to open the office door.

"Who's making that sound?" he asked.

The startled face of the receptionist looked up from her desk. Her eyes were wide and her mouth was moving. She made to stand but Stephen was already falling.

His eyes were closed before he hit the thinly carpeted floor.

§

Swayed by hazy days in the sweltering shade.
The farmer's drunk, slippery whistles in a shifting daze.
The harried hens slump in fitful, restless sleep.
The owl yawns at the coming dawn and settles down for oaken roost.

§

There were flickers of consciousness. Stephen saw white rooms. White lights. White coated men and women with clipboards. Then there were the shades of blue. Blue-clad people bustling, most not paying him any mind. A blue-tied, blue-eyed familiar face he couldn't place. The cloudless blue sky of a late autumn afternoon. The depth of a cerulean pool he couldn't fathom his relationship to.

Then there were sounds. Horns and brass. Bassoon and flute. The distinct buzz of an alarm. The soft click of closing doors. The shuffling of chairs and the squeak of tennis shoes on an uncarpeted floor. The clink of cheap, metal eating utensils on cheap, ceramic dining sets. The constant hum and knocking of a radiator. The smell of overcooked oatmeal. The thickness of his tongue and the acidity of pulpy orange juice. Little ovals on his tongue. A numbness washing out all things around him. All the things he couldn't make sense of. His name disappearing in the mist. The sun, heatless and white, melting and spreading across the horizon. A dark-less, starless night.

Stephen slept.

§

He was prompted awake several times. Hands clasped his arms. Moved his chin upward. Lights flashed in his eyes. He saw the vague shapes of faces, eyes wet and large, cheeks drawn and pale, mouths closed and open. The smell of stale coffee. The sting like the bite of an insect somewhere on one of his useless arms.

Stephen slept.

§

Rivers stood leaned against a towering streetlamp.

Rivers Stanton.

Great blankets of fog shifted like untucked swaddling in some eternal night. A dull yellow shone down from the lamp. A loose corn kernel holding the last of the sun's harvest warmth. An anglerfish's waiting surprise.

Stephen's not sure Rivers can see him. Flytrapped and sticky in some glued-in darkness. He must speak to him. It is overwhelming, this sense of needing to communicate with Rivers Stanton.

"Rivers," he calls.

The man shows no sign of having heard.

Who is he waiting for? It must be me. It has to be me.

Rivers! I'm here. I'm right here.

His mouth isn't working. His brain tells his mouth to make the sounds but they scream out only in his head.

Rivers! Rivers Stanton!

Stephen sees the flicker then the flash of a light in the obscurantic night then the amber glow of a cigarette sending languid smoke up into the serried clots of fog.

"And how are we feeling this fine morn, Mr. Paul?" a cheery voice asked.

Stephen blinked. Nothing came into focus, so he blinked several more times.

"What?"

A rough wetness pulled at his cheeks then began rubbing at his eyes. Stephen tried to pull away but didn't have enough energy to move.

"Let's get you cleaned up for breakfast, shall we?" the voice crooned.

Stephen felt thick clobs of eye-crust break away from the sensitive area around his tear ducts.

He tried to speak but a fuzzy moan was all that he could muster.

"There," the mother cat's tongue licked him clean once more. "All better."

Stephen blinked and opened his eyes. The bright light of a nearly mid-day sun shone in a straight shaft, a column of radiance as captivating as a lava lamp, dust mites and other particles flashing in myriads of glints and twirling languorously in its incandescence.

Stephen breathed through his open mouth.

"Wow."

"Aren't you talkative this morning?" the voice said.

Stephen moved his eyes, his head felt too heavy to even consider turning, towards it. Two magnified eyes stared down at him. They were kind eyes. The kind eyes of an elderly person, someone's grandmother maybe. There was a twinkling in them indicative of happiness. Genuine happiness.

Stephen wondered when he'd last been truly happy and couldn't find an answer.

"Wher—" he tried to speak.

His open mouth felt full of cracks and cotton. His tongue some foreign reptilian usurper bathing in the slanted sunlight.

Stephen, with a herculean effort, forced his mouth to close and his heavy tongue to move around, searching for any moisture that hadn't evaporated in his slack-jawed daze.

"Thirsty?" the kind eyes asked. "Here. Open up."

Soft fingers opened his mouth for him and a trickle of cool water filled in the cracks. Stephen splashed it around with his tongue and coughed when some snaked down his throat unexpectedly.

"Easy now," the eyes said.

Stephen's eyes filled with tears and a sense of relief. He hadn't realized how dry they'd been.

Stephen coughed weakly a few more times.

"Thank…" he tried to speak.

"Ready for breakfast?"

At the sound of the word, Stephen's stomach rumbled. Yes, he was hungry. Very hungry.

The eyes disappeared. An abrupt sense of motion jerked Stephen's head backwards. It came to rest on something stiff but padded. He watched the column of light, the dancing particles still prancing, move away and a thin breeze of motion cooled his face, still slightly damp.

Stephen tried to focus his eyes on what was before him. He found his lids were heavy and the steady motion was making them harder to keep open. He saw a dully shining hallway lined with doors. He saw a wooden bench and a shape huddled there. He saw an alcove of great windows crystalline in the afternoon's gentle sun.

"Where?" he croaked.

"We're almost there, Mr. Paul," the kind eyes said from somewhere just behind. "Don't you fret none. There'll be plenty of chow for you when we get there."

Stephen couldn't help it. He slept.

§

His mouth was moving. Something warm and soggy and tasteless was being ground down by his teeth. He was chewing, he realized. He was eating something with no conscious will of his own. Some rote reflex, this eating. He was amazed that could happen.

Stephen couldn't open his eyes. He tried.

Stephen tried to lift his hands to his face to pry the lids open but found he couldn't do this either. He tried to wiggle his fingers, sent the appropriate brain waves to signal this response, but couldn't.

His mouth worked.

He slept.

§

There is a darkness more blue than black.

§

The rubbing woke him. His eyelids fluttered several times before he could get them under his control and open them.

Darkness. Quiet.

More rubbing.

The sound of stiff fabric friction. The scrape of a cat's tongue.

Stephen saw a huddled shape around his waist level. He was in a bed, he saw. Covered by sheets pale and creamlike in the dim light. He tried to focus on the sensation, what was happening, but his mind was slipping, sinking back into some deep blue-hued pool, some water so deep it seemed black.

"Wha—" he tried to speak.

The shapes seemed to flinch and pause. Then the rubbing intensified followed by a wet slurping sound. Stephen felt wetness spread across his groin area but at a distance. The sensation was there but it felt like touching your lips after a dental appointment: numb and torpid.

What is happening? he wondered.

Stephen sank back into sleep.

§

The cat plays with its prey
Another limbless gift deposited
Before the first golden light of Reaping Day.

§

The voice of the kind eyes woke him. Stephen blinked then closed his eyes as the wet rag came into focus heading for his face. His head felt fuzzy, a hayloft of field mice: tiny, scratching feet and itchy, prickling stalks.

"Good morning, Mr. Paul."

Stephen moaned. He felt thirstier than he'd ever been in his life.

"Would you like a drink of water?"

"Mm hm."

"Here you go."

Stephen drank.

"Thank," he said, his mouth still awkward and unwieldly like some new appendage.

"You're welcome," the kind eyes said, the voice rising with enthusiasm at his words. "You're quite welcome."

Stephen opened his eyes.

The woman with the kind eyes was in her late sixties or early seventies, Stephen surmised. Her face was painted heavily with makeup. Her lips a crimson twist. Her eyes a clouded, twinkling sunset.

"It sure is good to hear the sound of your voice," she said. "Think you're up for a little stroll around the garden? Roll, I guess I should say."

She chuckled. It was a light, musical thing.

Stephen felt warm all over.

"There's a smile!" she said. "I'll take that as a yes. Well, come on then, let's go."

Stephen's body moved. Windows and doors and walls breezed by. Then there was a brief stopping, something buzzed then popped, then movement again. Stephen was jostled, unable to control his body, his head lolling to the right, slumping against his shoulder.

"Oops," she said. "Sorry about that. Here, let me straighten you out, Mr. Paul."

Soft hands moved his head to a more centralized location.

Stephen tried to get his eyes to focus. Little snatches of sensation came to him. He drifted on the border of unconsciousness. He felt a cool breeze touch his face. He felt the warmth of unobstructed sunlight on his closed eyelids. He heard the twitter of a bird somewhere near. He felt his quiescent, unresponsive body move smoothly forward.

"Beautiful day, isn't it, Mr. Paul?"

Stephen tried to answer but couldn't even muster a groan.

I'm in a wheelchair, Stephen realized. *I'm in a goddamn wheelchair. What is happening?*

He felt his stomach drop, that rollercoaster feeling of pinpricks and butterflies, with the understanding.

I can't move. I'm in a wheelchair. Did I have an accident? Am I paralyzed? Where am I?

"Oh, no, no, no, Mr. Paul," the kind eyes said. "Sit still. You don't want to go falling out of the chair, do you?"

Stephen wanted to scream. He wanted to thrash his way into motion, mobility of his own accord, but he couldn't. He wanted to cry, to bawl like the helpless baby he felt like, but he couldn't do that either.

Something was pulling at him. Blue caressing hands from the deep were stroking him, tugging at his consciousness, pulling him under. Stephen realized he was going to sleep again and there was nothing he could do to stop it.

From somewhere in the not-too-distant surroundings, Stephen heard a young woman singing. The voice was not beautiful exactly. It had a rusty quality about it. Catgut strings on a classical guitar badly in need of changing. The melody rose and fell. The voice working at it with abandon, unselfconscious of its tenor.

Again, Stephen slept.

§

The rubbing woke him. The sound of cotton friction. The rough wetness about his groin. He felt it more acutely this time but still strangely at a distance from how things should've felt.

Stephen opened his eyes and saw the shape about his waist. There was more light in the room this time. The moon hung suspended like a cigarette burn from the window to his right.

A tangle of black hair bobbed about.

Are those cat's ears?

Stephen felt himself stiffening but it was uncomfortable and remote.

Somebody is trying to blow me.

A.S. COOMER

The thought blossomed like the sudden explosion of fireworks. He saw it there in his mind, the sentence appearing and holding a luminance then slowly fizzling into smoke and ashes, the smell lingering but the understanding fading too quickly to hold.

Stephen slept.

§

The cat tore him open and left him for the farmer to find.

§

He woke to hushed voices. He didn't try to open his eyes. He listened instead.

"Trina found her."

"Three-thirty in the damn morning."

"And she was in the bed with him?"

"She was down about this level. Mouth just a-working."

"Jesus."

"Three-thirty in the damn morning. Just rounded the corner and saw the door cracked."

"Jesus."

"Better call HR. This could be a CMS complaint."

"Should we go ahead and inform the family?"

"Jesus."

"No family listed in the recs."

"Well, that's something, at least."

There was a silence.

"Was he even awake?"

"No. Didn't so much as flinch when I flicked the lights on."

Sounds of discontent.

"I tried to talk to him after I pulled her off. Gave his shoulders a little shake. Nothing."

"Think he could feel anything?"

"He wasn't exactly limp."

"Jesus."

The sound of a door being pulled to.

I wasn't dreaming.

Then, despite his best efforts, he was.

§

The moon shook and shone. It pulled itself inward then glowed fiercely. It shrank in on itself and became the glowing tip of the cigarette under the streetlamp. Rivers Stanton took one last drag and sent it arcing into the darkness. The fog quickly swallowed it.

Rivers.

He pushed himself away from the lamppost and shrugged his shoulders several times, then pulled the collar of his leather jacket up around his neck. He set out walking off into the darkness.

Wait! Rivers! I'm here! Right here!

In the pale glow of the street light in the fog, the shape of Rivers Stanton seemed to shrink smaller and smaller with each of his steps. He didn't appear to be moving away, per se, but something more akin to shrinking.

Wait!

Rivers Stanton diminished until he was no longer there.

Stephen felt more alone than he'd ever remembered in his life. This despite the years of estrangement from his family. Despite an almost nonexistent social life since his early undergrad days. Despite the life-clearing devotion to the man and story that had just disappeared before his eyes.

Stephen Paul felt alone, there, in the hazy darkness. He knew he was somewhere in between dreaming and wakefulness. Part of him was motheringly reminding him that he was dreaming, that he would wake soon and this wrenching feeling swelling to bursting in his stomach would soon be over. Another part reminded him that he'd wake and still not fully be awake. That he was trapped in his body, unable to provide for himself in the most basic ways, in some foreign, unknown place.

Rivers. Rivers come back.

§

"I'm not sure he'll be able to answer you, officer."

Stephen blinked.

"He's quite medicated."

"Why's that?"

"He's psychotic, sir. Been here for, what? Three months now? Betty, check the chart for me."

"That's not necessary right now."

Stephen opened his eyes.

"Mr. Paul?"

His eyes closed against his will.

"Mr. Paul, can you wake up for me? I need to ask you a few questions."

It was a man's voice. A young man by the sound of it.

Stephen's head was scooped up and several pairs of hands and arms lifted him into a sitting position in the small bed.

Stephen opened his eyes.

A clean-shaven face, unsmiling, hovered into view.

"Can you hear me, Mr. Paul?"

Stephen licked his cracked lips.

"Yes."

"Good. I'm Detective Thorpe with TPD. I'm here to ask you a few questions about last night. Do you remember last night?"

Rivers.

Stephen's eyes closed slowly and filled with tears.

"Mr. Paul," the officer said, "I need you to stay awake for a few moments, OK? Did anything happen to you last night?"

He left. He's gone.

"Open your eyes for me, Mr. Paul. This is important."

More important than anything, he thought. Watching Rivers Stanton disappear felt like a watershed moment in Stephen's life. It coated his entire being in a slate grey meaninglessness. It was the weight on his arms and legs and eyelids. It was the haze in his brain. It was all-consuming.

Nothing matters now. The story is gone. Rivers is gone.

Stephen imagined a blank screen and a flashing cursor big enough to blot out the sun.

He willfully slipped into sleep.

§

The henhouse is an abattoir painted red, red, red.
The fox cleans his teeth with the bones of the dead, dead, dead.
The farmer kicked the bucket clutching his chest, chest, chest.
The owl snatches the field mouse & returns to its nest, nest, nest.

§

The days slipped silently by.

Stones skip and slide, by and bye,

off to hide on the other side of the frozen farmer's pond.

Stephen stopped speaking. He ate when fed. He drank when prompted. He did not dispute or question anything. The police officer returned once more but Stephen did not speak to him. He did not listen to the words the man said. He watched a little sprout of stubble on the man's upper lip, just below his nose, that he'd obviously missed shaving. It was an oily black. Something remarkably tarantulaen about it.

The woman with the kind eyes, Stephen did not ask for her name, came several times during the week but not every day. Despite himself, Stephen felt a sense of disappointment on days she was not present.

Give up, he told himself. *Quit. Don't wish for anything. Don't want. This is what's left of life now. This is it.*

He was watching the motes in the column of light shining through the large bay windows. Several others were around him.

Other crazies.

They were seated in wheelchairs, like he was, or in shabby armchairs and couches. There was a constant hum of inarticulate human noise about the place. It took Stephen several days to notice it. It operated on a level just to the point of madness.

Toeing the line.

Tongues wag and lips smack.

The taste of cornmeal could just be the bones of bats.

Stephen had no more nighttime visitors. He returned to the fog nightly, but Rivers Stanton was nowhere to be found.

Stephen tried to cry but couldn't. He wanted to bleed but felt empty.

Cease. Cease being. Cease. This is my life now.

§

He discovered the change of the season when the woman with the kind eyes stopped taking him for "walks", as she called them. Stephen did no walking. He couldn't remember the last time he had. Instead, she began reading to him.

Her voice was as kind as her eyes.

She brought all sorts of books, unsure of what he'd enjoy since he'd stopped talking or making any preferential determinations at all.

He listened to some of it.

Sometimes, he wasn't there.

§

The henhouse, the slophouse, all cleaned out.
The farmer getting nibbled on by the coyotes and the fox.
The wife had gone off a long time since.
On the arms of a younger man, a bruiserman who calls her "Miss".

§

And on it went.

§

"I think it's time for a shave, Mr. Paul?" Kind Eyes said.

Stephen felt a long strand of drool bounce, stretch, then snap and fall into his lap.

"Oh, dear," Kind Eyes said. "You're especially groggy today, huh?"

The rag. The wiping. The feel of radiator heat on his damp face. The crust from his eyes scratching. Tears. Blinking. More wiping.

"Have they upped your meds, Mr. Paul?"

Stephen did not know. He did not answer.

"I might have to talk with Linda."

Stephen watched the motes twirl. They were thick today. Much thicker. Coming in with more regularity. They moved in a slantwise, downward direction. This was new. Stephen tried to focus with more intensity.

"Ah," Kind Eyes said. "Yes. It's supposed to keep on for the next few hours."

There was a uniformity that baffled Stephen.

Sugar plum fairies?

"Yessiree, I'm glad I live pretty close," Kind Eyes said. "Or else I'd of skipped coming over this afternoon."

Snow.

It's snowing, Stephen realized. *It's snowing outside. It's winter.*

It was the first string of conscious thought he'd had in several days. It made his stomach flutter.

The hatching of moths.

It's snowing outside. I'm in the looney bin. I've been here since the end of Summer, at least.

Stephen felt the stinging in his nostrils first. Then it was burning and his open, dazed eyes filled with tears.

"Oh, Mr. Paul," Kind Eyes said. "Are you OK? Are you in any pain? Let me get the nurse."

Stephen heard Kind Eyes' hurried footsteps amongst the clatter of crazed chatter and the hiss of the radiator.

§

"I think he may be on too much medication."

"Are you a doctor now, Martha?"

"No, of course not. You know that. No need to condescend."

A huff.

"I just think he's trying to be more communicative, but he isn't able to with his current level of medicated-ness."

"Medicated-ness."

"Or whatever the proper medical term for it is."

"Medicated-ness. OK, Martha. I'll inform Doc Shwartz that you think Stephen Paul might not be able to chat with you because of his level of medicated-ness."

§

Stephen was gently jostled.

"Mr. Paul?" a woman's voice said. "Wake up, Mr. Paul. The doctor is here to see you."

Stephen opened his eyes. The same cracked, creamy ceiling. The dimness of it told Stephen it was early morning sometime. Long before he normally woke.

"Mr. Paul, I'm going to check your pupils," the doctor said.

He smelled of chicory coffee and cigars.

A light blossomed and filled his vision. Stephen tried to blink but a hand was holding his right eyelid open.

The light moved to Stephen's left eye. It, too, was held open.

The doctor made affirmative noises.

"Can you sit up for me, Mr. Paul?" he asked.

Stephen tried; found he couldn't move the weight of himself.

"I see."

Stephen blinked several times. The light's afterimage filled his vision, with his eyes closed and with them open, like a negative of a failing sun.

"I think we could make some changes," the doctor said.

The nurse and the doctor said several things to each other. Stephen tried to listen but couldn't. It felt like trying to turn a doorknob with wet hands.

The hens are all gone.

The fox is on the run.

A new farmer comes a-whistlin',

Sighted, sober eyes staring down the barrel of a gun.

§

Gradually, like the sun burning off the mountain mist, Stephen came back to himself.

First, he found he could flex his fingers collectively. He could just make the faintest claw of a fist. Then, he could move each of his fingers individually. It took time. So much time. He worked at it.

One.

He moved his thumb around in its circular orbit.

Two.

Stephen curled his index finger until it grazed his palm.

Three.

He extended his middle finger upward then downward.

And so on.

It filled the days. It filled some of the nights too. He'd begun to wake long before sunrise, staring at the ceiling, seeing for the first time the old cigarette stains there. Seeing the cobwebs in the corner and the spider-webbed cracks and watermarks.

He felt the rough linen of the bed. Felt the over-starched pajamas against his dry, flaky skin.

Stephen itched all over but did not trust himself to scratch. He knew he wouldn't stop.

He worked on regaining control of his facial muscles. He wiggled and grimaced until he could lift his eyebrows. He blinked each of his eyes individually. He stretched and scrunched his mouth.

He did not smile.

The days seemed longer. He was wheeled out of his room to the bay window or the cavernously empty room with the television and the card tables.

He set about working on his lower extremities. He clenched and grunted until he could move his toes. Then he could, with a strain tight enough to make the pulse beat in his eyeballs, lift his left foot off the wheelchair's footrest. Then the right.

He hadn't noticed he'd shit himself until the disgusted sound came from behind.

"Oh, yeah," one of the older nurses said. "Mr. Paul is ripe. Better change him, Mary Ann."

From behind him, he assumed it was Mary Ann that sighed.

§

Stephen found himself cringing. Cringing and cringing and cringing.

Life on the knife's edge, he thought, grinding his teeth at the off-time beating of a metal spoon on the plastic card table nearby. *It wouldn't be so bad if it weren't so sporadic. One. Two. One. Clang-clang. Clang.*

Off.

Everything felt off. Stephen's head was clearing. The fog rolling out as the sun rose, revealing just how crooked the stairs were—and down and down and down they went, the steepest descent with no end in sight.

He grimaced at the spoon ladling out more lukewarm, tasteless oatmeal, at the wiping of his face, the once-a-week shave he was given, the clipping of his fingernails, the wiping of his ass, and, *oh God*, the sponge baths.

The nurses liked to talk while they worked. A ceaseless prattle on the weather, on their husbands and children, their vehicles, their overtime al-lotment and shift schedules. The careful avoidance of eye contact helped, especially when they were cleaning him.

The stairs. The swirling mist and clinging fog. The descent back into reality.

They've changed or modified the medication they're giving me, he realized. *Either that or my body is building up a tolerance.*

He thought about how long he'd been away. How many days and nights, weeks and months he'd been an empty shell.

How many? How had this happened?

A corn husk in the fall.

Stephen could lift both his feet off the wheelchair at the same time. He could lift his arm high enough to scratch his nose.

He tried to speak but found the thoughts spinning in his head did not settle into coherent words when he opened his mouth. His tongue felt over-sized, thickened by inactivity or some monstrous transformation into something reptilian and useless.

The oatmeal.

The hotdogs.

The instant mashed potatoes.

The inanity becoming unbearable.

He's painting the henhouse.

He's bringing in the hatchlings.

He's putting up the chicken wire and the lights.

He's got a plan for a running machine in a fortnight.

Stephen worked.

§

The pills came in latex-gloved hands. They came with a pouring of mineralized water from paper Dixie cups. Sometimes they got stuck in his throat and he choked, splashing droplets of water on annoyed nurses. Stephen found he could now operate his tongue well enough to cheek the pills, if the nurse was distracted enough.

He pissed himself on purpose just as the pill was dropped into his mouth. He clenched his stomach muscles and pushed the stream with all the force he could manage. Warm, streaking streams spread across his pajamas, a darkening stain spreading and smelling, something not to go unnoticed by the hovering nurse.

"Really?" the nurse Stephen came to recognize as Mary Ann, younger by several years than the rest of the staff, said. "Now?"

Stephen tucked the pill under his tongue and let his mouth hang open.

Dolt. I'm just a poor, idiotic dolt pissing himself. Not in control of my bodily functions, Stephen thought.

He didn't know when, but he'd begun directing his thoughts at people as if he were speaking. Willing them to believe what he was showing. Begging them to forget about him, leave him unnoticed.

I'll get out of here.

He didn't know when, but it became his mantra.

I'll get out of here.

He refused to think further than that. He refused to think about the apartment he surely no longer had. All his belongings probably unceremoniously tossed—stomped on, spit on, broken by a raging Wren Risner, who'd had to cover that broken window after all—into the street and long since scavenged by the students and adjuncts.

He was wheeled, rather roughly and without concern for his lolling head, to the large, bleach-scented bathroom area. The nurse huffed as she turned the knobs and readied the bath. Stephen spit the pill silently into his lap. He used his numb, clumsy left hand to brush the pill off his thigh down onto the floor and out of sight.

He gritted his teeth and repeated his mantra as his pants were jerked down his piss-slicked legs.

I will get out of here.

All his clothes were removed.

I will get out of here.

Another member of the staff was summoned. Stephen sat unmoving in the damp wheelchair completely naked, goosebumps prickling nearly every inch of his skin.

I will get out of here.

He was lifted by uncaring hands and dropped into a scalding tub. Water splashed over the edges onto the two angry faces' clothing.

Curses.

I will get out of here.

They pulled his hair when they washed it. They pinched his arms and stomach as they sponged.

I will get out of here.

Stephen ground his teeth but showed no outward emotion as his penis and testicles were slapped and pinched, as the insults were hurled. Out of sight, he rolled the pill between his thumb and index finger, feeling it dissolve slowly in the cooling but still far too hot water.

I will.

§

He waited until the place was quiet. He heard the soft squeak of rubber-soled shoes of the night staff in the hall outside his room descending. Little squeaks fading off into the night.

Stephen swung the covers off his body. He sat up. His body felt more his own than it had in a very long time. He curled the toes of his feet and flexed the muscles in his thighs. He pulled the fingers of his hands into fists then relaxed them.

Close, he thought. *Almost there.*

Stephen stood and stretched. The popping of his back sounded like muted firecrackers in the wash of silence.

He took the seven steps to the window, looked out. The night was clear. Punctured needle wounds of shining diamonds in the sky.

Must be way out of town, he thought. *No light pollution.*

Stephen turned slowly, still not confident in the responsiveness of his body, and walked the seven steps back to the bed. He leaned forward and tried to touch his toes. He got about as far as his shins.

Stephen rose, unsteadily, and walked back to the window.

Seven steps.

Seven steps.

The moon hanging like an illuminated hangnail in a tub of Prussian blue.

Seven steps.

Stephen's body ached with the effort. His legs quivered, and knees buckled but he did not fall. He would not allow himself to fall.

I will get out of here.

Somewhere just below the surface of that thought was another. Stephen did his best to avoid looking it square in the face, instead, he kept it just below the surface, refusing to acknowledge it directly.

What does it matter if I do get out of here?

§

Active nights and patient days.
The strain of the crazed on a waking brain.
The henhouse, a nightmare, becoming just another forgotten dream.
The new farmer cracks open a new bottle and drinks deep.

§

Stephen waited for Kind Eyes to visit. He sensed she was on his side. He knew that if he could just speak to her, show her that he was not insane, that he was functional and not a danger to himself or anybody else, then she would help him.

She's already spoke up in my defense once. She'll help me get out of here.

But Kind Eyes hadn't visited in several days. In his forgotten state, he was treated as if he didn't exist as a person but more along the lines of some strange new plant that had to be moved into the sun a few times a day.

Stephen kept track of the staff. He gleaned names and patterns. He learned to gauge mood by tone of voice. He did not take the medication they put in his mouth, once in the morning and again at night.

Four days passed and no Kind Eyes.

He thought about asking another patient but understood the futility of this right away and did not risk exposing himself to do so.

That was the word they used for them. *Patient.* As in: another unruly patient on the East Wing. Patients but not patience. Stephen watched the staff jerk wrists, pull hair, pinch. Always the slamming of a door. Always the whimper of a stifled sob. He saw the barely concealed anger at dealing with helplessness. The frustration of it a coat of lacquer on the shining brutality of institutionalization. He did his best to continue going unnoticed.

§

Kind Eyes returned on the fifth day. She looked thin, frail. Stephen wasn't sure if she'd always looked this way and he just hadn't been able to notice, or if she was ill.

He carefully took stock of her.

Old and getting older. Frail and getting thinner. Can she really help me?

"Good morning, Mr. Paul," she said.

Stephen had to restrain himself from answering. A full concerted effort was required to keep his face placid, to have just the right amount of drool pooling and overflowing from his slackened jaw, to have just the right dullness in his eyes.

Where have you been? he thought.

"It's a bit warmer than it has been these last few days," Kind Eyes said. "I think I might be able to get permission for a stroll in the sun. How does that sound, Mr. Paul?"

Stephen thought that sounded wonderful. The sterilized smell of the place was becoming unbearable. He'd tried to open his window at night, but it was sealed shut.

Kind Eyes left him by the large, definitely in-need-of cleaning bay window. Stephen watched the dust motes in the sun and felt awash in déjà vu. His skin prickled at the sudden onset of it.

This isn't going to work, he thought. *She's not going to believe me. I'm going to die here.*

Tears filled his eyes and he desperately tried to blink them away. She wouldn't take him out in the cold, winter's day if he was already upset, already crying for no discernable reason. He lifted his hands and wiped his cheeks with the palms of his dry, cracked hands, then each of his eyes.

Keep it together, he told himself.

When he lowered his hands, Kind Eyes was staring wide-eyed before him, her eyes, magnified by the thick lenses she wore, looked mousy and alarmed.

"Mr. Paul?"

Shit, he thought.

§

The sun was a warm kiss. It hit his bare face and hands like a mother's caress. He closed his eyes and felt it warm and red on his eyelids.

Kind Eyes stopped them at the end of the garden walk, within sight of the black iron gate and two-lane road beyond. A great weeping willow stood vibrant in its solitude, boughs waving in the light, variant wind glinting ice crystals in the bright, midday sun.

"Mr. Paul..."

Stephen opened his eyes. Kind Eyes was before him, her veined hands on her thin knees, mole's eyes scanning his with concern. It felt like something out of a children's book: the concerned grandmotherly mole's paramount beneficence keeping the gossamery, the field mice and hens, from the fox's teeth.

Stephen smiled.

"Mr. Paul, are you..."

"I'm here," Stephen said.

The sound of his voice struck Kind Eyes like a slap. Her head jerked backwards on her neck and she took a slight step away, reeling.

"You're...you're..."

"Full cognizant."

"How?"

"They're keeping me drugged, Kind—" Stephen stopped himself.

He'd heard a name. He'd heard this woman's name said aloud when he was still thought of as the vegetable he wasn't.

Martha.

"Martha," he said.

Her eyes widened further.

"I need your help."

New Moon

"You can speak?"

"Yes. I haven't been taking the medication they give me."

"What? You haven't? For how long?"

"I need to get out of here. I'm not crazy. This has been a terrible mistake."

Kind Eyes—Martha—didn't reply right away. Stephen wondered what she'd been told about him, about why he was there, why he was *institutionalized*. He, too, wondered what happened, what he'd done to end up there. His memory was a blank void filled with some strange farmscape.

"Have you told the doctors?"

"They won't listen to me," he said.

Stephen's voice sounded tired, strained. How long had it been since he'd spoken this many words? Weeks? Months?

Too long.

He felt like some sleeping mountain opening its eyes for the first time in centuries. Everything was sluggish, out of practice. His tongue. His throat.

"What do you mean they won't listen?"

Doctors are here to make you better is the thought process here. She's oblivious to the nature of this place; the placating use of pills to tame the waves of insanity, a still pond glistening and halcyon, not frozen but immobile. I'm just a stone's throw, a skip on the ripples.

"I have to get out of here, Martha. I can't live like this."

"Of course not," she said, her face brightening. "You're getting better, Mr. Paul! This is fantastic."

Stephen offered her a weak smile. He was getting cold, the blanket that'd been wrapped around him didn't do much for the wind that seemed to be picking up.

"Let's get you inside and tell everybody the good news."

She was behind the chair and pushing before he could offer up a reply. He closed his eyes against the added wind of movement, tears stinging in the cold, cheeks blossoming fresh patches of crimson. A sack of spiders opened in his stomach. He felt them crawling around, toying with his insides, making him queasy and uneasy.

§

Martha took him directly to the nurses station.

"Is Dr. Shwartz in this afternoon?" Martha asked Mary Ann, who had her attention turned to the cellphone held in both of her hands.

"Nope," she said without looking up. "You know he's not in on Thursdays."

Thursday. How long had it been since he'd last thought of time in terms of the specific day of the week?

"I think we might need to call him, hon," Martha said, her voice nearly bubbling with positivity.

Mary Ann looked up, her face a cat's unreadable judgment.

"What is it now, Martha?" she asked.

"Mr. Paul is getting better!"

Mary Ann turned to Stephen. He felt himself shrink under the glare. He kept his gaze above and just beyond the nurse's eyes.

"Oh?" she said. "He looks about the same as he always is."

"He's talking now."

Mary Ann's eyebrows raised but her face remained blank, feline.

"Aren't you, Mr. Paul?"

Both women turned to Stephen, hunched forward, shrouded in a coarse blanket, sitting in the uncomfortable wheelchair.

The spiders intensified their investigations of his intestines.

"Yeah, he's super talkative today," Mary Ann said, returning her attention to her cellphone.

"Come on now, Mr. Paul," Martha said, bending down to look into Stephen's face. "No need to be shy. Go ahead and tell Nurse Mitchell."

"I heard you'd been under the weather, Martha," Mary Ann said, still not looking up from the phone, her thumbs working away at the screen. "Maybe you need a few more days at home? Maybe you're volunteering a little too much? At your age, your health really needs to be your number one concern."

Stephen saw Martha straighten.

"Mr. Paul," she said. "Why won't you speak up?"

"Because he's crazy," Mary Ann said. "Because he lost his mind under the strain of some cushy professorship. We both know he's uncommunicative. Would you like me to look up the definition of 'uncommunicative' for you, dear?"

"I'm not crazy," Stephen said.

Marry Ann looked up from the phone. Her eyes found his and they widened. Her mouth hung slightly agape.

"What?"

"I'm not crazy, Mary Ann," Stephen said.

"Holy shit."

Stephen heard Martha smile. It was the sound of paper-thin, dry lips moving. He turned to her.

"Please don't let them drug me."

"Oh, I don't think they'll have any need for that," Martha smiled as she reached down to pat Stephen's shoulder.

"Mr. Paul?" Mary Ann's voice was small and astonished. "You're—you're—"

"Cold," he said. "Could I have a sweatshirt or another blanket?"

The cellphone dropped down onto the desk.

"I think you'd better call in Dr. Shwartz, dear," Martha said.

Mary Ann stood, staring down at Stephen in the wheelchair. She opened her mouth to speak but found nothing to say and closed it again.

Stephen felt uncomfortable, both women staring at him. He shifted himself in the wheelchair and readjusted the blanket.

The nurse's eyes widened with his movements.

"I'll call him now," she said.

§

"How long have you not been taking your medication?" Dr. Shwartz asked.

Stephen thought he looked more annoyed at being called in then cheered by his patient's recovery.

"I don't know."

"Just today? A few days? A week? What?"

"A few weeks."

The doctor looked piqued.

"You shouldn't do things like this, Mr. Paul," he said. "You need to take your medication."

"So I can be just like a goddamn zombie all day?" Stephen said. "I don't think so. I'm not crazy."

"Nobody called you crazy, Mr. Paul."

Stephen snorted.

"I'd like to call my attorney," Stephen said.

The doctor stiffened.

"And why would you need to talk with your attorney, Mr. Paul?"

"I don't belong here. You've been drugging me. I want out and I want out now."

The doctor leaned forward and rested the tips of his fingers against each other, forming a triangle, an extended form of supplication or prayer.

This is the church; here is the steeple…

"Yes," Dr. Shwartz said. "I think it's time for a change of medication."

"Change? I don't need a change. I don't need *any* of your medications."

"I see. And are we having any strange thoughts or ideas, Mr. Paul?"

"Strange? What do you mean 'strange'? Other than the thought that I've been poisoned here for months with little to no actual medical basis or reasoning."

"No reason? Come now, Mr. Paul. I'm glad you're feeling better, but do you not recall your actions and behavior leading up to your stay with us?"

Spiders' feet. Thousands of tiny, prodding spiders' feet.

"I don't," Stephen said.

"I see."

Stephen felt the blush, hot and stinging on his neck and cheeks.

"Mr. Paul, I think we're due for a change in your medication," Dr. Shwartz said, quickly lifting the palm of his left hand to still Stephen's response until he'd finished speaking. "It would not be good to stop all medication, Stephen. You had a serious break with reality. You were quite sick. I'm glad you're feeling better, but I don't think we're out of the woods just yet."

Stephen ground his teeth.

Only doctors use that damn phrase: out of the woods.

"I will speak to my attorney, Dr. Shwartz."

"As you wish, Mr. Paul," he said and sighed. "But you're bound by the court order regardless."

Stephen felt his mouth drop.

Spiders everywhere. Spiders and spiders and more spiders.

"Ah," Dr. Shwartz said, remaking the steeple with his fingers. "I see you don't recall *that* either."

§

"What are they saying I did?" Stephen asked, then after a second added, "Martha?"

She looked away. Stephen followed her gaze to the big bay windows. The angle of the light showed several smears and finger smudges. In one spot near the flannel couch, it appeared someone had pressed their entire face into the glass, as if they'd taken in the entirety of the "activity room", then smashed their face to the glass imagining escape.

"I'm not sure, Mr. Paul," Kind Eyed Martha said.

Stephen felt she was holding back.

"Please, Martha."

She sighed.

"Well."

"Come on now," Stephen said. "I need to know."

"You have no recollection?"

Stephen shook his head.

"Well, the paper said you were arrested for making terroristic threats at that doctor's office."

"The paper?"

Kind Eyed Martha nodded her head.

"Said you'd 'threatened bodily harm to yourself and others' and had to be restrained."

Stephen mouthed the words to himself: *threatened bodily harm* and *restrained*.

He, indeed, had no recollection of those things. He'd remember hearing something and seeking the source of the sound and then a smeared blackness that, when remembered, felt more blue than black.

Martha turned away from the window. Her eyes were kind, so soft and full of warmth. A smile stretched her frail, lined face.

"But you seem to be getting much better, Mr. Paul," she said.

Stephen tried to return the smile; it was weak, a poor man's cup of re-used teabags.

"I have to get out of here."

Martha nodded and patted his knee.

"All in good time," she said. "They have to make sure you're well first. That's the important thing."

"I can't stay here."

"This place isn't so terrible," she said. "I've been helping out here for, oh...twenty-three years now, it is."

"Twenty-three years?"

Martha nodded. The smile stretched a bit further. Stephen saw it spelled out: S-A-T-I-S-F-A-C-T-I-O-N.

"How?" he asked.

Martha laughed. Stephen saw it typed out as: chortled. He'd never imaged he'd actually hear someone chortle in his life. He'd taken it for granted that that word was just one writers used to avoid a plethora of 'laugh's' in their work.

"It's easy, Mr. Paul. I just keep coming back."

§

"Mr. Paul?" Mary Ann called.

Stephen inched himself forward in the wheelchair. He didn't necessarily need the thing, but his legs were still too weak for him to stand waiting in the medication line. Plus, he wasn't sure just how much of himself to show the staff yet. He didn't trust them.

"I don't want that," Stephen said, jutting his chin up and away from the small, white paper cup containing three pills.

"I'm sure you don't," Mary Ann said, her face tightening, "but since we're under doctor's orders here and not our own dictates, I guess we'll just have to grin and bear it, huh?"

When Stephen still made no move to take the cup, Mary Ann rattled the pills around in three short shakes of her hand.

He sighed and took the cup.

Mary Ann smiled. It was not pleasant.

Stephen emptied the contents of the cup into his mouth and tossed his head back. He made his Adam's apple bob down and return. He'd slid the pills under his tongue for the swallow then worked them to the inside of his cheeks when he returned his eyes to the nurse's.

"Better wash 'em down, Mr. Paul," she said, another paper cup extended his way, this one full to the brim with water. "Don't want them getting stuck now, do we?"

Stephen took the cup and hesitated.

If I just throw it back fast, the pills should be fine, he thought.

In one fluid motion, Stephen upturned the cup into his open mouth and swallowed.

"Here," he said, making to hand the cup back.

"Oh, those are particularly hard to get down sometimes," Mary Ann said. "Let's have another, shall we?"

The cup was refilled and placed back in Stephen's hand.

Shit, he thought.

Stephen looked at the nurse. Mary Ann's eyes were alight.

She knows.

Stephen tried to get the water down with minimal mouth exposure but the pills, bitter and dissolving, spread through his mouth. He tried not to screw up his face, but the taste was horrendous.

"What's the matter, Mr. Paul?" she asked, that smile still painted there, a facsimile of honesty. "Need another drink? I know those can be hard to take sometimes. Horse pills, I've heard 'em called."

Stephen waved his hand and tried to smile but it was a grimace through and through.

"You know, if you'd rather, Mr. Paul," Mary Ann said, "we could give you your medications intravenously. You know, if they're too difficult for you to take on your own."

She leaned forward, a tightness pulling her face smooth and leering.

"Would you rather we do that, Mr. Paul?" she asked.

Stephen swallowed the bitter mess in his mouth. He shook his head.

"Good," Mary Ann said. "Have a wonderful afternoon, Mr. Paul."

Stephen turned himself around in the wheelchair and wheeled himself away from the still-smiling nurse.

"Mr. Holloway," she called, rattling another cupful of pills.

§

He made sure he wasn't eyed by the staff, then wheeled himself to the bathroom. He left the chair standing empty just outside the door. He frantically turned the cold water tap all the way on and splashed palmed cups of water into his mouth. He spat and swished, spat and swished. The bitter white foam spreading and dissolving.

Stephen had managed to forgo taking the full amount of the medication given. Three-fourths of one pill remained whole, little specks and foam of the other two washed down the drain.

Shit, he thought. *Shit.*

He wetted his right index finger and used it as a make-shift toothbrush, scraping around the inside of his cheeks and gums for any missed pill residue. He swished another mouthful of water around and spat.

He looked at himself in the mirror. A pale, gaunt face stared back. Deep pockets of purple hung under his wide eyes.

I can feel it coursing through me, he thought. *No, shit. Come on now.*

That's ridiculous. They can't be that fast-acting. Can they?

Stephen splashed some water on his face then dried it with a rough paper towel. He shivered when the image of a gigantic cat's tongue flashed
in his head.

He opened the door, got back into his wheelchair and made for his
room. Halfway down the long hallway, he changed his mind.

They'll think something is up if I just go sit by myself all day, he thought.
They'll keep even closer tabs on me.

Stephen paused there, both hands on the rubber tires of the wheelchair, thinking.

*No. I better go sit with the rest of them. Wait and see how the drugs affect
me there.*

Stephen turned the wheelchair around and headed back for the room
with the blurry bay windows.

§

Stephen wheeled himself to the window. He sat staring out at the crisp
winter morning, spits of snow fell in wet clumps but did not stick and no
real snowfall seemed likely. His breath fogged the window slightly and he
turned himself in the chair at an angle to look out the clearer portions of
the window.

It's starting to kick in, he thought.

He felt clammy, sweat beginning to appear and tickle his upper lip and the back of his neck.

I won't let it, he told himself. *I won't let it. I am present. I am here.*

Stephen clenched then unclenched his fists. He took a deep breath and held it for as long as he could. Little star-specks danced across his vision, mixing with the varied snowflakes in a cheap theatrical manner.

Wouldn't that be nice? he thought. *If this were all just some fucked up, melodramatic play? A dream sequence?*

Stephen let the breath go and sucked in stale air, slightly tinged with disinfectant.

Where's the denouement? Where's the hero's return? Where's the happy ending?

He blinked away tears.

Fuck, he thought. *Fuck.*

§

It slid into his brain like a cotton knife. It was comfort. It was bland. It was numbness.

Stephen, without any shock, saw that it was nearly dusk. He'd sat, a cooling sun, a thawing pond sent back to freeze, watching the intermittent snow flurries, for hours. He knew he should feel...something.

Concern.

Terror.

Anger.

Stephen felt nothing. If anything, he felt a little hungry.

§

The meatloaf had little globs of freezer-burnt peas in it. They smooshed in an unpleasant way when you bit into them. A little tension as the freezer hardened shell resisted the pressure then finally gave way to a dully soured mush.

The cafeteria, a cavernous room painted, of course, a slate-grey, was full of the sounds of mouths working. Lips smacked. Tongues lapped. Juices were sucked. Stephen felt the hair on the back of his neck and arms raise at the sounds. He'd always hated them, the sounds of eating. There was something obscene and indulgent about those sounds.

He cringed involuntarily but quickly relaxed. He focused on the sound of his pulse beating in his ears. A steady *beat-bat beat-bat* of certainty. He changed the pace of his chewing to match the rhythm. *Beat-bat-smoosh. Beat-bat-smoosh.*

Someone behind him was laughing. It started as a giggle. Something Stephen registered but on an unconscious level, but the giggling turned into a slow-rising guffaw. Stephen turned around in the uncomfortable plastic picnic-esk table and craned his neck to find the laughter's source.

A man in overalls stood leaning on the doorframe, his hands wrapped about his stained, denimed middle. Big blue tears cartoonishly streamed from his eyes. Wisps of a month-old beard hung about his chin and cheeks and a single, green spikelet of wheat protruded from his cracked lips like a cigarette or toothpick.

The man saw Stephen looking at him and his laughing intensified. He leaned forward and slapped the thin knees of his overalls.

His voice was high and traveled far. It seemed to grow louder with each, new peal of laughter.

Stephen looked around at the others eating their dinner. Nobody batted an eye.

The farmer was crying in his mirth.

Stephen looked down to find his plate in his lap. Congealed pieces of gravy-coated meatloaf slid out from under the upturned plate down the curve of his thighs onto the plastic bench seat and onto the floor.

"Will somebody please shut him up?" Stephen screamed.

He scraped up a handful of instant mashed potatoes from his lap and plopped them down onto the tabletop.

"Hee hee haw," the farmer laughed.

"Shut the fuck up, goddamn you."

Stephen tried to focus on removing his dinner from his overly-starched clothing.

"Hee haw hee."

Two strong hands lifted him from the bench and set him down in his wheelchair.

"Wha—"

A sharp pain stung the bicep of his left arm. He turned to see the stern face of Mary Ann looking down at him. There was a cold fury in her eyes that stilled him.

He wanted to apologize and hated himself for it.

The room, dozens upon dozens of sets of crazed eyes topping slanted faces, was watching him. His skin tried to crawl off his body. The spiders returned to life in the innermost sections of his stomach.

Then the room was rushing by. Dizziness and nausea swept over him. Stephen passed by the smirking farmer on the way out of the cafeteria. He shrank lower in the wheelchair but couldn't avoid looking. The tall, gaunt man smiled down with eyes blacker than anything Stephen had ever seen in his life.

Stephen was screaming before he even registered the sound as human.

§

"Just a little setback, Mr. Paul," Kind Eyed Martha said. "It happens. These things take time."

She was patting Stephen's hand. It was like the touch of dried paper, papyrus or a mummy's linen.

Stephen sat quietly in the wheelchair, a rough blanket about his lower half, staring at the stains in the window. He realized they'd been there for days. The same stains, the same partial left hand, the same greasy face print—Stephen thought it was a woman's face by the press of lips but in a place like this all bets were off. The same willow tree standing hunched over with the weight of itself out in the expansive green.

He hadn't seen the farmer since "the episode", the term Dr. Shwartz used, in the cafeteria. His medications had been changed again. Mary Ann had given them to him not an hour ago, her face stony and seeming to revel in some quiet way in his ruin.

"These should help you get back on track," she'd said.

As if his psychological state were just a child's train set, a little smoke machine and flashing sets of red lights. Stephen saw his crumpled in a jangled heap of melted plastic and broken tracks. Someone had thrown a switch, got the routes confused, something.

"Not very talkative today, are you, Mr. Paul?"

Stephen wasn't. He didn't know what to say. He didn't know how to broach the fact that he'd seen somebody— a farmer, bib overalls and all— that wasn't actually there. He didn't know what plane of crazy he was considered as being on. He knew that the person he'd seen existed only in his imagination, but he'd still seen him, felt his presence as real and foreboding and actual. Now he sat in a wheelchair he didn't need waiting for the new antipsychotics to slip between his thinking self and his acting self like a sleek, sliding, pharmaceutical garage door.

Automatic, baby.

The spiders were walking. They didn't seem overly troubled, just exploring. Stephen wondered when they'd spread throughout the rest of his body.

Stephen saw himself as a penitent dog, tail between his legs knowing he'd done wrong but knowing it was probably just his nature. Nothing he could do about it, really.

§

"Mr. Paul?"

It's all nothing anyway. I shouldn't complain. Maybe the drugs will be nice. I can act up if they're not. Throw a fit to get the good stuff.

"Mr. Paul?"

Nothing, nothing and more nothing, right? Hemingway's old waiter was right all along. What's the point? The great American existentialist novel.

Stephen let loose a derisive bark of laughter.

What was I thinking? Even if I did write the damn thing, what difference would it make? The world is a wash. A whiteout before the blackout. I could've wrote the most beautiful prose anybody had ever seen, draped it up in a plot so commonplace every person could relate, and it still wouldn't mean anything. Nothing. Nothing, nothing and more nothing. The old waiter was right. Or, maybe, that old drunk sitting up late in the well-lighted café was right.

A.S. COOMER

"Mr. Paul?"

Who knows? Doesn't matter.

"Mr. Paul."

Stephen looked up. Kind Eyed Martha was standing, hunched over, eyes wide with concern.

"Huh?"

"Mr. Paul, are you OK?" genuine concern in her voice, a slight quiver there, the rasp of age and kindness like drying leaves clinging to the boughs in the fall.

The room was still. The seemingly ceaseless chatter had stopped. All eyes, crazed and demented and hopelessly morose or blank, were turned to him in his cheap wheelchair.

Stephen shook his head to clear it. It felt full of gauze and cotton balls.

Something wet and sticky smacked his cheeks. He lifted his hands and found his nose to be bleeding a strange, thick mixture of blood and snot. Tears were flooding down his eyes. How had he not known?

"I'll go get a nurse, Mr. Paul," Kind Eyed Martha said. "Don't you worry. You wait right here."

Stephen was laughing and crying and not sure he cared either way.

§

A long strange trip strapped to a bed. The jangling faces of nurses and men with stethoscopes and needles a country-mile long. A sleep without rest. Slips in the great turning cogs of reality. Waking sleep. Days and nights and more days.

A spot just below his left shoulder blade where the spiders were trying to tear their way to freedom. Can't let that happen. They are his spiders. They belong to him. If they leave, who will keep him company?

He feels the farmer watching him. Knows he's close but the man never shows his face. Stephen hears him chewing on the spikelet of wheat. Smells the dried shit on his bootheels. What's the man planning? Why won't he just leave Stephen alone?

§

The henhouse is a spreadsheet.
The eggs are the formula.
Little Martha went on back to her momma's.
The farmer skinned the cat then left him out for the coyotes.

§

Stephen was laughing. He felt so empty that it made sense that he was laughing. Sometime in the night, during a window in time the size of a keyhole, the spiders had escaped. They'd come out crawling and covered in his insides.

He was alone in a new room in an old building. The nurses came and went. The doctors did too but on a more glacial schedule. He saw the ice in their eyes. The pair of them interchangeable like cubes in a glass.

Stephen thought he could see the cracks in the ceiling slowly growing, tributaries in the desert filling with the unseen, unfelt rains upcountry, some cooling oasis curing the parch of others. He hoped the thing would open up and drown him.

§

Stephen stopped counting days. He stopped fighting nights. He let the needles enter his arm. He let the pills slip down his throat. He let the oatmeal mush move around until it was cool enough to swallow. He let the strangers bathe him. He let them wipe his ass.

§

"You're making progress, Stephen."

Stephen didn't respond.

"It might not seem like it, but you are."

He met with her twice a week. She was young, a recent graduate Stephen guessed. First job out maybe.

"Are you having any side effects with the new medications?" she asked. She had to slip the 's' on at the end of 'medication', probably because she didn't have his medication list in front of her but assumed he was prescribed and taking more than one, making her sound strangely sibilant or somewhat intoxicated.

Does life as a sleepwalker count?

He didn't offer her a reply.

"You know, Mr. Paul, these meetings would be more productive if you'd speak your mind."

Stephen held his breath.

I have no mind to speak from. The spiders left and I think they took it with them.

"Could you kindly tell the farmer to leave me alone?"

"What?"

Stephen hadn't meant to speak.

"Nothing," he said. "Sorry."

"Mr. Paul, you should really consider letting me in. I'm here to help you, but I can't do that if you don't pull your own weight."

His own weight too? Wasn't the weight of his failures enough to lug around? He was already in a goddamn wheelchair. The axles would break if he added any more weight to the thing.

She studied him. He ignored her. The room was small but pleasant. She'd some sort of air freshener hidden about the place, making it smell of cinnamon and apples. He wondered how many aroma therapy classes she'd attended in undergraduate or graduate or medical school. He pictured them all sitting together discussing the potential psychological effects of lavender on the psychotic.

"What about Robert Wilkins?"

Stephen was suddenly alert.

"What?"

"He was your friend, right?" she asked. "Colleague at the University of Toledo? Hell of a writer. *Winter's Teeth* was a hard but important read, wasn't it?"

Robert.

"*Bones and more* was published by the Atlantic too, wasn't it? Pretty impressive."

There are certain things you keep to yourself, he remembered. *Every thirty-sixth step. The dance.*

"That must've been interesting to be around? All that buzz and excitement your friend was garnishing. Clout and prestige."

The thing had been written in blue. Robert's last written words. *Blue.* There was something so profound about this remembrance.

There is a darkness more blue than black.

"Did you ever feel jealous of Robert, Stephen?"

"Yes," he said. "Of course."

She nodded, and Stephen thought he saw the slight up-curl of her lips in a smile.

"How did you feel about your friend's success?"

"I was very happy for him," Stephen said. "For Robert. Very happy."

She nodded.

"His death must've been shocking for you. Hard to deal with."

Stephen nodded, twice. Slight little forward motions that required a lot of himself to retract. His head felt bandied down, his neck a taught rubber band or constricting spring.

The silence stretched out like some pagan hand, an offering to something obscured and unknowable.

"Mr. Paul, tell me a little bit about that night."

That night. What night? Oh, that *night.*

"I don't remember much, really."

"What do you remember?"

"There was a fire in a barrel. A man in rags. There was this blue that was not quite black but really dark, you know?"

She nodded. She waited.

"There were cracks in the concrete. There were many stumbles."

A.S. COOMER

"You fell?"

"Yes. I think in more than one way. I think there might have been drugs involved. I'm not sure."

"I see."

"I have no clear recollection of taking any drugs but there's this…this gaping expanse of time that I can't explain. I have holes. I don't know what happened. What I did. What happened to me. It's all this blankness that's absolutely terrifying."

"I bet."

"Is there anything else you can remember about the night you were arrested?"

"The hawk'll take the dive when the timing's right."

"Excuse me?"

Stephen relaxed the muscles of his face. He hadn't realized he'd been scrunching them up until he felt a quiver just below his left eye. The concentration of remembering had been all-consuming.

"I'm not sure. But that's something from that night."

"Is that from a story or poem or something?"

Stephen shook his head.

"I'm not sure. I think it's like some fucked up nursery rhyme or something. I've been having these little snatches of them for a while."

"Nursery rhymes?"

Stephen nodded.

"There's usually a henhouse, a fox, a cat, and a farmer involved."

"A farmer?"

Is he here now?

Stephen paused, his senses alert. He sniffed the air but did not smell fertilizer.

The pause was telling.

Bit off more than she can chew with me, he thought.

She checked her watch.

"Well, that's about it for this afternoon, Stephen. I think we're making excellent progress. Don't you?"

She didn't wait for him to reply.

"I'll be back on-site Thursday. We'll meet then. OK?" she ushered him out the door and into his waiting wheelchair.

He rolled himself down the hall in a fog. The farmer didn't feel close, but Stephen felt the prick of eyes on the back of his neck.

Stephen wheeled himself to the smudged window and watched the willow dance in a wind he could not feel.

§

"Oh," the voice said.

It was nearly nails on a chalkboard. Rusted nuts and screws in a blender.

Stephen looked up to see the attorney standing before him, looking like he'd stolen his oversized suit from his father. The attorney looked startled at Stephen's current appearance.

Corey Streeter cleared his throat and pulled up a plastic chair to sit next to Stephen in his wheelchair.

"Good afternoon, Mr. Paul," he said.

Stephen felt like crying. He did not answer.

"I'm here because we had another hearing in your case this afternoon."

"What?"

"A hearing, Mr. Paul," the attorney said, opening an unmarked manila folder across his lap, "in your case. You know the one where you were arrested and charged with being intoxicated in public, resisting arrest, disorderly conduct, failure to comply with the order or signal of a police officer, and present risk of harm to—"

"Jesus. I know," Stephen said, his stomach clenching with tension. He spoke through gritted teeth. "What I'm saying is I didn't know about the hearing today. Why wasn't I informed? Shouldn't I have been there?"

"Oh," Corey Streeter said, looking up from the papers. "Yes. You could've been there. It wasn't, like, mandatory or anything though. I figured it would've been a real hassle to arrange for transportation to the court house through these people. They're kind of hard to work with really. Anyway, it wasn't necessary, your being there."

That last sentence rang out in Stephen's head like a wrench dropped in an empty oil drum.

It wasn't necessary, your being there.

"It's my case," Stephen said. "I should've been there."

"Duly noted," the attorney said. He removed a pen from his coat pocket and clicked it. He began writing, the letters cartoonishly large and childlike. He read them as he wrote. "Client wishes to attend all court proceedings."

The tip of his tongue showed between his lips as he wrote. He clicked the pen again and said, "There. It's in there now, Mr. Paul."

Stephen flexed his fists together then relaxed them. He took in a long, slow pull of air.

"What happened at the hearing today, Mr. Streeter?"

"Ah, yes. Today," the attorney said, returning his gaze to the papers on his lap. "Today the judge continued the case for another three months out. The court heard testimony from several of the doctors and hospital staff via various reports and affidavits and the like on your current progress."

"And?"

"And the court will meet again on this matter in three months, Mr. Paul."

"Three months?"

"Yes."

"So, I just sit here in this...this...this place for another three months wasting away on medications I don't need or want? Is that what you're telling me?"

"Yes. The court will meet again on this matter in—"

"Three months, yeah. I got it," Stephen felt like hurling something through the smudged glass windows. "So what happens in three months? Exactly."

"The court will hear testimony from the hospital staff on your progress and make a determination on whether you've fulfilled your obligation of completing mental health treatment to ensure the safety and well-being of yourself and the community and deferred charges will be ruled upon."

"What happens if I haven't made any more progress?"

"Then the judge can either continue the case for another period to allow you to continue with your treatment, or the judge can send you to another facility. Or, if the judge rules that you're competent, sane enough

I should say, and still not making any progress in your treatment, then you can be sentenced to jail time."

"Jail?"

"Yes," the attorney moved his index finger down the sheet of paper. Stephen could see what looked like dandruff under the man's nails. "For an upward of ten years based on these charges."

"Ten years," Stephen shouted. "Are you fucking kidding me?"

"I am not, Mr. Paul," the attorney said. "There is no need to cuss at me. I did not charge you or make you do the things you're accused of doing."

Stephen let out an exasperated, strangled noise. The room seemed to be closing in on him. The walls pressing at his temples and forehead.

One hellhole to another, he thought.

"These doctors aren't helping me, Mr. Streeter," Stephen said. "I don't know how to make any progress or whatever they want me to do."

"You need to do what they tell you do to, Mr. Paul."

"They just tell me to take the medications and go to the counseling appointments."

"Are you doing those two things?"

"I am."

From somewhere behind Stephen, he heard a chuckling. He went cold all over.

"Then this should be no problem really. If all they're asking you to do is take medication and go to counseling sessions and you do that for the next three months, the doctors should be able to give a beneficial testimony to the judge."

Stephen heard the heel-click, heel-click of boots. He smelled a faint whiff of manure and freshly cut hay.

Oh God. Please no.

"Just try and relax, Mr. Paul," the attorney said. He slid the paperwork back into the folder and shut it. "We're doing everything we can for you. I think we're on track. We just need to make sure there's no more slipups."

"What if I can't help some of the things I'm doing?"

"What, Mr. Paul? I don't understand."

The laughing was getting louder, closer.

"What if I...need help."

"That's why you're here, Mr. Paul."

The attorney looked uncomfortable.

Stephen couldn't help it. He turned around in his wheelchair and looked over his left shoulder towards the laughing.

"Mr. Paul?"

No.

The farmer was leaning against the wall next to the dirty windows. His hands were stuffed in his overall pockets. He wore a stained baseball hat, a golden fishhook gleaming from the bill. His dark eyes seemed to be alight with a mirth that was terrifying. He was watching Stephen from across the room, the little spikelet of wheat bouncing with his laughter.

"Mr. Paul?"

Stephen forced himself to look away from the farmer. He felt his body shaking. The wheelchair moved about with his trembling.

"Mr. Streeter, please get me out of here," Stephen whispered.

"I can't do that, Mr. Paul," the attorney said. "You have to complete your court-ordered treatment."

Stephen closed his eyes and held his breath. He felt tears squeeze through his interlocked eyelashes and fall out onto his cheeks.

The farmer was chuckling. Not an out-and-out laugh. It was an amused sound. Something done for show.

Stephen opened his eyes and the farmer was gone.

The back of the attorney's ill-fitting suit was bobbing away toward the front door.

§

The farmer stood over his bed for the entirety of the night. He made no comment. He just smiled and watched Stephen.

Waxing Crescent

The henhouse, the whorehouse, the shithouse, the rain.
Another chance broken up by chance and pain.
The farmhouse, the workhouse, the alehouse, the rain.
Another night's shaky hands caress the rest from the insane.

§

"Stephen, let's talk about your friend some more. Is that OK?" she asked.

Stephen nodded.

Whatever you want. I'm working towards progress, he thought.

"OK."

Stephen realized he didn't even remember this doctor's name.

"Ma'am, I'm really sorry. I feel terrible about it, but I can't remember your name."

He cringed at himself for asking the question.

Does that make me sound crazy? I've meet with this shrink for two weeks now and I can't remember her name.

She smiled.

"Nothing to be sorry about, Stephen," she said. "I'm Dr. Holt."

Stephen nodded.

Dr. Holt. Dr. Holt. Dr. Holt, he repeated, trying to hold onto the name.

"You can call me Rebecca, if you'd rather," she said.

Rebecca Holt. Dr. Rebecca Holt.

Stephen always had trouble with the names of people in real life. Fictional characters often seemed more real and, therefore, easier to remember.

"Stephen, let's talk some more about Robert Wilkins."

"OK."

"You worked together, were friends."

"Yes."

She waited for Stephen to elaborate.

"Uh, yeah. We also went to undergrad and graduate school together."

"Did you meet in undergrad?"

"Yes. University of Cincinnati. Then we both applied to and were accepted into Miami's Low Residency Master's program."

"You must've been close."

Stephen nodded.

He was the closest friend I ever had.

She waited.

"We were close."

"The feeling was mutual?"

Can you ever really know? Stephen thought. *All those nights sitting across great hulking library tables, eyes flicked up and caught, smiles warmer than the sun they hardly saw, much less felt. The stacks of books between them like cities in miniature and the central focus of nearly all their talk.*

"Yes. I think so."

Dr. Rebecca Holt seemed to weigh her next line of inquiry.

"I think we need to discuss Robert's death."

Stephen saw the words in blue: *You exist within your limitations. You spread your wings finding the enclosure more cramped than you remembered.*

The hand of his friend. The writer of the words he could never find.

"OK," he said, his mouth a hollowed-out log rotting in some piney wood.

"He committed suicide."

Stephen nodded.

There are certain things you keep to yourself. Secrets, private musings, urges. Burdens, shames, acknowledged shortcomings. You carry them across your shoulders closely.

"Was that a shock to you, Stephen?"

Stephen nodded.

You carry the weight as if it needs protecting, stopping every so often, if you're like me it's every thirty-sixth step, to make sure a zipper hasn't slipped, a stitch hasn't broken, not a flap of your flak has flurried the streets, peppering your insecurities under the noses of the unkind, the unaware, the unappreciative.

"Hindsight being 20/20, as they say, did you see anything in your friend's recent behavior that hinted at any such rash action?"

Stephen thought. The weeks preceding Robert's death were a haze, as was much of his life he realized. Little jags of memories glinting like glass shards in a great wash of blue and black and stillness. A great conveyor moving him through time at a pace that was impossible to see in real time.

"No," he said. "I can't recall anything that would've made me think he was going to…to do what he did."

"I see. So, it must have come as a complete surprise to you to learn of his passing."

Passing. Stephen always hated that term. *He passed on. His passing.* He thought it sounded prudish and concealing. Something older folks told each other to lighten the blow of their own rapidly approaching mortality. The thought occurred to him that he might've been viewing the term in the wrong light. Maybe passing was more apt than he realized.

"Osmosis," Stephen said, not meaning to speak aloud.

A.S. COOMER

"I don't follow," Dr. Holt said.

Stephen blushed and cringed.

"I'm sorry," he said. "My thoughts are all jumbled. I was thinking about the term you just used: passing. All of my life, I've despised the term. I thought it avoided the heavy truth at hand."

"You don't hold this view any longer?"

"I'm not sure," Stephen said, shifting himself to a more comfortable position in the chair. "I think maybe there's some truth in it."

"Could you elaborate for me, Stephen. I'm still not following."

The letters in blue. The void in black. *You start to think that maybe there is a place without limitations. Maybe there is a place where you can exist freely. Maybe there is a place where you are complete, where you can make the things you see shining out into the dimness of everything that surrounds you, encases you in stagnant pools of disquiet and uncertainty. There is a place. There must be.*

"I can try. I guess maybe there could be some truth in the term if there's something beyond this," Stephen said, taking in the entirety of existence with his left palm upturned, his arm sweeping the room slowly. "Maybe when you die, you just pass through this plane, or whatever you want to call it, into something else. A freer state."

"I see."

Stephen didn't know what else to say. He felt himself blushing again. He was embarrassed at his existential nakedness. He'd only discussed matters such as these with Robert and through his writings with Rivers Stanton.

"Does that thought help you deal with Robert's passing?"

Stephen narrowed his eyes and thought about it.

"Yes," he said. "I think it does."

"Do you believe it?"

"I'm not sure."

"You know, I've read some of your work, Stephen."

"Oh?"

She nodded.

"I have. I read three of your short stories. I found them online in the electronic editions of the journals they were published in."

"Which ones?"

"I read," Dr. Holt paused to flip back a page in her legal pad, "*Swayed in the Belly of the Gale.*"

Stephen nodded.

"Interesting story," she said. "How would you describe the premise of it to a potential reader?"

Stephen always hated that question. He hated the idea of distilling the essence of something vibrant and alive into a four-line epitaph for a story now killed. It felt like a little blasphemy every time.

He sighed.

"I'd say it's the story of an agnostic fisherman blindsided by a rogue wind out in the middle of Lake Erie. He's out there alone, in the dark expansiveness, afloat. He's pleading for assistance from a god he's not sure he believes in. He makes promises to be a better person. To be kind. To be generous. All that."

"But he drowns anyway," she said.

"Yes."

"What's the message there?"

"Nothing matters."

We are alone. Everyone. Me. I am alone.

"I see."

Blue from the black: *You stifle the quaver in your words, the meaning barely concealed behind platitudes, rearing its ugly head like a hidden, burdensome child, the blighted fruit of a love gone wrong. The child wanting to cry out for light, for love, for acknowledgement, for a chance to be whatever everyone else gets a chance at.*

"Can we discuss that a little more?"

Stephen shrugged his shoulders.

"I guess so," he said. "I'm not really sure what to say."

"If nothing matters, why write?"

Stephen looked out the little window. A small, gravel parking lot with a handful of vehicles parked there. A weak winter sun reflected dully off the metal bumper of a rusted-out Chevy pickup. Stephen could see the little motes of a crystalline snow land on the sanguine and black hole, the rust hole like an aching cavity.

"I guess, I didn't see any better use of the time?"

§

He didn't feel like talking.

She looked like a fisherman about to call it quits.

"Well, you're stuck here for a time."

Stephen turned back to Dr. Rebecca Holt. She was reeling in the line.

"Court-ordered treatment. Job depends on it."

His mouth felt very dry. An arid waste of useless fleshy bits. He still wasn't used to speaking so much.

"English professor to pay the bills but you're a writer at heart, yes?"

Stephen nodded, slowly.

"Well, how about this," she said, setting the pen down on the legal pad and leaning forward in her chair, "as part of your Treatment Plan, let's have you start a diary. Journal, whatever."

Stephen cocked his head slightly to the side. He hadn't considered writing since the loss of Rivers Stanton.

"A detailing of your thoughts and memories. A running log. Freeform at first, I think, to get you back into the swing of things. Might find yourself a tad rusty," she smiled. "Just twenty minutes of straight writing. You know the drill: keep the pen moving until the time elapses."

Stephen had used the exercise in his Creative Writing 101 classes and during Stream of Consciousness lectures.

"OK," he said with hesitation.

Woolf, Beckett, Joyce, Faulkner. Face and book covers pinged around in his head like some literary pinball machine. He thought of the parts where Kerouac was onto something, then all the times he needed a hard-nosed editor.

"Don't treat this as a new manuscript, Stephen," Dr. Holt said. "This is part of your Treatment Plan. If you have to think in terms of deadlines, do that, but this is something I think will be beneficial for you. Seeing what's transpiring or, at least, the translation of what's transpiring in your thought processes anyway will help you reshape your perspective, deal with some of this baggage we're circling around, and get you on the road to a healthier life."

Stephen saw a wolf in a suit, raven-black hair slicked over, a hard-part, white teeth gleaming as he read from "the defendant's diary" to the court. He couldn't hear the words, but he saw the cringing and the shock and the amusement. He saw the charges stacked up like weights on a bench, like cards on a deck, like shackles and chains.

"I'm not sure…" he faltered, searching for the words, the right words, "how this will help me get out of here."

She smiled again.

"Fear is part of the problem, Stephen," Dr. Holt said. "You're afraid of failure, like most people, I remind you. Plus, this is not up for debate. This is officially a part of your Treatment Plan, and therefore, one rung in the ladder out of here."

§

An hour before medication time, one of the oldest of the facility's nurses, Theresa Marks, strolled over to where Stephen sat in his wheel-chair watching the weeping willow.

"Mr. Paul, it's time for your journaling," she said.

"Oh," Stephen said. "OK."

He let her wheel him down the hall to the nurses station, where a small foldout card table had been set up. The faintest stub of a pencil sat atop a half-empty legal pad.

Suicide risk, the term flashed like fading neon in the night.

Stephen wheeled himself around the table and got comfortable.

"Now, you just sit there and write," Theresa Marks said.

There was something in her voice, a maternal diction, something passed down from on high, the expectance of acceptance of her directions, that felt vaguely pacifying to Stephen. Nurse Marks sat down at the nurses station desk and resumed some sort of paperwork.

Stephen looked down at the pencil and the empty yellow page. The burnt orange line running the length of the left-hand side. Blue-green lines running across in straight, hard lines.

He picked up the pencil and looked at it. It felt like rubber. He squeezed it in his hands and felt it give. Holding the orange-bodied thing between his fingers, he bent it again. It bowed into a lower case "u".

"What the—"

"Bob Barker makes those," Nurse Marks said.

Stephen saw that she'd been watching him fiddle with the pencil.

"Called a flexible jail pencil. That one's been about used up. We got some more coming though."

Stephen looked at the pencil. He saw Vanna White in his head and immediately realized that she hadn't been on television with Bob Barker.

"Not the *Price Is Right* guy though. Some other guy. Doesn't seem right to name your company the Bob Barker Company and not be *the* Bob

Barker, right?"

Stephen didn't answer.

He heard the shuffling of papers and knew the nurse had gone back to her work.

The blank page seemed to stare back at him. The yellow was a caution. The blue lines flashing with malevolence, daring him to try and put something between them that was worthwhile.

What the hell am I supposed to write?

"You better get on to writing, Mr. Paul," Nurse Marks said. "You got less than forty-five minutes 'til medication time. Go on now."

Stephen put the pencil tip down and started writing.

§

There is a farmer here. He's not real. I know this. I do, but he's here nonetheless. He wears threadbare bib overalls and is always chewing a spikelet of wheat or some such grain. He likes to laugh at me, at my misfortune, at my current predicament. I know I should not acknowledge that I see a person that is not there, that is, in fact, imaginary, but I am trying to be honest. And if I'm being honest, I want out of here. I do not feel like this place is conducive to my mental health. I do not like the way these medications make me feel. I think they are keeping me numb and trackless in a dark wood.

§

A.S. COOMER

Stephen set the pencil down and popped each of the five fingers of his right hand. He looked up at the nurses station and saw Nurse Marks still hard at it.

He picked the bendy pencil up and continued.

§

The medications kept me passive and dark for far too long. I've been resigned to use this wheelchair because of my physical decline and weakness due to ~~weeks~~ months of inactivity as a result of these medications. My legs shake but carry me now, just not for extended periods of time. I can't wait for warmer weather, so I can take walks in air that doesn't smell like lemon-scented disinfectant and urine. I miss the sunshine. I miss the rain. I miss walking unmonitored and free.

§

Stephen was crying. He hadn't realized it until he saw the little splatters on the page. He sat back in his wheelchair, set the pencil on the card table, and wiped his eyes with the palms of his hands.

I'm a mess.

He steadied his breathing then picked up Bob Barker's bendy pencil.

§

"Med time, Paul," Mary Ann said.

Stephen intensified his scribbling. He didn't look up.

"Come on," she said, taking a step closer to the card table. "I don't have all day now."

He finished the sentence with a stabbing period. A spear cast out into the night. The flicker of the flames and the pounding of tribal drums. It was new again.

He used his legs to push himself in the wheelchair out from under the table, then followed Nurse Mary Ann down the hall to the medication room, where a line had already formed, bits of hair extended in odd places, eyes glazed, mouths agape and drooling.

Stephen couldn't stop his smiling. He couldn't stop the shaking of his hands and the nervous energy making him bounce his legs and feet in the wheelchair's footrests. The squeak in the wheel, an annoyance from days on end, was nothing to him now.

He traced the sway of the words he'd left on the page. The smudgy graphite river funneling across the blue-green lines. Tributaries leading to something larger. Stephen could feel it. Something immense. Something profound. Something meaningful in a world completely devoid of meaning. A light in the dark.

He swallowed his pills without so much as an afterthought.

§

He couldn't help it. He looked forward to the writing.

He wrote and wrote and wrote without thinking. He crafted sentences as quickly as they came to him and did not second guess himself, something he'd never done before.

Must be the pills, he thought.

He wrote about not taking the pills and walking around his little room at night. He wrote about the hazy molestation by another patient, which he'd initially mistook for a gigantic cat eating him alive. He wrote about his treatment by the nurses and the doctors and the rest of the staff.

He did not think about the reaction these sentences, slanted and crazed with the need to get them down and out of him, would have on others. He wrote because it felt there was some new mechanism about him. A drive-train connecting the wellspring of his mind to the hand holding the pencil.

His thoughts changed shape. They were sentences again. Inky black things in type he could read and rearrange. Things pulled from a darkness more blue than black. Even when he wasn't writing, he thought about writing. He saw each facet of his day as it would appear in written form.

The way Nurse Mary Ann Mitchell walked.

The smell of cigarettes hung about Nurse Theresa Marks.

The doctors, the food, the writing itself: everything.

Stephen felt himself coming alive all over. He took to walking the halls. The wheelchair sitting beside his bed under the cracked, water-stained ceiling of his little room like a monument to a war recently waged.

Stephen stood at the window, the boughs of the willow bending in a breeze he could almost taste, all crisp crystals of the coming snow, and smiled. Using the sleeve of his overly starched pajamas, he wiped clean one half of the smudged face there.

§

"Mr. Paul, you look…" Kind Eyed Martha looked him up and down. "How are you doing, Mr. Paul?"

She pulled up a chair and sat down.

Stephen turned from the window and sat on the lurching tweed couch beside her.

"Hi, Martha," he said, smiling. "I'm doing OK. How are you?"

"Well," she said returning the smile. "I'm just fine. You seem awfully chipper this afternoon."

Stephen fought the blush, but it blossomed anyway. He smiled despite himself.

"I feel all right."

"That's wonderful."

He nodded.

A silence.

"I brought a book," she said, motioning the paperback in her shaky hands. "Hadn't been in in a few days. Been a little puny."

She waved the hand not holding the book in his direction.

"Nothing major," she said. "Just a little cold was all."

"I'm glad you're feeling better."

"Thank you," she said. "Anyway, I brought a book to read to you since you were awfully quiet the last time I was in."

"Yes, I was."

Another silence.

"What did you bring to read?"

"Oh, it's…" she held the book up to read the title then decided against it and extended it to Stephen. "Well, here. Take a look your own self. You seem well enough."

Stephen noticed a look of stifled embarrassment on the elderly woman's face.

How to Beat Back the Sadness by Reverend Jim Schlub. With a new foreword by Reverend Timothy Gluck.

Stephen looked up, the smile fading on his lips, to see Kind Eyed Martha studying his face. He quickly turned his eyes to the back of the book.

> With over a million copies sold, How to Beat Back the Sadness by the empowering Reverend Jim Schlub has helped cure people of their depression without the need to turn to habit forming medi-

cations. In his simple, straightforward, Gospel approach to treating depression, Rev. Schlub proves he is God's messenger of happiness. This groundbreaking self-help book has been translated into over twenty languages and is in frequent use in hundreds of countries worldwide.

There were several blurbs about the book's practicality and effectiveness following this. Stephen pretended to read each of them.

He felt embarrassed for Kind Eyed Martha. He felt embarrassed for her as if she were his own well-meaning grandparent. He saw by the sticker covering the book's barcode that she'd purchased the book used from the campus bookstore.

"I thought it might be something good for you to hear, if you were having one of them lowly days," she said.

Stephen forced the smile.

"Thank you, Martha," he said. "That's very kind of you."

"You can borrow it, if you'd like."

One blue strand in the quiver of her frail voice. It vibrated on a wavelength of purity Stephen could hear.

"Thank you," he said, not trusting himself to look her in the eye. "Thank you very much."

§

Stephen took the book back to his little room.

He stood at the window and watched the flakes of snow flit and jive under the halogen lights. He bent his knees then raised himself up on his tippy toes periodically.

Stephen left *How to Beat Back the Sadness* sitting in the seat of his wheelchair when the lights were turned off. It felt like something obscene lurking in the dark. He reached over and picked the book up, leaned over the side of the narrow bed and slid it underneath.

He smelled the farmer before he heard the bootheels approach in the quiet of the hall outside his door. Dried shit and hay. Something warmed far too long under a heavy, summer sun, unprotected.

Stephen tensed but did not get out of bed. He saw the outline of feet, twin blocks of black on the tiles under his door seemingly sucking in all light, all perception, all thought.

You're not real. I'm imagining you.

At first, Stephen thought he heard the farmer sigh. A rustling of brittle leaves in a late autumn breeze. After a moment, he realized the farmer was, again, laughing at him. It was a low, breathy thing. Barely audible. A chuckle in sighs; laughter in breaths.

Go away. Goawaygoawaygoaway. Go.

The faintest of raps on the door.

Tap. Taptap.

Stephen pulled the covers up over his head with shaking hands. He couldn't keep his eyes closed. He could feel the twin blocks of black pulling him as surely and constantly as any other gravitational force.

Go away, Black Hole Farmer. You're not real. I'm getting better.

The laugh. The rap. The pull.

Stephen did not sleep all the night long.

§

He flinched when his door was opened.

"Rise and shine, Mr. Paul."

The door was left open and the speaker moved to the next room down the line.

Stephen sat up and threw off the covers.

The dawn was bleeding into the night sky. The stain of morning blossoming.

He kicked his legs over the edge of the bed. He rubbed the thick crust from his eyes. He stretched and yawned and scratched.

Sitting on the seat of his waiting wheelchair was the book. *How to Beat Back the Sadness.*

He reeled, shook his head.

"No," he said.

The twitch of the bag hanging just below his reddened left eye was the Black Hole Farmer's whispered chuckle.

In a whirl of gnashed teeth and wild eyes, Stephen snatched up the book and flung it across the room. It struck the open door and clattered to the floor in an open heap.

This is not happening. This is not real. You're getting better. I'm *getting better*, he told himself.

He stood up, his eyes riveted on the book on the floor. He pushed the chair away from the bed and turned to the window.

The stain intensified, spread.

Stephen could see the book out of the corner of his eye. He turned around and slowly walked over to where it lay. He leaned forward to pick it up then stayed his hand. He made to rise, then reached for the book again. He couldn't pick it up. He stepped back to the wheelchair and sat down heavily. The weight of a sleepless night. The weight of unseen, mirthful eyes.

Stephen rubbed his eyes with the palms of his shaky hands.

God.

He wheeled himself past the book and out into the hall. He could smell the weak coffee and bland oatmeal already. He thrust himself down the hallway in an unsteady pace. He parked himself before the window

and watched the morning come, doing his best to keep his mind blank
and clear and unfocused.

§

"Here you go, Mr. Paul," Nurse Marks said.

Stephen saw the extended hand. It held out *How to Beat Back the Sadness* for him to take.

He shook his head.

"Come on now, Mr. Paul," the nurse said. "You can't just leave your
things laying around on the floor."

She held the book out for Stephen to take for several beats longer,
but when she realized he wasn't going to take it, she sighed and stepped
around the chair. She let it drop into the little pouch behind the wheelchair's backrest.

"Grumpy this morning, huh?" she said, walking off down the hall towards the nurses station.

Stephen watched her go, feeling the book through the chair like a tick
on his back. It felt cumbersome and heavy and unwanted.

The bag under his left eye twitched. Stephen cringed.

Nervous tick. Shit, Stephen leaned forward in the chair, plopped his
chin on his waiting upturned fists, his elbows on his pajamaed knees.
This can't be happening. I'm getting better.

A.S. COOMER

How to Beat Back the Sadness shifted a little lower in the pouch with Stephen's movement.

"Breakfast," Nurse Mary Ann called into the room.

Stephen turned himself in the chair and wheeled into the cafeteria.

§

He mushed the oatmeal. He ate the burnt bacon. He sipped the weak, already stale coffee. He felt the book like a cocklebur on his lower back.

How to Beat Back the Sadness.

Stephen wanted to write. He wanted to slip into that all-consuming flame and stoke the fire from within. He wanted to forget he was crazy, in a loony bin, seeing things that weren't there. He wanted to exist outside himself. Or, was it that he wanted to exist wholly within himself, in those inky black letters from the darkness more blue than black?

The bag twitched. Stephen cringed, then swallowed the lukewarm mush.

§

After breakfast, he wheeled himself to the nurses station and waited for Nurse Marks to give him paper and the bendable pencil the Bob Barker Company made.

Vanna White's toothy smile. Help control the pet population. Have your pet spayed or neutered.

His feet tapped an incessant rhythm on the wheelchair's footrests. It made the book move a little in the pouch, tapping his back again and again. The bag twitched. Stephen cringed.

"You're making me nervous, Mr. Paul," Nurse Theresa Marks said, from behind the desk of the nurses station. "Stop with all that tapping."

Stephen stopped, for a moment, then started right back up again without realizing it.

Nurse Marks sighed.

"Hold on, hold on," she said, opening a file cabinet drawer with a key from her lanyard.

She stood up with the legal pad and Bob Barker pencil. She handed them across the desk to Stephen and said, "Give me a minute and I'll get the table ready for you."

"Don't worry about the table, Nurse Marks," Stephen said, squeezing the pencil.

She raised an eyebrow and stared down at him.

"You better not make me regret this," she said.

Stephen looked up from the blank page and smiled a hurried, forced smile.

"I won't," he said. "I'll just be over by the window."

He pointed with bendy pencil to the spot.

She nodded her head.

"I'll be watching, you hear? Don't do nothing stupid."

Stephen nodded, already wheeling himself towards the window.

§

He stood outside my door like a plague. Death incarnate. A black hole sucking everything I've worked for away. The Farmer. The mother fucking farmer that doesn't exist that I can't help but see and hear and smell and hate and fear and oh God I'm never going to get better. I'm going to spend the rest of my meager existence in a wheelchair I don't need in a facility that doesn't even know how to make coffee properly.

§

Stephen looked up and saw the huddled shape of Kind Eyed Martha, wrapped up in hat and scarf and gloves in a heavy but frayed jacket, slowly making her way up the path towards the front entrance.

He held the bendy pencil aloft and watched her for several moments. She moved as if against a great gale.

Stephen turned away. He went back to the writing.

§

How to Beat Back the Sadness, a self-help book by some religious nut, was given to me by the very kind volunteer Martha O'Connolly. She's been wonderful. I can't say enough nice things about her and her presence here and the effect it's had on my recovery (God I hope I'm recovering). I can't help but hate this book. I haven't read it. It feels like a soft slap in the face. Every time I look at it or feel it poking me in the back, which it's doing now because it's in the back of the wheelchair that I don't need, I am awash in shame. Shame. That blanketing sourness. That cringe of cringes. That pain. That suffering. Shame. I feel like I've disappointed the world, but I know the world doesn't care. It's odd, this— if this were a play, the direction would be something along the lines of "the writer turns his palm up to the uncaring world and slowly presents it to the audience." It's odd. I'm out of sync but, then again, I've always been out of sync. I've never made sense. Nothing has ever really made sense to me. I've wanted Truth. I've wanted Understanding. I've found neither.

§

Stephen saw Kind Eyed Martha walk behind the nurses station, slowly removing the layers of winter clothing, toward the backroom marked: Staff Only.

§

My friend wrote, "You learn how to make the steps look normal. It's a dance. You don't dance but you can learn, and you can emulate and immolate in time with those not burning." He wrote it in blue on a piece of tracing paper that nobody else has ever seen, save me. Me. The finder of nothing. The writer of nothing. The believer of nothing. The doer of nothing but the wrong things. Things I can't even remember. I am crazy. There. I wrote it. Said it in my head as my hand moved Bob Barker's— not to be confused with the gameshow host— pencil across this legal pad. I see things that are not there. A farmer. He laughs at me and this is frightening for some innate reason I cannot understand. I don't know why he's a farmer. I'm not particularly scared of farmers or agriculture or rural life. Never had any bad run-ins with those kinds, that I can recall— but there's a lot I can't recall, so there's always the possibility. I hear nursery rhymes, if I listen. They aren't any nursery rhymes parents read to their children. They aren't taught in schools. They are nonsense. They are weird. They must be the creation of my subconscious. Why? I do not know. All I know is that I don't know. I am Socrates in a straitjacket. Or wheelchair, I should say.

§

Kind Eyed Martha was walking down the hall towards him. Stephen looked up to watch her. She smiled. He returned the smile.

She looked from his eyes to the pencil and pad in his lap and changed her course. She mouthed the words: I'll leave you to it.

§

There is a darkness more blue than black. There is a hopelessness that swims in the night. There is a henhouse and a farmer fighting drink and a wife that leaves and returns and leaves again. There is a fox and there are coyotes. I do not understand but I know they are all there, somewhere, and I am their creator and, somehow, created by them. I think they are all connected in their respected disjointedness to a breakage somewhere inside of me. I want to know I want to understand why I am broken. This was not of my design.

§

"Med time," Nurse Mary Ann called.

Stephen looked up, then back at the legal pad. He read then reread the last four sentences he'd written. He raised the pencil to write more, hesitated, then decided against it. He wheeled himself the short distance to the nurses station and handed the pad and bendy pencil over the desk to Nurse Marks.

"Thank you," he said.

She didn't look up from the paperwork.

"I think it's time for your meds, Mr. Paul," she said.

§

"I read through some of your journaling this morning, Stephen," Dr. Holt said.

Stephen sat up straighter. He was back in the undergraduate workshop with Robert, Dr. Bell, and the rest of them. They'd been assigned three stories to read: one of Robert's, one of Stephen's, and one from Gabriela Francisco.

He'd read each of them, including his own, which he read after reading the other two and with as objective a set of eyes as he could manage. Stephen thought his story was better than the other two. He couldn't help it. He told himself that he was being prideful and reread the other two. Then he read his again.

Mine's better, he told himself. *Objectively. It's a stronger story. There's an actual plot* (this was a critique of Robert's story, which traced a young man's thoughts after his ATM transaction ends with the knowledge that he has overdrawn his account after a night of drinking) *and sentence-for-sentence it is well-written* (this was regarding Gabriela's story, which had a fine plot but was clunky and stagnant throughout).

The discussion of his story was saved for last. Stephen took this as a sign that Dr. Bell held it in much higher esteem than the other two, which were given multiple suggestions for improvement and asked to be rewritten before final submission at the month's end. He'd participated in the discussion, including giving some soft-handed advice on plot for Robert and some suggested sentence changes for Gabriela.

"OK," Dr. Bell said. "On to Stephen's story."

The room, filled only with the eight participants in the workshop, seemed to bristle with noise. Everyone was speaking at the same time. Stephen suppressed a smile, assuming the chatter was glowing praise of a story masterfully told.

"OK, OK," Dr. Bell said. "Round robin we go. Let's start with you, Robert."

The room quieted. Robert gave Stephen an uneasy sidelong glance then started into it.

"The execution is well-crafted, but I can't get away from the hokeyness of the thing. It was a frivolous story told well, which I can't understand," Robert said.

Stephen saw several heads nod in concurrence. His stomach dropped through the chair, through the floor, on down to the basement, where it smoldered in ruin.

"I mean, I'm not trying to sound mean or to bash you," Robert said turning in his chair enough to face both Dr. Bell and Stephen. "I know you're a good writer, a hell of a writer, but this—"

He picked up the printed, stapled pages, Stephen's robbery-gone-wrong story, and shook them.

"Isn't worth the effort you put into it," he finished.

"Gabriela?" Dr. Bell said.

The class shifted to face her.

"I agree," she said. "The story's been told a hundred times before and with more intriguing changes to the plot. It's like instant potatoes or something. It's a facsimile of the real thing. You're obviously very talent-ed. Some of your sentences are straight poetry but I don't see the point of having them in a story that's not worth telling."

It went on this way. Each of the students either adding to the denigra-tion of his story through vocal outpourings or through tacit head-nod-ding and smirks.

After the last of the students had spoken, after Dr. Bell had stepped in with his own, though less brutal criticisms, after the spark had turned into flame had turned into complete annihilation and loss of everything, Stephen was given the opportunity to speak.

"OK, Stephen," Dr. Bell said. "You've heard the workshop's remarks. What do you think we've got right? What have we got wrong?"

Stephen remembered the failing of his throat. He tried to swallow but the weight of his failure seemed lodged in his Adam's apple like a strangler within. He tried to play it calm, keep his face composed as the air dwindled and the fluttering spots of lights began, on the peripheries at first, slowly spreading across his entire field of vision, but when a full minute had gone by and still Stephen had offered up no reply, the shifting of chairs and the stray throat clearing showed the discomfort of the workshop.

Stephen opened his mouth, a strangled cough emanated.

"Are you OK?" Dr. Bell asked.

It was a question Stephen could never answer, not on the brightest of days. The unsurety of existence, the incertitude of one's place in the grand scheme of things, the false-calm of the pre-dawn hours knowing the praise was forthcoming, knowing that his genius would soon be recognized, were gone in a puff of air that, for the life of him, Stephen could not get back into his lungs.

He coughed, reached for his throat, slumped over in his chair.

Stephen woke sometime later. It couldn't have been much later. When the workshop had gotten around to scalping his story, it had already been close to the end of their allotted time. College students will watch a calamity. They'll watch it blind-eyed to reason, to political motive, to the harm it causes themselves or others, but they will not watch it if it makes them stay after.

Stephen slowly sat up.

Dr. Bell laughed an uncomfortable but clearly relieved laugh.

"Jesus, Stephen," he said. "There you are. Are you OK, man?"

Stephen nodded his head without questioning, without actually making sure his windpipe was dislodged of the silent intruder that had just tried to kill him.

"Ever choke on your own spit to the point of passing out before?" some wise-ass asked.

It was probably Mooney; Richard Mooney was an asshole who thought he was the next Thurber.

Stephen was cold. He shivered and fought against the shivering. He didn't want to show any more weakness than he had already.

"I'm fine," he said, his voice not more than a whisper. "Sorry about that."

"Anybody got any water?" Dr. Bell asked.

Water was provided. Stephen sipped.

"Well," Dr. Bell said. "I guess that's it for today. See you all next week."

"And?" Stephen couldn't help but ask Dr. Holt.

"I can tell you've missed it."

Missed it? As in: the mark?

Stephen felt a wash of anxiety that was akin to nausea. It was happening again. Here he would choke on his own shortcomings and wake up on the floor.

"The writing," Dr. Holt said. "It's like a floodgate opened up. I can't believe you wrote this much in such a short amount of time."

"Ah," Stephen said.

The clicking of an engine cooling down. Stephen gave himself a moment to idle down and cool.

"I think it shows how far you've come, Stephen," Dr. Holt said.

I was writing all my life, but it took a breakdown to show how far I've come, Stephen thought. He tried to formulate what to say. Did she like it? Did she relate? Did it make him clearer in the vast murk of reality? Did what he wrote hold even the faintest semblance of reality? Was he inundated in complete absurdity? A vague stranger shipwrecked on the Isle of the Void?

Dr. Holt was nodding and making little notes in her legal pad. She then flipped open a manila folder and held several loose pages up for Stephen to see. He could tell it was his handwriting, remembered writing what was presented.

He couldn't help feeling like a child before the proud parent: *See what you've done! Just look at what you made!* The voice higher in pitch than any adult would speak to another adult. The tone reserved for the child or the child-like.

But what did you think? Stephen wanted to ask. He knew this was the wrong question. Only the insane, or, at the least, the most clearly self-conceited would ask their therapist, the person providing their court-ordered mental health treatment, if their diary entries were "good literature".

The words in blue: *There are certain things you keep to yourself.*

Stephen realized Dr. Holt was watching him. He could feel the measuring quiet of her gaze.

Had he lost track of time? How long had this silence ensued?

Stephen nodded, for show.

"I think you're right," he said. "I think I'm making progress."

This seemed to satisfy her. She smiled.

"Same time, same place?" she asked.

Stephen nodded and returned to his waiting wheelchair in the hallway.

§

"How are you today, Mr. Paul?" Kind Eyed Martha asked.

Stephen hadn't heard her approach. He'd been sitting in the wheelchair watching the weeping willow, still as a summer pond, in the great tundra outside. There was a shimmer about the boughs, a coldness that seemed to breathe but not stir that fascinated Stephen.

"Oh," he said, turning away from the window. "I'm well. How're you,

Martha?"

Martha smiled but it changed to a wince as she lowered herself into the cracked armchair beside Stephen's wheelchair.

"I'm fine," she sighed.

Settling into the chair, the wince morphed back into a smile.

"Just fine," she repeated.

"Good," Stephen said.

They both turned to the window. There was still no wind. The bright blue sky hung like a hotplate in reverse; the world a flash frozen miniature perched and waiting for the white in a snow globe.

"How're you liking the book?" she asked, after some time.

"I'm still, uh…" Stephen shifted uncomfortably in the wheelchair, "working my way through it."

Kind Eyed Marth nodded, taking this for the truth she assumed it was.

"It's hard going for you now, Stephen," she said, "but you'll make it. You'll get through."

Stephen didn't turn his head from the window but looked at the elderly woman out of the corner of his eye. She was smiling that faint smile of the old, something that was either natural to the gradual accrual of wisdom, or hard-won understanding of axial points of reference.

She believed what she said. Stephen believed Kind Eyed Martha was incapable of deception.

I will read that damn book, he told himself. *If for anything, just because I owe it to this woman.*

§

Troubled? World got you down? News depressing? Job soul-sucking? Times hard?

The Lord can help! Jesus Christ had the same feelings and he died on the cross for your (and my) sins. Think on that. You can't be having that bad a day, now can you? I mean, you didn't just get persecuted for your sins and the sins of the people your father created to the point of your execution! Things are looking up after all, huh?

§

Stephen set *How the Beat Back the Sadness* down on his lap and shook his head.

This is going to be painful, he thought.

He picked it back up and continued reading.

§

If you, like me and countless others, have struggled with depression, sadness, melancholy and all the rest of it, consider yourself lucky! This book can and will help!

I know some of you reading this right now are doubtful. Sure, the world is a-drenched in the doubtful. That's why the Good Lord put people like myself on this world, to cure the world of the disease of doubt. To instill in your mind the Truth and Understanding that you serve a purpose, a Higher Power. There is reason to all this madness. There is hope in all this despair.

Believe!

§

Stephen turned the page and saw that he hadn't even gotten to the introduction by Reverend Timothy Gluck yet. This was an introduction to the introduction apparently.

For fuck's sake, he thought.

He looked up from his bed and out of the small slit in the window. Between the bars, charcoal clouds were gathering on the horizon. A great heap of them.

It's going to snow. Really snow.

"Fuck it," Stephen said, returning to *How to Beat Back the Sadness*.

He flipped the book open at random and read.

§

The door to experience should remain open

AT ALL TIMES.

§

Stephen sat back in the chair and looked out the window again.

Although he agreed with the sentiment, he despised the use of all caps. It was the literary equivalent of drunken speech: too loud, rash, defeating itself in the process. Even if you had something incredibly insightful to say, you probably condescended to whomever you were drunkenly preaching to.

You lose them in the over-explanation, Stephen thought. *You have to leave room for people to stumble into understanding on their own, when they'll be less likely to toss your meaning out offhandedly.*

He flipped several more pages.

§

Understand that you are not alone. God has provided man with the ability to understand and to comprehend for a reason. There is a panoply of experience and those experiencing, you are one drop in the bucket. That bucket is life. You are a part of it. You are a drop in God's bucket of hope, truth, understanding, love, everything. You matter. Everyone does. God created each of us with our own unique

skillsets, pitfalls, loves, and lives for a reason. There
is a reason. Trust in God.

§

That strange mixture of allure and distaste. The co-mingling of ideas
abhorrent and longed for by his rationale and preference.

He laid himself bare to his thoughts.

I want to belong. I want to matter. I don't want to blink and cease to be.

He picked up the book in his hands, holding the spine cradled in
his right hand. He let several pages flip, his thumb feeling each move
like a rustle of brittle leaves, the sound they make scraping across a
night-shrouded sidewalk late in the fall.

He read at random.

§

There is Truth in all things. There is Understanding in the tree stump, the sidewalk and streetlamp,
the grocery store cash register, the pills your doctor
prescribes for high blood pressure. I repeat: There
is Understanding and Truth in all things.

§

Another trick of the trade that Stephen disliked: capitalizing things
that did not require it for the sake of emphasis.

This man is not writing about Truth like Plato, he thought. *This man is no Aristotle.*

The clouds were there. Just outside the window, Stephen watched the first flakes of snow begin to fall.

Is he?

Stephen pursed his lips and scowled at the oncoming storm.

What if there is truth in everything? he mused. *Would that mean context isn't important? Or would everything be in context already and it's just a re-alignment, a re-adjusting of the lenses that brings all into perception?*

Stephen closed the book. He let his thoughts unwind. He imagined them as a kite. He let it run up into the storm clouds.

I mean, the door to experience should remain open AT ALL TIMES, right?

A series of experiments, rules governing their research, practical methods of ascertaining their validity, were all beginning to form in his head. Crystallization. Chrysalis. Crisis.

A study in Christian self-help roulette.

Stephen opened *How to Beat Back the Sadness* in earnest for the first time.

§

**God provides us with the ability to conquer all
the challenges he presents us with. He does not**

256   A.S. COOMER

give us hurdles we cannot jump, no mountain we cannot climb, no storm we cannot weather. All we need to do is learn to unleash our abilities.

Think of each new trial and tribulation life sends our way as God showing us areas of our life that can be improved, weaknesses that need fortifying, holes that need plugging up.

§

Stephen forced himself to stop cringing at the prose. He made himself look past the overwrought examples, the clichés upon clichés, and just search for truths, for understandings, for anything at all that he could use to help himself.

That's the purpose, right? he thought. *I'm reading this ridiculous book to better myself. There's no other real reason to even give it the time of day.*

He refused to acknowledge that there was a sense of shame involved with reading the book. The fact that Kind Eyed Martha had taken the time to hunt it down, purchase it, and give it to him personally to read and cognize was painful in a special way.

Should I ask for Bob Barker's bendy pencil and the legal pad? he thought. *Maybe I can write a paper on this. A critical review in practical use for the nonbeliever.*

He went through several possible titles and perspectives before he realized he was avoiding processing the information.

Just read the goddamn thing. Do the experiment. Write it up later.

He looked back down at the page he'd been skimming.

God provides no mountain we cannot climb, the author is alleging, Stephen thought. *Fine. That's an affirmative view of challenge-facing. The proverbial: You Can Do This. Nothing so much wrong with that. It helps you get through tough times. It helps you to believe that there is an end to the suffering, to the heartache, to the sense of being forever lost. A shining arrow emerging from the directionless void: This Way.*

But why that *way?*

Stop it. Work through it. Find some meaning. Do the experiment.

Maybe I need a new definition of God. Maybe that'll help me stop tripping all over myself and these tripe sentences.

Redefining God: he saw the new title for the article that would surely come from this.

Focus.

God is the pursuit of happiness? God is the feeling of completeness? God is the underlying sense of security and validation of one's place in the world?

What is God?

The storm outside the window was raging. Gigantic clumps of wet snow fell in torrents.

Ash after the blast, the stray thought ran across his mind like a newsreel headline. *Ash after the blast. This isn't snow. This is ash after the blast.*

A.S. COOMER

God is security? God is a pact men make to make it through? God is...

The overhead lights, harsh and white, flickered once, twice, three times but did not go out.

God is freezing to death in a loony bin?

Stephen forced a smile and acknowledged that he was too sleepy to proceed with the experiment. He closed the book and settled down for bed.

§

The ropes were the first thing to come into a hazy focus. The ropes under the light. Swaying in a slight breeze. Swirls of fog curled and unfurled around him.

Stephen stepped into the pale circle of the streetlamp's light.

"Hello?"

God is the rope.

"Huh?"

Stephen took a hesitant step forward.

"Anybody there?"

God is the rope of the damned.

"What? Who's there?"

Stephen stood blinking in the dimness. He squinted out into the swirling darkness all around him.

The light of the lamp above pinged and buzzed.

"Rivers?"

The wind sounded like a muted trumpet's laughter at a distance.

§

"Rise and shine," the voice called into Stephen's room.

He stirred but did not wake right away.

The overhead lights were turned on.

"I said, 'Rise and shine, Mr. Paul'," the voice repeated, louder.

Stephen opened his eyes. The last vestiges of a midnight lamppost dissolved with the crust from his eyelashes. There was a paleness about the room he recognized as new immediately.

"Morning," he said.

"Morning to you," the voice said, leaving the door open.

Stephen sat up and stretched. He turned to the window and stared in open-mouthed amazement at a grey madness. It was an oil painting of a blizzard. It couldn't be real. The window appeared to be coated in a sheen of ice that gave everything visible through it the hazy glaze of Renoir's liquidly blurred *Road at Wargemont*. A dreamlike quality of unreality. A drunken perception of landscape and space.

Stephen rubbed his eyes then looked again.

"Jesus," he whispered.

He moved himself to the wheelchair and made his way down the hall. It was amazingly cold. He forced a puff of air out his mouth and was surprised that he couldn't see it.

Several other patients were awake and moving about in the room with the bay windows. Most were still wrapped in their blankets. Stephen saw three space heaters had been brought out from some internal closet and turned on. People were milling around these, talking to themselves, to people that weren't there, to people that were there but were incapable of responding or uninterested.

Stephen wheeled himself to the window and looked at the impressionistic glaze. He could just make out the outline of the willow through the ice and the snow that was still coming down.

"Jesus," he whispered again.

"Jesus!" a bearded man took up the word as if it were the battle cry of a last-ditch battalion hell-bent on fighting to the last man. "Jesus! Jesus!"

Stephen ignored him.

He leaned forward and placed the palm of his right hand against the glass. It was unbelievably cold. He pulled his hand back and there was the slightest hesitation, as if his skin had been in the process of bonding to the glass.

Stephen shivered. He opened his mouth and let his breathe out. The faint outline of a cloud formed then dissipated.

He moved himself along the window until he could feel the warmth of one of the space heaters. He stared out, shifting his gaze from one portion of the window to the next. It was every bit of that painting he's seen at the Toledo Museum of Art, *Road at Wagemont*, not four months before he went crazy.

The Toledo Museum of Art was a gem. He'd stood in front of the painting so long that one of the blazered men came up and asked Stephen if he was all right. He'd seen prints and digitized photos of the painting but neither did the thing any justice. The landscape, some banker's retreat in the northern portion of France, looked awash in fresh tears. Stephen found himself physically there, he stood on the top of a rolling hill in Wargemont blinking back tears.

What was he crying about?

Through the ice-shroud, Stephen watched the wind pick and prod the willow. One bough, in particular, was loaded down with ice and snow, clumped together like meat on a string. It swung like a hung body in some winter's desolation.

God is the rope of the damned.

There was a commotion emanating from the nurses station. Moans and sighs and exclamations.

Stephen turned in his chair to see three of the nurses, Mary Ann, Theresa, and a newer nurse Stephen thought was named Megan, huddled together. Theresa had the phone cradled between her right shoulder and her ear. She said something into the receiver then hung it up. The three nurses looked at each other in silence for a moment.

Stephen wheeled himself over to the nurses station slowly.

The nurses were talking now. Hushed tones. Tight faces. Concern. Sadness.

Something awful's happened.

Stephen approached without either of the three nurses noticing.

"Is it time for my writing yet?" Stephen asked.

The three nurses jumped at the sound of his voice.

"Jesus," Mary Ann said.

is the knot in the rope of the damned, Stephen couldn't help but think.

Nurse Marks studied him, a slight tremble in her lower lip and a tightness around her normally sagging cheeks.

"Yes," Nurse Marks said, finally. "Yes, I think it's time for you to do your journaling."

She ducked down and retrieved Bob Barker's bendy pencil and a legal pad from the locked file cabinet drawer. She handed them across the desk to Stephen but when he made to take them, she held onto them.

"Mr. Paul…" she said, seeming unsure how to proceed.

"Yes?" Stephen said.

They were holding opposite sides of the legal pad. Bob Barker's bendy pencil had slipped down the pad, but Stephen lifted his index finger and trapped it.

"Never mind," Nurse Marks said, letting go of the pad. "You go on and do your writing."

The other two nurses looked everywhere but at Stephen.

"What's going on?" he asked.

"Go on and do your writing now," Nurse Marks said, turning away from him.

Stephen wheeled himself back to the bay windows slowly, taking looks over his shoulders back at the nurses station. The three nurses watched him go. He could hear them talking but could not pick out a single word.

§

The ice's glaze shines in the murky haze of a winter's day
The fluorescents flickered three times but stayed on
There's a henhouse somewhere that's cold to the touch
A fox holed up, nestled and waiting and sleeping
A bucktoothed farmer laughing, I know it but do not hear it or see it

The spikelet gleaming like a pagan torch or an assassin's dagger

§

Stephen stopped writing.

The nurses were still huddled together at the station. They were talking. They were looking at their cellphone screens. They were making phone calls.

Stephen saw that it was nearly time for medications to be distributed.

§

God is the rope of the damned
God is the question asked but never answered
God is the reason for the season

§

Stephen smiled and looked up at the window.

A fuzzy lightness somewhere in the east beyond the hangman's weeping willow. The snow had not slackened.

§

God is the rope of the damned
There is a darkness more blue than black
The experiment continues

§

Stephen laid bare the outline of his experiment with *How to Beat Back the Sadness*. He thought about Dr. Rebecca Holt reading about this and her reaction. He wondered if it would hurt or help his chances of getting out of there. He wondered if her testimony at his next hearing would be favorable. He wondered if he should start lying, start making himself more normal to her.

Then he thought about the farmer. The misplaced time. The overwhelming reality of his situation, the unreality of it as well, dictated that he needed to be completely honest.

I need help, he thought. *No point in denying it.*

"Time for your meds, Mr. Paul."

Stephen looked up to see Mary Ann standing there, staring down at him. She seemed composed of less edges somehow, something in her eyes and facial features had softened.

"Huh?"

He'd heard her but thought he heard something else in her tone.

"Time for your medication, Mr. Paul," she repeated.

Yes, he thought. *There's something like pity there. She's feeling sorry for me.*

"OK," he said, setting Bob Barker's bendy pencil on the legal pad and extending both upward to her.

"Thank you," she said, taking the legal pad and prison pencil. "I'll put these up and meet you over at the med room, OK?"

Warmth? he thought. *Oh, God. What's happened?*

She waited for his response. She never waited for his response to anything.

Stephen nodded his head and avoided her prying eyes. He turned himself in the wheelchair and made his way down the hall, feeling the sting of her eyes on the back of his neck like hot pinpricks. He forced himself not to turn and look.

§

"Stephen, I've got some bad news," Dr. Rebecca Holt said.

Stephen was preoccupied. He was looking out the little window of Dr. Holt's office and thinking about human perception.

A camera wouldn't see what I see, he thought.

He saw the view, from his perspective in the armchair, of the window, the ice smeared across the surface like a heavy-handed lacquer, but imagined it from behind the lens of a camera.

The golden glow of the sun hitting the ice wouldn't look as warm, he thought. *It would look more clinical. You'd have to add filters and effects to see what a human being sees.*

He knew he'd been holding his breath, off and on, since the morning. A tenseness spread across his body and he felt that he was just waiting for the rain of blows. He thought the restricted air vessels and low amount of oxygen in his bloodstream had something to do with the way he was seeing things, especially the sunlight, finally shining, coming in through the little slit of a window.

"Stephen?"

Stephen turned away from the window and made eye contact.

"Sorry," he said.

"You seem a bit distracted this afternoon, Stephen."

He nodded.

She paused, sized him up.

Stephen knew she was making the determination whether she thought he was fit enough to handle whatever bad news she had to give.

"Stephen, I've got some bad news," she said, having made her decision. "Martha O'Connolly was in an accident."

Kind Eyed Martha.

"As you can see," Dr. Holt said, motioning towards the ice-glazed window, "we've had some inclement weather. The roads are bad. They're saying that only those that absolutely have to be out on the roads should risk it."

An accident. Kind Eyed Martha was in a car accident.

"She died, Stephen," Dr. Holt said.

Stephen saw those eyes, Kind Eyed Martha's, looking down at him that first time he was conscious of another's presence since his troubles. They embraced him with their warmth. They felt like the last warm breeze of summer dancing across your face in autumn. The last reminder of hope and kindness and a sweetness that was nearly impossible to define.

Dead. Gone. Another blank space stretches the void. Drops in the bucket of nothing.

"Stephen?"

How to Beat Back the Sadness or How to Lie to Yourself to Make It Through a Hard Time in a Lifetime of Hard Times. Martha.

Stephen was crying. A silent weeping that did not hiccup, that did not gulp for breath, that did not screech out the hurt for all to hear. Stephen wept in painful sighs, in long shuddering arcs of the spine that stabbed pinpricks into his heart.

He closed his eyes and made his hands into fists until he felt the bite of his elongated fingernails into his palm. Then he relaxed his fingers until the tension was overwrought and had to be squeezed out through the fists like some sadness juice.

First Quarter

They clipped his fingernails that afternoon. Mary Ann did it at the request of Dr. Holt. They usually clipped them once every week and a half or so. The schedule was hard to remember but Stephen was sure there was a chart somewhere.

After the nurse was finished, Stephen stared down at his open palms in his lap. He sat in the wheelchair and thought that each red-ringed blood crescent was a moon. A moon for an uncountable series of losses. A lifetime of losing. A life of loss.

Stephen wept.

§

The farmer was sitting on his bed. Stephen stopped short in the door when he saw the dirty overalls stretched across his bed linen.

"This here is a shitty bed," the farmer said.

Stephen swallowed, hard.

"Yessir. I've slept in many a-shitty bed but this one right here," the farmer drove the shit-flecked heels of his weathered boots into the quilt and sheets, "takes the cake."

Stephen blinked. Swallowed. He opened his eyes and the farmer was still on the bed.

"What do you want?"

Stephen cringed under the farmer's shining eyes.

Wrong question, he thought. *He's not real. It doesn't matter what he wants.*

The farmer chuckled. A spikelet of wheat appeared between his lips. He set about grinding it slowly between his teeth. Stephen watched it spin in little uneven spirals. It was hypnotizing.

"So, your little old lady friend bought the farm, huh?"

Stephen felt like he'd been slapped.

The farmer continued a low-level chuckling.

Stephen's stomach churned. The muscles of his neck screamed with tension.

"Martha," Stephen said.

"I guess we'll see if you know how to beat back the sadness, huh?"

Stephen screamed.

§

"He was in my bed. Right there. Shitty bootheels and all," Stephen said.

Nurse Marks looked from Stephen, sitting hunched over, his arms wrapped around his knotted stomach, to the bed, freshly made and def-ecation-free.

"Mr. Paul, I don't see a thing on that bed," Nurse Marks said.

Stephen saw the empty bed, he saw that it was clean and made. He blinked and saw the after-image, like a sunspot, of the farmer sprawled out there, his hands behind his head, the hat cocked at an awkward angle, jutted out like some rock pile crag.

"He was there," Stephen said, depleted.

He felt so tired. So beaten.

How to Beat Back the Sadness.

Sand. Time and sand and loss and a farmer that won't leave me the fuck alone.

"You sit tight, Mr. Paul," Nurse Marks said, turning and exiting the room.

Two of the them returned. Stephen was given a pill to swallow and ushered into the bed.

"Now you just lay there and relax," Nurse Marks said. "You just need you a nice little nap is all. Big shock you had today. You'll be OK."

The medication worked quickly. Stephen felt gravity change, force his eyelids lower and lower until they felt like they stretched all the way to the tips of his cold toes.

He smelled the shit though. He smelled the shit and the hay and the fuzzy sun-soaked smell of the farmer's skin. He did.

§

The rope was swinging. The wind had picked up.

Stephen watched the swirls of fog dance around the rope hanging down from the streetlamp. It looked like some great ghost ritual, swirls of worship surrounding the holy.

Black and blue and twine and time.

Stephen knew he was alone but called out anyway.

"Hello?"

His voice seemed muted, boxed in by the dancing flutters of mist.

Ghosts.

I am haunted.

Stephen was crying. He felt he was always crying, that it was his natural state, his status quo, his idle.

"Is anybody there?"

There was no reply.

§

He sat watching the ice melt off the big bay windows. Little rivulets of crystalline tears smearing arcs across the willow.

How to Beat Back the Sadness sat open in his lap. He'd tried to continue his experiment. He flipped the thing open at random four times but couldn't force his eyes to make sense of the type. Just stains of ink slowly dissipating from black to blue.

There is a darkness more blue than black.

"It's time for your writing, Mr. Paul."

Stephen did not answer. He did not turn away from the window. He did not even register who was speaking, just that words were spoken.

He felt himself wheeled away from the window and closed his eyes. He felt two hot tears slip through the teeth of his lashes and spill out onto his cold cheeks.

Martha.

Kind Eyed Martha.

Into the Big Empty. Filling the void with another blank. A darkness more blue than black.

Motion ceased.

Stephen opened his eyes. Nurse Marks was speaking, her eyes locked down on his. Her mouth moved, noise issued forth, but Stephen heard no single word, just the collection of vowel and consonant sounds, the wet smack of lips, the blurred movement of tongue, the wisp of breath as punctuation.

Nurse Marks handed down the yellow legal pad and Bob Barker's bendy prison pencil. Stephen took these objects and held them. They felt foreign and unreal, more atom than object, little dots in the ether, a collection of the invisible colliding and reeling and coming together to make the visible shape of something, enough to show but not enough to feel real in his hands.

He set them on his lap and closed his eyes.

The sound of voice and the sound of movement. A faint breeze on his face.

Stephen slept.

§

The streams run, the river and the creek
The buck in rut and the fickle moon's sad-eyed sweep
The farmer is gone, lo, he is gone
On the run or roam, somewhere, far from home

§

There is

Stephen opened his eyes.

a darkness

He closed them again.

more blue than

"Time to wake up, Mr. Paul."

black.

§

A vast spread of inky blackness. A small shape somewhere just off-center. A huddled form. A mass of atoms shaped like a huddled form.

Something.

Nothing.

The fog slowly setting in. The swirls, ghosts in their pagan ritual, the carrying off and the carrying on, grey and white and steadily growing. There is a huddled shape just off-center. The emptiness is filling.

The lamplight buzzes but does not produce any illumination.

§

"Mr. Paul?"

§

"Stephen?"

§

The chair is wheeled. He is between the wheels, not at the wheel.

§

Stephen opened his eyes. It was late afternoon, early evening.

"Mr. Paul?"

Something was stuck in his throat, not quite choking him but keeping him from speaking. He swallowed. It moved.

"Yes?"

"Can you sit up for me?"

The light was weak. A pale cup of creamy afternoon tea gone cold.

Stephen used his elbows to prop himself up. He was having a difficult time focusing his eyes. The light was all he could see and acknowledge. There were shapes there but he could not place them.

"Mr. Paul, how are you feeling today?"

Stephen did not know.

"Tired," he said, finally.

"You've been asleep for quite some time."

Have I?

Ghosts and their pagan rituals.

"OK," he said.

He lifted his hands to rub his eyes. They were heavy, made of some wa-ter-logged wood.

Tropic rot.

His bones were disintegrating. His flesh petrifying, slipping back to dust or ash after the blast.

He rubbed and rubbed his eyes. There was an oil there, something that smeared but did not come clean.

He opened his eyes and there was the light and the shapes, but he could not distinguish them beyond the fact that there was light and there were shapes.

"Mr. Paul?"

Stephen felt himself sliding back down. The ghosts weren't finished with him yet. Unseen hands wrought and wrung and pulled.

§

How's it gonna be?

How's it gonna end?

Does it ever really end?

Stephen felt himself slipping into something less. He felt his arms stretch, lapse back into some older, fundamental form, an oddly satisfy-ing semi-illusoriness. Stephen stretched and thinned and became transparent. He could see through his arms. He could see through his legs. He could see beyond himself into the black expanse.

There was a metallic tinkling, a rattle, a buzz. Then a great pale light, nearly orange but tinged with a soft yellow, shining down from somewhere above.

Stephen saw that he was mist. Swirls. Bits and pieces of himself catching and flitting on the hands of something unseen but constantly moving. He was a ghost. He was among ghosts. A collective.

"Rivers?"

There was an answer from somewhere very far away.

§

Stephen opened his eyes. The little room was dark.

He wiggled his toes and felt glad they responded, the scratchy, starched sheets rough against his skin. He sat up, feeling hunger and emptiness growl in his stomach, and looked out the window.

The bright white scythe of the moon shone with an intensity that Stephen had never before witnessed.

It's beautiful, he thought. *The moon.*

He turned on the bed so he could lie still and inert and stare.

§

"It's often a long road," Dr. Holt said.

A long, hard road, he repeated to himself. He heard Woody Guthrie singing it.

"There are up's and down's," she said. "You can't just snap your finger and be better, Stephen. I know this is hard, but this is the reality of your situation."

I's walkin' down this road feelin' bad, bad, bad, he sang to himself.

"But you need to stay positive. There is no need to sink within yourself. You're making progress, Stephen," Dr. Holt leaned forward to emphasize this point. "You are. It might not seem like it, but, you are."

She leaned back and adjusted her grip on the pen.

Stephen noted that it was not one of Bob Barker's bendy prison pencils.

He didn't know what to say. He felt dirty and tired and had. Had, like the butt of some cosmic joke. His skin prickled with the unseen but pungent flakes of shit from the farm.

"Stephen," Dr. Holt said.

She was staring at him.

How long have I been quiet?

"Sorry," he said. "I'm...I'm a bit off today."

She smiled.

"That's OK, Stephen," she said. "Let's talk about your family today, OK?"

Stephen sighed but nodded.

§

Have you always been this way?

Yes.

I have always been a wreck.

What's your earliest memory?

Crying after a man stubbed a cigarette out on my stomach for eating some dollar bills that were left on a dirty coffee table next to an overfilled ashtray.

A tick. A second's pause too long and the cause was another brick in the wall. Closing off and knowing it's wrong. Wrong. Stupid. Futile. Doing nothing to help himself.

The fox was restless in its den. Its stomach growled but the winter was bitter, the winter was cold, and the henhouse was well-lit.

Tell me about your stepfather.

The farmer had returned. The farm never slept. There's always work to be done.

There's a level of misunderstanding rooted deep that goes well back before I can remember. I never trusted him. I never loved him. I couldn't. He's unlovable. I guess, I might be too.

Why would you say you're unlovable?

The porch creaks with the pulse of the rocking chair. The beat of the farm. *Tap tap whoosh. Tap tap whoosh.* The farmer has a jug. He drinks. It'd been a long day of chores and winter maintenance, but the spring was coming. That vast arctic tundra would thaw and the fields would yield up their bounty. The earth would be tilled. The seeds would be sewn. The crop would rise as sure as the sun.

§

There were pockets of hopelessness. Stephen tread carefully. Sometimes, he couldn't help but getting tripped up. Sometimes, he fell headlong into a darkness more blue than black.

He watched the days slowly stretch. Longer. Longer until there was the hint of something sweet on the horizon. Something pure and green on the breeze. Something ticklish about the mornings. Something promising about the dusk.

He waited. He didn't know what else to do.

§

Stephen returned to the experiment.

§

When the road is rocky, tread carefully but do not stop! Keep going! The path may not be clearly marked but Trust in the Lord and He will show the way. God will untangle the maze. Sure, you may find yourself facing many a dead end but remember that God provides! He works in Mysterious Ways—mysterious only because we are incapable of seeing the Big Picture—but He works with your best interests in mind.

§

Don't that road look rough and rocky, Woody Guthrie sang. Don't that sea look wide and deep.

He saw the book as some cryptic grimoire now. The keeper of secrets in a faulty translation. Or, more probably, a coded book of insights into the inner workings of a collective motivation: a glimpse between the lines of "Everything happens for a reason" and "God doesn't give you more than you can carry."

God is the pen on the page. God is the act of creation. God is the realization that choice exists, and actions matter. God is the endgame where there is nothing you can do.

Stephen felt like a kid with swimmies adrift in the deep end. No lifeguard. Enter at your own risk.

He was groping for a handhold, something sure and steady and constant.

God is the rope of the damned. The lapse into blind faith. The trust in a boldfaced lie. The path doubled back. The snake eating its tail.

God is the path through the maze. God is a metaphor for pursuit of understanding. A name for an action, a way of life. A collection of myriad mini-courses in the process of coming to know. Gleaning and bleeding understanding.

God is a metaphor for the crack in the ceiling. The slip in the seam. The ethereal made tactile.

He knew it was bullshit but what wasn't? He had nothing if not time. He had nothing if not a drugged mind.

§

"Time for your writing, Mr. Paul."

§

"Time for your medications, Mr. Paul."

§

"Rise and shine, Mr. Paul."

§

"Lunchtime, Mr. Paul."

§

"Let's talk about your journal, Stephen."

"OK."

"The style of your writing is very intriguing," Dr. Holt said. "I've been following the changes. You're getting very experimental with your approach."

Here's the critic, he thought.

Stephen nodded. It was true. He'd thrown caution to the wind, left stylistic formality on the line knowing the storm was approaching.

"There's a liberating feeling in writing," Stephen said.

He opened his mouth with no idea what was going to come out but nodded in agreement with himself after hearing the sentence. It was a fundamental truth of writing. It was the creative act of chasing the thread.

You have to find it first, he thought. *This is more than half the battle.*

"You're working through some things," Dr. Holt said, her eyes skimming a yellow sheet from the legal pad, "in a very obscure but beautiful way."

Stephen couldn't help it. He smiled. He forced his face smooth before Dr. Holt looked up from the page though.

"Thank you," he said.

"You're welcome, Stephen," she smiled.

§

The forest for the trees. The topsoil from the tilled. The rope from the vine. The time for the bind. The twine for the rhyme. A penny for the road; save the thoughts.

§

The spring came suddenly. There was one warm spring morning then another and not a single frigid slip.

Stephen's medications were changed. He was told this was minor tweaking. A lower dose of this. An introducing of that. The cigar smell and white coats agreed: Stephen was improving.

Stephen stopped thinking about it. He stopped willing himself to improve. He let it happen. He did what he was told. He wrote. He conducted The Experiment.

§

"The hearing's next week," Corey Streeter said. "I'm working with Dr. Shwartz on arranging for your transportation. He thinks you're well enough to be accompanied by Dr. Holt and myself."

The lawyer was watching Stephen sidelong. Appraising him.

He wonders if I'll try to run away, Stephen thought. *Thinks I'll try and slit his throat and run off into the night in his Mercedes.*

"What do you think the outcome of this hearing will be?" he asked.

"Well, that depends on the testimony," the lawyer said. "If you're present, you'll be called to testify. You don't have to, if you don't feel up to it, but showing that you're in control of your faculties will go a long way with the judge."

The attorney closed the folder and looked at Stephen full-on for the first time since the start of their supervised meeting—Nurse Marks was steadily punching the keys on a laptop with only the index fingers of each of her claw-like hands.

"Do you think you're, uh…" Streeter looked over to the nurse then back to Stephen, "ready to testify in a courtroom setting?"

Stephen nodded.

"Because if you don't," the attorney added quickly, "that's fine too. The testimony of the staff here seems to be all positive. It might be enough to get you out on supervision. If not, we could get the hearing postponed a few more weeks."

"No," Stephen said.

The attorney looked startled for a split-second.

"I'm ready," Stephen said.

The attorney walked Stephen through several lines of inquiry he supposed the prosecution would try. Stephen bit his tongue and answered appropriately.

§

Nurse Marks came into his room with a bundle of clothes draped over her arm.

"Change up," she said, passing the clothes to Stephen. "You all will be leaving in the next half-hour."

The nurse left, the door pulled to behind her.

Stephen looked at the clothes. They were not his own. Not in a style he would've worn had he any choice in the matter. He'd been told they had been provided by his attorney.

Streeter would've picked these, he thought.

The khakis were stiff and cheaply made. The button up shirt was an old man's argyle. He opened the shoebox then slipped his feet into the uncomfortable leather slippers.

There was no mirror in his room to gauge his appearance. He walked down the hall to the bathroom and studied himself from different angles through the toothpaste specks, hardened pimple excretions, and snot-coated mirror above the sink. The bathroom smelled of stale piss and bleach.

I look like somebody's costumed attempt at a professor.

§

The trees, great pines and oaks, spectral and bare but hints of a looming spring shown in the fresh splash of green here and there, whirled by the clean windows of Dr. Holt's Land Rover.

Stephen sat in the passenger seat. He'd tried to take a seat in the back but Dr. Holt informed Stephen of the facility's protocol, which called for at least two adults, one of which had to be a member the facility's staff, and the strict seating arrangements, one beside and one behind.

He did not question her. He did what he was told.

He had never been out in this part of the county. He watched great stretches of farmland mix with tall strands of second-growth forest as they rolled down the nearly empty two-lane highway.

No one spoke for some time.

Corey Streeter sat in the backseat of the Land Rover, directly behind Stephen, and breathed heavily. There was a high-pitched whirr, something hard partially blocking his nasal passageway. Stephen heard the attorney tapping away on his cellphone.

The landscape scaled back. Less and less trees. Less wild places. More farmland.

Stephen tensed. It took him some miles to realize he was tensing.

Quit being ridiculous, he told himself, embarrassed. *The farmer isn't real. He isn't.*

He forced his muscles to relax. He let out a low, soft sigh then took each breath consciously in, held it, then let it out. He did this quietly, hoping neither Streeter nor Dr. Holt noticed.

Farms began to be interrupted by other forms of industry. A rock quarry. A farm machinery shop. A car dealership. Warehouses in various forms of disrepair and use.

Then they were on the outskirts of the city. Stephen recognized where they were and watched the familiar cityscape pass.

Along with this environmental familiarity, he felt the spiders returning to his stomach. It was an odd homecoming and he couldn't help but feel thankful for their company.

An infestation to be thankful for, he thought.

Stephen smiled but quickly made his face blank again, making sure Dr. Holt wasn't watching him out of the corner of her eye.

They started with only the rustling of a few tiny legs but as they neared the city center, Stephen felt the webbed sack open and hundreds of new spiderlings took their first hesitant but excited steps in the darkness of his belly.

Welcome, he thought.

Dr. Holt parked the Land Rover at a meter in front of the courthouse. The blue-green Spanish American War statue of a soldier with his sleeves rolled up greeted them as Dr. Holt fed the meter.

Streeter's demeanor changed as soon as his feet hit the sidewalk. He was in his element. One of the chosen. He moved with the sureness of a rooster.

Stephen found himself thinking of a henhouse at dusk. The skunk-like scent of the recently emerged fox had the birds nervous. They clucked and preened and jostled each other noisily.

"You'll be fine," Dr. Holt was telling him.

The attorney had been speaking. Stephen realized he hadn't heard a thing the man had said.

Stephen shook his head to clear it. He banished all barnyard images from his mind as they passed under the arched doorway into the courthouse.

§

They entered with the hushed sounds of the courtroom looming large. Some epic rite of terror told through whispers, the shuffling of thick, crisp papers, the signing of important names on important documents, stamps stamping away, the click-clack clatter of rapid typing. There were lots of unfocused eyes and several pairs that were as sharp as talons.

Streeter left them sitting on a pewlike bench that was nearly half-full. They watched him strut his rooster's walk to the large wooden table where several other men and women in the utmost business of attire sat or stood or leaned. They smiled and winked and nodded and talked in sibilance.

A pagan cathedral of itemized justice.

Neither Dr. Holt nor Stephen spoke. They sat, mute and still, and took in the happenings of this strange environ. The judge was not yet on the bench. The tall entrance doors of the courtroom opened and shut and people, in various stages of appropriateness, passed in and out. Stephen saw short skirts and fishnets, filthy baseball caps and sleeveless t-shirts, oversized or undersized suits and dresses that had obviously been purchased for other events—funerals, weddings, court dates years in the past. He marveled at the dichotomy of the setting and the innate make-up of several of the individuals.

Sinners and saints and the pulpit of on-lookers passing judgement like communion wafers.

The room was like a refrigerator. Stephen counted four massive ceiling vents pumping down arctic air. He shivered but was thankful for Streeter's choice of cheap but thick clothing.

A man in a Toledo Rockets football jersey walked down the aisle scouting for a place to sit. Stephen took note of the rumpled condition of the quite old jersey, stained, holey jeans, and duct-taped work boots. Their eyes met, and Stephen offered up a weak smile. The man returned a terse nod and sat down a few feet away from Stephen.

The bailiff, a barrel-chested woman with short, stiff hair, entered through a door near the front.

"All rise," she called.

The rest of what she said was lost in the shuffle of dozens of people rising to their feet. A collective groan and sigh peppered with joint pops and even a loud, wet-sounding fart from somewhere just behind where Stephen sat. He had to force himself not to turn around and look for the culprit.

"Be seated," the judge's microphoned voice said.

The voice came from above. Stephen felt like Dorothy as he scanned the ceiling searching for the speakers. It took some time, but he saw them, carefully camouflaged by wood paneled siding that matched that of the walls.

The voice from on high, he thought.

Stephen followed the words for a while then stopped. The voices, lawyers and police officers and court staff and medical professionals and those entangled with the former, slipped into a white noise. His eyes wandered, as far as they could without making a scene of his visual exploration, lighting on a very young breast-feeding mother, a shabbily dressed man somewhere in his mid-fifties unapologetically picking his nose with the precision and whole-hearted devotion of an archeologist, a woman with some sort of downstairs discomfort who danced a strange jig in her seat on the bench, a father with a gaggle of frenzied children. Stephen watched the man's face flicker like a channel slipping between grainy stations. He was stern. He was adoration. He was threatening. He was exasperated. He was loving. But always he was tired. So tired.

An hour passed. Two. Dr. Holt began to tap a light beat with the right leg she had crossed over her left. Stephen counted the rhythm off in his head as his eyes roamed.

One two three one two three

The breastfeeding mother had to switch breasts.

One two three one two three

The nasal archeologist became enamored with the cache from his most recent dig.

One two three one two three

The bailiff moved with a controlled malice to a crying woman in orange and ushered her out of the courtroom.

One two three one two three

One of the children broke from the pack and ran up the aisle. A remonstration was issued from the bench and the father, red-faced and shaking, sat the child down firmly in the seat next to him with apologies and raised palms.

One two three one two three

Streeter was kneeling down beside them, hunched over in the small space between benches, whispering something into Dr. Holt's ear. She nodded and rose to follow the lawyer.

Stephen made to stand too but she turned and leaned forward to whisper down to him.

"Sit tight, Stephen," Dr. Holt said. "I'll be right back."

Stephen eased himself back down and watched the two of them walk over to the great wooden desk of the lawyers.

Streeter opened a folder and several papers were looked over and discussed. Dr. Holt nodded and nodded and signed one sterling white page and nodded some more. She kept stealing glances back to Stephen. He made it a point to be looking elsewhere when she did.

§

There was a brief recess, twenty minutes or so for the judge and several attorneys to disappear back into the judge's chambers to discuss some case privately, then Stephen was called before the court.

He listened to his name drift down from the overhead speakers.

Once. Twice. Stephen saw that both Dr. Holt and Streeter were staring at him with eyes like SOS flares. The bailiff, scowling with muscled arms crossed, made to cross the room to the bench where Stephen sat.

He rose on shaky legs and apologized to four different people as he sidled out of the narrow space between benches.

He felt all of the eyes on him as he walked up the aisle, pushed open the swinging gate, and made his way to Dr. Holt and Streeter. A chair was offered for him to sit down at the large table. He sat.

Streeter whispered something to Dr. Holt then approached the bench, the judge preoccupied with a document she was reading, held one finger up for Streeter to wait.

Stephen looked over at Dr. Holt. She smiled and patted the top of his left hand.

He tried to smile back but the muscles in his face felt hijacked. They fidgeted, jittering up and down to some syncopation Stephen did not recognize.

"Approach the bench," the judge said.

Stephen made to rise but Dr. Holt stayed him with another pat of the hand.

"Not us," she whispered.

Stephen watched another attorney move across the floor in some of the

A.S. COOMER

highest heels he had ever seen. She moved with the grace of some wild creature.

The judge held her hand over the microphone and spoke down to the two attorneys.

"What's happening?" Stephen whispered.

He couldn't help it. He didn't want to speak but he felt he might explode if he didn't do something to ease the tension.

"Just wait," Dr. Holt said.

This discussion took several minutes.

Stephen began bouncing his right foot to a frenetic pace. Something jazz fusion or beyond. He forced himself to stop but it took right back up again on its own accord as soon as he stopped thinking about it.

Somewhere a man sneezed. It was an elongated thing. It started low in the register, the receding of the gentle, beach-lapping waves, a rumbling intake of breath, then exploded with a fierce wail, the tsunami crashing down over the hushed room.

A child laughed but was quickly quieted. Without turning around, Stephen saw the red-faced father squeezing the arm of the child and issuing threats through clenched teeth.

One two three one two three

His own feet with the beat. The beat intensifying, picking up pace.

Onetwothreeonetwothree

The three of them, the judge, the prosecutor, and Streeter, all turned to look at Stephen and Dr. Holt sitting at the oversized table.

Stephen's face went white. He felt the color drain like a bath, all dredges and foam and scum sucked away leaving only the exposed fear and uncertainty there.

Oh God, he thought. *Oh God.*

onetwothreeonetwothree

The waltz of terror.

"Mr. Paul, please approach the bench," the bailiff said. Her voice carried like a bugler's blow.

He rose too quickly and knocked both of his knees on the underside of the table.

"Shit," he said.

His face filled with red at his own utterance.

Ohgodohgod.

onetwothreeonetwothree

From somewhere behind, Stephen heard chuckling. He tried not to focus on it, but he recognized the voice.

Please not now, he thought. *Please God, not now.*

onetwothreeonetwothree

"Be calm," Dr. Holt whispered.

She tried smiling but her face was tight, the lips barely able to upturn with the pressure.

Stephen nodded, a jerk and pull affair that must've looked like a donkey's awkward buck and pushed the chair back from the table. He put one foot in front of the other and felt tripping was a very real possibility.

The laughing.

onetwothreeonetwothree

He stopped beside his attorney, who leaned in and patted Stephen's arm.

"Mr. Paul, the court has been informed of your tremendous progress since our last hearing," the judge said.

Stephen heard the microphoned voice issue from behind and above. The room felt upturned and loaded onto a massive spinning top picking up speed.

God is the rope of the damned.

God is the voice in the sky.

God is the verdict of death.

Stephen took in a quick wisp of air, held it, then let it out after the stars began dancing their structured flit and flutter in his eyes.

The farmer is here.

Stephen cringed at the thought but did his best to minimize its appearance on his countenance.

The laughter was steadily though nearly imperceptibly increasing in volume and toneless mirth. Stephen could smell the faint whiff of shit in the room.

The spiders were not a comfort now. They spread through his stomach with little furry bellies, needle-prick teeth, claws and tarsi dragging and poking and prodding.

onetwothreeonetwothree

"I think you've proven you're on the road to recovery, Mr. Paul," the judge said. "Do not make us regret this decision. We'll reconvene in two months to evaluate your progress."

Stephen watched the judge lift a gavel and rap it on something he couldn't see from where he stood. Stephen flinched at what he expected was going to be a thunderous boom but the sound was lost in the restive sounds of the courtroom.

Streeter was smiling at him and pulling him by the arm away from the bench and back towards the table where Dr. Holt rose smiling.

"Congratulations, Stephen," she said.

From the corner of his eye, Stephen spotted *him*.

"That went about as well as possible, I think," Streeter said.

The judge's voice called a name and number from on high.

onetwothreeonetwothree

The farmer stood near the door, his back to the oaken frame. He was steadily working the spikelet between his stained teeth. A smile like a rotten apple's core. A smile like the putrid inside of a forgotten jack-o-lantern. A smile like a skeleton. He pulled his left hand from the pocket of his overalls and waved a dainty two fingered salute, which he punctuated with a snort.

"Stephen?"

The courtroom pixelated, blurred into something remotely familiar but not quite in focus.

"Mr. Paul?"

onetwothreeonetwothree

Stephen blinked, hard and fast. He shook his head to clear it and re-opened his eyes. The room was back in focus. He could hear the murmur of voices. Someone sniffled near at hand. The shuffling of papers like dust in the wind.

Stephen turned to see twin sets of worried eyes. Dr. Holt and Corey Streeter were no longer smiling.

"Be seein' ye," the farmer called.

Stephen shrank from the loudness of the voice. He couldn't help it. He knew it was only in his head, but the volume struck him like the snap-pop of a wet towel.

onetwothreeonetwothree

"Stephen, are you all right?" Dr. Holt asked.

He saw Corey Streeter take an unconscious step away.

Stephen looked back to where the farmer had stood but he was gone.

Waxing Gibbous

"**I** know it must be a bit overwhelming for you, Stephen," Dr. Holt said.

They were back in the trees now. The road seemed impossibly straight to Stephen. A slash through stabs of trees and splatters of farmland. A rising, twirling mist of fog rose from the road in ghostlike wisps. Hands outstretched. Faces upturned. Mouths agape. Eyes closed and open and dazed and unseeing. A pagan dance for the whole thing to come crashing down. The sky electric, not a single cloud, blue and impending, colossal and watchful.

Stephen nodded.

The farmer had been there, and Stephen thought his face had changed.

Changed or had I finally recognized it? Stephen thought. *Am I dreaming? Is this real?*

Streeter was punching away at his cellphone in the backseat. He'd just gotten off a phone call, Stephen assumed with one of his superiors at the law firm, all laughs and yes's and thank you's.

He'd been there. The whole time. Just waiting. Watching. Why won't he just leave me alone? Why's his face so familiar now?

"I know there are some big changes on the horizon for you, Stephen," Dr. Holt was saying, "but I think you know you have the tools to deal with them. Don't you?"

Stephen nodded. He hadn't really heard the question. Just the rise in inflection at the end of the sentence and the slight turn of her head and eyes from the road to where he sat, dumbfounded and reeling.

What am I even thinking? He's not real. There wasn't a farmer in that courtroom. Well, there might've been—another rural domestic violence or boundary dispute case—but not The *Farmer.*

The road was turning to the left slightly. A long, graceful arc leading away from a massive farming operation, all silos and ponds and heavy machinery, acre upon acre of cleared land. Cows dotting the horizon like the spots on their hides.

The road slipped into an opening of towering oaks. Stephen looked up into the faceless trees. Shafts of sunlight found pine needle, pine cone, great expanses between the trees where the snows of the past few weeks were crusted, a diamond's twinkle to the hardened edges, but untouched.

"You won't be on your own," Dr. Holt said. "You'll have meetings every evening. You'll be in constant contact with your new therapist. You'll have regular appointments, most likely on a monthly basis, with your new psychiatrist to make sure the medications are remaining effective."

Stephen nodded. It was expected.

Why is he bothering me?

Stephen clenched then slowly, purposefully unclenched his teeth. His jaw hurt. The tendons and muscles of his face felt like they'd just run their own marathon. Stephen opened his mouth to relieve some of the tension and an audible pop issued from the left side of his jaw. It sounded like a pistol report so near his ear.

A.S. COOMER

But then what's the point in questioning insanity? Because I am insane, aren't I? Shuttled to and from courtroom proceedings, predicated by insane actions, by your shrink, no less. Protocol in place to avoid harm to self and others. Two-person transports. Nobody else has figments of their imaginations, creations so unlike anything related to their existence but somehow a somewhat rational figment—I mean it's not a three-headed chicken monster or unicorn or centaur, just a normal, if somewhat antiquated, farmer—following them around and making them embarrassed for something they have completely, absolutely zero control over.

Stephen blinked, hard, holding his eyes closed a half-second longer than he needed to rewet them. He leaned over and pressed his forehead against the cold passenger window. He sighed and watched his breath fog the glass.

I mean, why the fuck a farmer? Why not Steinbeck or Hemingway? I'm a writer for Christ's sake. Or even a pompous, showy Fitzgerald. By-the-word Dickenson, even. Shit, I'd take a passive aggressive and morose Sartre.

"You're awfully quiet over there, Stephen," Dr. Holt said.

Stephen closed his mouth and tried thinking of a suitable response. The fog on the window receded into itself. Some just off-center point of departure and dissipation.

"I mean, I know it's a lot to take in," Dr. Holt said. "After all this time in a carefully controlled environment, the thought of being on your own must come with a little anxiety but you must not let yourself worry too much. You're progressing well, Stephen. You're making tremendous progress. The court acknowledged as much this morning."

She rushed from one sentence to the other as if the house of cards would come crashing down if she didn't stack another on quickly.

Streeter snickered at something from his phone.

What do lawyers laugh about?

Stephen listened to Streeter's fingers tap the screen. He listened to the man's breathing wheeze in and out of a constrained nasal cavity.

Stephen's body felt like it was vibrating. A great tuning fork struck. A static ringing. Blood rushing in a campanologist's design in his ears. Tolling, tolling, tolling. A great wave of fuzz. Thousands upon thousands of atoms shaking, jostling against each other. The fabric of himself like a sheet in the wind. Snapping and slapping and whipping against the unseen.

"Stephen?"

He didn't know what to say, so Stephen said nothing.

§

It was to happen in three weeks.

Baby steps.

Stephen was assigned a social worker from the community mental health center. They met face to face once a week in preparation of Stephen's release from the hospital. Living arrangements, weekly therapist meetings, a 24-hour helpline, twice monthly in-home visits from the social worker as well as weekly phone calls, monthly psychiatrist appointments, and more were discussed.

There was a screen of condescension that Stephen did his best to look through and not address.

"Do you know how to balance a checkbook, Mr. Paul?"

Stephen bit his tongue and nodded his head.

"Good," Mr. Clark Dennison said, moving his pen down the list of things he had to discuss and checkoff that he'd discussed with his client. "Visitation. Do you have any children that we need to set up some sort of supervised visitation with?"

Stephen shook his head.

The social worker nodded and went on down the list.

§

He looked forward to his time with Bob Barker's bendy pencil and the legal pad more than anything else. The sense of his looming freedom was still too foreign for him to process. Too remote for complete consideration. Besides, there was the new frequency of his tuning.

Stephen wrote ceaselessly every morning. A stream of consciousness was not quite the apt term, but it was the best he could come up with. New boundaries, new territories. Stephen worked on blending poetry into the prose of memoir. Thoughts as metallurgy. Words as primer. Scenes as emotional landscapes, stark and encompassing.

Stephen thought his style had shifted, morphed into something claus-trophobically beautiful. The governor he'd been riding with all his life was uprooted, jerked from the engine to lie still and useless by the side of some forlorn highway. He wrote with abandon. He wrote whatever came into his head. When his mind was blank, he wrote without process.

> Throw the ball.
> Chase the ball.
> Be.
> Do.

Dr. Holt seemed more and more confirmed in the belief that Stephen was making tremendous progress. He knew in his heart of hearts that she'd been on the fence after his little spell at the courthouse.

Stephen felt naked but comfortable when he wrote. He felt stiff and out of practice when he spoke with his social worker. The process of in-teracting with someone with guided expectations was tiring, exercising for the first time after a long period of overindulgence.

The days ticked off like a cooling engine. Stephen waited and vibrated and wondered how no one could hear the song of his bell.

§

"Employment?"

"I teach at the University," Stephen said. "Well, I used to teach. English."

The social worker flipped back several stapled pages, nodding all the while, and read.

A floating system of organization. A real-time data processor.

The social worker's brow knitted closer together. The fabric of understanding pulling threads both individually and collectively. He looked up from the papers at Stephen.

"You're still employed by the University, Mr. Paul," he said. "You'll start back at the beginning of next semester. You've been on unpaid leave pending your completion and compliance with this program."

Stephen nodded to answer something resembling a question in the man's eyes.

"We'll have to set up an appointment with the University's HR to make sure they're aware of the in's and out's of your release. Monitoring requirements and all that."

Stephen, again, nodded.

"You teach English there, you said?"

Nod.

"Huh," the social worker said.

He let his eyes study Stephen a tick longer, then, with a slight shrug of his shoulders, he went back to the questions.

They came in torrents. They came in floods. An inundation of ask, ask,

ask, scribble, scribble, scribble, check, check, check.

The stream of data collection. The processing of a life down to a series of boxes, a line or two in a clearly marked area, an encapsulation for a report for a supervisor who then had their own report to forge.

How many times has this man asked these same questions? How many times has the person asked not been able to respond? How many times had the answers come with a hidden cost? Some slight wear and tear of the soul. The eventual washing out of the soul's stone?

"Great," the social worker said. "Thanks, Mr. Paul. We're nearly there. See you on Thursday."

"OK."

The wheelchair had been pushed against the wall beside the door. Stephen watched the social worker's eyes flick towards it on his way out of the room.

Stephen sat on the made bed, his ears ringing with the sound of the man's voice. A muted replay through an empty can. All treble and static and the haze of something ill-remembered.

The sun was a weak bulb sprouting from a flooded field. The next crop would fare better.

I'll be out of here this time next week, Stephen thought. *On my own.*

A speck of black on the horizon. Drifting. Buoyed in the receding flood waters. The silt of time and the grains of a life on pause.

A.S. COOMER

It was a bird. It slowly shifted into focus, carried closer to the hospital on some unseen wind. Stephen watched the way it sidled and shifted, moving itself only enough to stay afloat. Against the receding current. The great pulling back. The draining, the emptying, the abating.

Stephen wondered what would be left in its wake.

§

Planning. Discharge Planning. Treatment Continuity Planning. Relapse Prevention Planning. Community Reintroduction and Stabilization Planning.

Boxes were checked. Questions were answered. Steps were put in place.

§

"Mr. Paul?"

The woman standing looked haggard and annoyed.

"Mr. Stephen Paul?"

Stephen wondered how many times she'd called his name. He could barely focus on his thoughts with all the noise of the waiting room. Screaming children—so many screaming children of various ages—and intrusive cellphone conversations and snoring and laughing and cursing.

Stephen stood up and made his way across the room to the woman in the doorway. He had to sidestep a crawling child who appeared to be coated in a thin layer of some sort of dust.

"Mr. Paul?" the woman asked once Stephen was within an arm's length.

Stephen nodded.

The woman turned on her heels.

"Follow me."

The door, Stephen saw it was nearly two inches thick, closed behind him, shutting out the din of the waiting room.

She walked the way she looked. Taking long, slow strides. Each punctuated with an audible groan or moan tuned to the frequency of her wheezing.

Stephen saw the seat of her khaki pants was nearly threadbare. It shone with a thinness that Stephen couldn't help but study.

The halls of the Lucas Metropolitan Housing Authority were prison grey. Slate and impending. Slate and without emotion. Slate and all-consuming.

There was thin carpet on the floor. Visible pathways had been etched into it by years of steady tramping.

They rounded a corner, took another turn, and Stephen couldn't tell if they were back where they'd started or in another part of the building.

The woman walked through an open door to a small, windowless office. She sat down behind a scuffed, laminated desk. There were three great piles of stapled papers, a keyboard and computer monitor, and a constellation of ringed coffee stains.

The woman woke the computer, rapidly slapped several keys on the keyboard and began clicking with the mouse.

Stephen sat down in one of the two battered chairs in front of the desk.

"All right, Mr. Paul," the woman said.

Stephen saw the glint of polished wood and gold peeking out from under the edge of a packet of papers. He lifted it carefully and saw it was a name plate.

Veronica Shepherd, it read.

"So, the process has been expedited for you due to your situation," Veronica Shepherd said, without looking away from the computer monitor.

"OK," Stephen said.

"The process usually takes anywhere from a few days to several weeks depending on how much information is readily available, tenant vacancies, and whatnot," she said. "Due to your situation, we'll get your application processed and approved as quickly as possible."

There was something of mild annoyance in Veronica Shepherd's tone.

Stephen forced himself to ease back in the chair.

"We'll get your application submitted this morning and I'll do the legwork on the background check, the tenant agreement forms—"

Stephen felt powerless to control his waning interest. The sound of her voice was smoke blowing through a hive of bees. A lazy drone and buzz. A crackle of static in an open-windowed rainy evening.

"—due to your situation—"

Stephen leaned forward and extended his driver's license and the printout Dr. Holt gave him towards the woman. Stephen heard her voice and saw her mouth moving but felt he was hearing a public-address recording in some other language. A train station in rural Russia perhaps.

Organic animatronics.

Stephen held the objects together in his right hand. His thumb pinning the plastic card to the crisp white papers. A slight tremor in the extension. Muscles unused to extended periods of usage.

The woman's eyes still on the computer screen. Her mouth and fingers working away. Speaking and clanking, buzzing and droning.

"Here you go," Stephen whispered.

No response.

Stephen cleared his throat.

"Here you go," he said again, with more force.

The woman's fingers stopped, her eyes stayed on the screen for a moment longer, then she turned and looked at Stephen.

"Oh," she said, leaning forward and taking the papers.

The license slid down the page then clinked down onto the coffee-stained constellation of documents.

"What's this?" she asked, her eyes skimming the pages.

A new star.

Stephen saw his unsmiling face staring up at him. His pale, white cheeks punctuated by two purpled holes with twin periods.

"I see," she said.

She flipped through the pages, looked up once, then went back to computer.

Buzz and drone. An unsmiling star, cold and distant.

Stephen sat back in the chair and crossed his left leg over his right and waited.

§

She led him back through the maze of slate to the waiting room. The transportation assistant sat waiting by the door. Stephen took the papers, the printouts he'd come with and some new pages from Veronica Shepherd, and followed the assistant to the waiting minivan.

The assistant spoke but Stephen did not hear what was said. He watched the cityscape delve back to farmland then the woods. The towering oaks greeted the van with a gentle jostling. A winter's whisper of snow on the ground. The gleam of a fading sun refracted and heatless.

The flicker of a shadow behind a passing trunk caught Stephen's eye. He thought he smelled shit but decided that it might just be the van or the driver.

§

There was no fanfare for his departure. He'd made no friends. The patients were steeled off in their separate and impenetrable worlds of delusion and secrecy. The nursing staff were formal and distant. Stephen put on the clothes Corey Streeter had purchased for him for his court proceedings and waited for the taxi by the nurses station.

He waited for the feeling of exuberance. The wind in the face of freedom. The warm buzz of that intoxication did not come. He stood by the desk and felt the faint longing for something he'd missed. He found himself leaning most of his weight on the desk and forced himself to stand erect and still.

No more props. No more crutches.

He felt like spitting on the wheelchair sitting unused in the room he'd just left. He felt that it had robbed him of something essential in himself.

Nurse Marks was at the computer. She did not look at him.

Stephen wanted something. He wanted to speak.

An island. Untouched. Isolated. Alone.

"Nurse Marks?" he said.

She stopped typing and looked up. Her face, winter dried and wrinkle-aged, softened.

"Yes, Mr. Paul?"

"Can I ask a small favor of you?"

The lines etched firmly back into place.

"Maybe, Mr. Paul. What is it?"

"Can I have that Bob Barker bendy pencil?"

"Wha—"

Then she smiled. It was like the first plugging in of a recently decorated Christmas tree. The laugh was the twinkling of twine and the jingling of jostled ornaments.

"Of course, Mr. Paul," she said. "Let me get it for you."

The taxicab arrived just as Nurse Marks placed Bob Barker's bendy pencil into Stephen's upturned palm.

§

The driver was uneasy. He kept looking over at Stephen sitting in the passenger seat in his ill-fitting clothes. He rapped the steering wheel with both thumbs in drums rolls not syncopated to the pop country coming in through the speakers in the doors.

Stephen did not look back when they pulled out onto the county road heading towards Toledo. He felt the pull of the weeping willow but forced himself to look forward, out the dirty windows of the white minivan at the empty road ahead, the towering oaks getting taller and taller as they approached, at the farmlands then the successes and failures of industry, then the suburbs, then the city's outer ruined shell, then the complex of the projects.

Squat, four-storied buildings.

Clones of clones of clones of a building no one ever wanted to live in.

The driver read off the numbers as he creeped the van through the parking lot.

"9b."

A Camaro from the late 80's with a billowing tarp issuing from the T-tops.

"6c."

The hairy crack of a man's stretch-marked ass, his upper half enveloped by the open hood of a quilted Geo Metro.

"Ah," the taxi driver said, pulling the van into an empty handicapped space, "here we are. 4b."

§

The apartment was three flights up. The elevator did not work, and

Stephen was glad he had no belongings to lug up the rickety, ill-lighted stairwell. A little boy with a runny nose told Stephen it hadn't worked in some time.

The efficiency unit was furnished and had an odd, slightly burnt smell about it. There was an amazingly scuffed coffee table, an argyle couch that sunk heavily to the left, a twin mattress and box springs, and one fold-out lawn chair.

Stephen let the door close behind him and stood in the dark of the fading afternoon light. The heat was not on in the unit. He walked over to the thermostat and flicked it on. A dull pulse issued from overhead and the smell of burning dust leaked weakly out of the rusted vent covers.

Stephen walked over to the window overlooking the bald and littered yard and parking lot, and shut the parts of the blinds that still worked enough to be able to be closed.

This is it. This is where I live now.

He walked into the bedroom and sat down on the bare mattress. The springs screamed and groaned then settled to a distraught mumbling.

Stephen thought about the empty fridge. The empty cabinets. The weird smell of the place filling his nostrils. His stomach rumbling despite it.

I have to call Hagan tomorrow, he thought. *I have to call Hagan, meet with the social worker, get a bus pass, pick up the medications.*

He ticked each item off the list in his head with a foot tap on the dingy carpet. The bed squeaked out in protest of his movements.

He retrieved Bob Barker's bendy prison pencil from his pocket and squeezed it softly. He bent it easily back and forth and slowed his breathing. He let his weight carry him down onto the hard mattress and, eventually, he slept.

§

The streetlight standing like a silent sentinel. A pale glow in a dark sea. More lighthouse than searchlight but leaning both ways like a straight-armed drunk.

The fog swirling around all that inky blackness. More blue than black. A pagan dance of the already departed. Ghosts and ghosts and more ghosts.

It took Stephen what felt like a lifetime, time on end, time with no end, the snake and the tail and the fuzzy separation that becomes no separation, to figure out he was dreaming again, that he'd been right where he was, looking at what he now saw, again.

To know you're in a dream...

He stepped up onto the road, cracked, forgotten asphalt, another county road from nowhere drifting off into nothing, forever, from the damp ditch he'd been crouching in. His thighs screaming with the effort. His bare feet cold with a dew on just this side of frost.

"Hello?" he called.

The breath of his words crystalized and floated away, joining the collage of swirling grey and white and black. The ghost dance.

To know you're dreaming...

Something in the air, maybe the quasi-solidified particles of mist, caught and carried his voice, hollow and foreign, the way you hear recordings of yourself speaking. It echoed off the vast nothingness like a kicked can in an empty alley.

"Anybody there?"

To know you're dreaming while still in the dream is to be a spider caught in another's web.

A change in the air. Something heavier and darker and moving. More blue than black. A great intake unseen. The drain opened. The waters receding.

Stephen felt the pull. He saw the streetlight flicker and he was drawn toward it.

Moth to light. Bee to honey. Ant to syrup.

Insectile the drive. Insectile the bind.

An expansive sighing. A thousand little exhales. The slow dance of ghosts. The misunderstanding of presence and purpose.

"What is happening?" Stephen asked. "What is this?"

Pivot. Step. The flap of his clothes and hair in the current. A great white flag ignored.

"It's all happening all the time."

Stephen felt sure he'd spoken the words at the same time he was sure he hadn't.

He stepped into the circlet of light and looked up, squinting against the dull yellow orb that was nearly blinding for all the darkness that surrounded it.

§

Stephen woke sweating with shuddered breaths to shafts of light filtered through the cracked blinds. He gasped, coughed, noticed the yellowed ceiling and realized it was probably nicotine stains, then cried. The springs called out their mutual discomfort as his body quaked. A symphony of squelch and moan and shake and whimper.

To know you're dreaming…

Stephen's tears petered out to sniffles then the wipes of his nose and eyes. He made his way to the damp-smelling bathroom, which was vaguely moldy, and waited for the water to warm. It splashed down in the rust stained tub in globs of yellow-tinged brine for some time before it settled into a not-quite clear normalcy.

He took a shower without soap or shampoo, letting the hard water dribbled through the clogged showerhead until he felt bolstered enough by the warm encapsulation to face the day. He stepped out and realized he had no towel. He picked up the threadbare, second-hand rug and dried himself off with it. Yellow fuzzy specks dotted his skin when he was finished.

A.S. COOMER

A spider caught in another's web.

Stephen dressed in the only clothes he owned. He opened the front door and the sound of sirens wailing, distant and fixed, greeted him. A man skittered across the parking lot. All hoodied red and jeaned black. A blink and he was gone, slipped between faceless buildings like a knife in the night.

Stephen locked the door to his apartment and descended the flights of stairs shivering. His breath puffed from his mouth in clouds of pale white and, for the first time in a long time, he wanted some marijuana. It was a distant pang, the feeble beginnings of an empty stomach.

§

The corner store, Little J's Corner Spot Carryout, was half a block from Stephen's apartment. He walked with his head down, his eyes and nose stinging and running in the brisk wind. The building that housed the corner store and a check cashing storefront had rusted metal bars over all the windows but the spiderwebbed cracked glass behind several of them attested to their uselessness. A couple with a bundled-up crying infant, long-faced and miserable, opened the door to the check cashing business as Stephen passed.

The cars rumbled by, frames and shocks and wheels stamping and complaining at the potted and cracked streets. The sirens continued their wail and, like the distant cries of coyotes, were answered by more sirens from another part of the city.

Stephen pushed in the door of Little J's Corner Spot Carryout to the smell of stale deep fryer oil and overcooked chicken. A group of elderly men huddled and laughed near the counter, where a fat man in a pork-pie hat stood turning over nearly blackened pieces of fried chicken under heating lamps. An unlit stogie hung from his caterpillar lips.

Stephen slipped into the first aisle he came to, a shield between himself and the other people in the store and counted the few bills he had in his Goodwill wallet.

Twelve dollars.

The smell of the fried chicken, overcooked and greasy and long sitting under the constant glare of the lamps, made his stomach growl.

Twelve dollars.

Stephen found the bread and went about comparing prices until he found the cheapest Little J's Corner Spot Carryout had to offer. Then he did the same with peanut butter. At the end of the third and final aisle of the place, Stephen saw the faded black cover of a composition notebook. It was coated by a thin layer of dust and the orange price sticker looked bleached with age and sun exposure.

Stephen didn't pick it up right away. He imagined Bob Barker's bendy prison pencil vibrating like a tuning fork back at his apartment. He thought he could almost hear the ringing of the chime, the vibration sinking deeper between his ears.

He picked it up, the bread and peanut butter tucked under his arm to free his hands, and checked the price.

Three dollars.

He had enough. He smiled and made his way to the counter, the smell of the fried chicken nearly overwhelming.

"Find what you were looking for?" the man behind the register asked.

Stephen nodded. Watching the man punch in the amounts listed on each item.

"11.82," the man said.

Stephen retrieved the crumpled bills and handed them over. The man counted them out and made change.

"You new around here?"

Stephen took the plastic bag and nodded.

"Welcome to the neighborhood."

Stephen made his way back into the cold streets without a response, feeling the eyes of the old men at the counter on his back.

The sirens were still screaming their plaintive wail of justice and despair. A TARTA bus wheezed by in a plume of charcoal smoke. Across the street a man pushed a shopping cart with one crazy wheel in the back spinning like a top gone wrong.

In the parking lot adjacent to his building, a crowd of mostly younger men were huddled around a smiling man, teeth gleaming pure gold, his breath clouding out like a doused fire, sitting on a neon green motorcycle. Something nearly inarticulate was shouted by someone in the crowd and with several quick flicks of his wrist, the man with the gold teeth reeved the motorcycle's engine.

Stephen slowed but did not stop, noting several heads turn his way as he walked.

He thought he'd heard a sound just like that of the screaming engine before. The apartment he'd shared with Robert in Miami, just off-campus, looked out onto a little park. Several tall trees, oaks and walnuts and elms, stood spaced out with bird feeders and birdbaths and benches between them. Stephen had been napping. He woke late in the afternoon to a sound he couldn't convince himself was commonplace. He got up to an empty apartment, Robert was gone, he was always gone, and sought out the noise. He followed his ears to the back porch, a cheap set of sliding doors opening to the little park. The sound was worse here and there was a smell, a burning smell.

Stephen opened the doors and the smell and sound intensified. There was a prickling of his skin, the hair on his arms and the back of his neck rose. He looked up and saw a squirrel wrapped around the bug zapper hanging from the balcony of the apartment above theirs. There was the faintest flicker of a flame on the squirrels back and the continued sound of the zapper struggling to continue to zap.

"You got a problem, man?"

Stephen shook his head, realizing he'd stopped walking and had been staring without seeing at the group of people and the motorcycle.

"Better keep on walking then, huh?"

Stephen nodded, vigorously, and crossed the parking lot to the stair-well of his building.

To know you're dreaming while still in the dream--

He shut and locked the door, peeking out the cracked blinds at an empty landing.

--is be to a spider caught in another's web.

He made himself a peanut butter sandwich and ate it flipping through the empty pages of the composition notebook.

§

Stephen started writing. He did not think about what he was going to write, just that he must write. He did not have a character in mind. He did not have a story. He did not have the budding formation of a line to bring to fruition. He just had the urge, the absolute gaping need to write, something, anything.

He wrote until great, aching hand cramps seized his right hand and he had to set Bob Barker's bendy prison pencil on the coffee table and sit back on the slanted couch massaging his screaming hand.

He thought of the pages he'd scribbled in the hospital at Dr. Holt's or-ders. The slanted nature of the sentences on the yellowed pages kept or-ganized by the pale blue lines and how the coherence of the thing wasn't paramount. The cohesive nature and tone were what held it all together above all else. The not-quite stream-of-consciousness layered and lacking only an aim, some forlorn animal's winding path through tall trees.

Stephen rubbed the hand and remembered. He rubbed the hand and dreamed. He rubbed the hand and wished he had a keyboard but immediately was thankful he did not. He rubbed the hand and worried about Martha and beating back the sadness, the copy she'd given him now the only book he owned. He thought about the experiment and resolved to include the findings in his writing. He caught the faint syncopation of nursery rhymes jangling like exposed wiring in his head and wondered how far the nearest farm was from his apartment. His apartment in a squat building in a series of squat buildings in a part of town he hadn't known existed. His clothes the clothes his attorney had picked out at some discount department store. His couch probably picked up from the curb of another faceless squat building just around the block. The white bread sitting starchy and uncomfortably in his shrunken stomach. The peanut butter nearly separated in the jar, more texture than taste.

To know you're dreaming while still in the dream is to be a spider caught in another's web.

Stephen picked up Bob Barker's bendy prison pencil that he was sure Nurse Marks was going to refuse to give to him and went back to work.

§

The words came fluidly and without cessation. Page after page of the three-dollar composition notebook filled, top to bottom without regard to top and bottom and side margins. The blue lines were adhered to when they were present.

Stephen's hand cramped and seized and finally settled into a muted screaming that he found easier and easier to ignore. He wrote. He had the notebook filled in two days.

§

"Mr. Paul," Dr. Hagan said, holding the door wide for Stephen to enter. "Good to see you. Come in, come in."

Stephen offered up a weak smile and entered the sunlit office. He took a seat and watched Dr. Hagan cross the room and ease himself into the chair behind the desk.

I'm the dog with its tail between its legs, Stephen thought.

"I'm glad to hear you're doing better, Mr. Paul," Dr. Hagan said, smiling.

Stephen nodded.

"I'm glad to say I'm doing better, Dr. Hagan."

"Good. Good, good."

"I'm ready to get back to teaching, Dr. Hagan," Stephen said.

"That's great," Dr. Hagan said, the smile stretching further.

Stephen had seen saltwater taffy made before.

"The next semester should be starting back within the month, right?"

Dr. Hagan nodded, the smile never leaving his face.

Stephen felt the spiders crawling about.

He's going to try and dick me out of my job.

Dr. Hagan's phone rang and he answered quickly.

"Dr. Hagan," he said.

The Head of the English Department listened for a few moments then offered an "mmhmm" and a "OK" and a "fine, fine" then set the receiver back in its cradle.

"Sorry about that, Mr. Paul," he said.

"It's fine," Stephen said. "We were talking about my coming back to teach this next semester. You know, as my attorney told me I would be doing."

At the mention of the word 'attorney', Dr. Hagan's smile stretched to a point where Stephen was sure the skin of the man's face would tear.

"You know the policies of the University, Mr. Paul," Dr. Hagan said. "We're a very welcoming and accepting place. We strive to ensure the best environment for everyone: students and faculty alike. We have some of the best professionals in the world on this campus, Mr. Paul. Adept at helping those in need. Quick to help those seek out the right, best, most effective services to get them treated and to continue their treatment once unfortunate episodes happen."

He's going to dick me out of my job.

The spiders shifted and began making their way upward, climbing in a languid, searching manner towards his throat.

"Mr. Paul," Dr. Hagan said.

"Stephen," Stephen said.

Dr. Hagan seemed to relax a bit.

"Stephen," Dr. Hagan said, "I know you've been in a rough place. I know. I was here for your..."

He waved one uncalloused hand in the air, turning it slowly, sweeping it towards the door and the waiting room outside.

"Episode and, if anybody has sympathy," Dr. Hagan said, then quickly corrected himself, "empathy, I should say, for you and your predicament, it's me and this department."

The man seemed to require some sense of validation for what he said because he paused and looked at Stephen in a meaningful way.

Stephen nodded.

"But with the current complaints on file," Dr. Hagan said, "from several of your students, I fear, now is the not the time to bring you back into the classroom. I feel these issues must be resolved before I, as the Head of this Department, can with full confidence and assuredness bring you back on in a full capacity."

There it is, Stephen thought. The entire meeting had a dreamlike quality to it. One of those dreams that mirrored everyday real life but stretched the absurdities of your reality until they were painful in their blaring inconsistencies with the human spirit, with the expanse of hope and kindness that keeps us from tearing each other apart at first glance.

To know you're dreaming while still in the dream is to be a spider caught in another's web.

Stephen wanted to scream. He wanted to cry, to beg, to plead, to drop down on his knees and tell Dr. Hagan about the hospital and the shitty apartment and how badly he needed the money and normalcy back in his life, but he didn't. He didn't say anything.

Stephen nodded, once, curtly at Dr. Hagan and rose to his feet. He turned and forced himself to walk slowly from the office, open the door-knob and offer up another nod at the secretary behind her desk. He made himself keep the same pace as he walked across the waiting room, down the hall, and out of the building.

He wanted to run. He wanted to spring in whatever direction he was facing and run until his lungs exploded or he passed out. Whichever came first.

But he didn't.

Stephen walked, slowly, across the campus to the bus stop and sat down on the cold, hard bench and waited.

§

He called the attorney from the therapist's office.

"I can't believe this, Mr. Paul," Corey Streeter said, everything in his voice saying that he saw this coming. Expectance and deflection. "I just can't believe this. Don't you worry, Mr. Paul. We'll get this worked out."

They would sue, if it came to it.

There was a gleam in the way Streeter said it. The court-appointed sensing real money for the first time.

Stephen gave the phone back to Dr. Childers, his therapist at the brick, nondescript community mental health building on Nebraska.

"I bet that feels a little better," Dr. Childers said, "having started the process of resolving that particular challenge."

This was the way she spoke. Stephen tried not to focus on it.

"I guess so," he said. "It means I still don't have a job in the meantime."

The therapist nodded, giving Stephen plenty of time to add or elaborate or change directions and when he didn't, she spoke.

"But your living situation is settled for the time being and your basic necessities are being met, so there are things to be thankful for."

This was true. Stephen couldn't deny it. He couldn't deny it, but he also couldn't particularly care for his current mode of existence.

To know you're dreaming while still in the dream is to be a spider caught in another's web.

"How's the writing coming along, Stephen?"

"Good."

"Good."

§

He met with the psychiatrist after his counseling appointment with Dr. Childers. Same building, same waiting room, same shuffle of papers and the same sitting in uncomfortable chairs.

"Your bloodwork looks good," Dr. Heidelberg said.

"Good," Stephen said.

"How have you been feeling?"

What a question, Stephen thought. *Suffocated in my newfound liberation? Shackled by poverty and joblessness? Isolated and adrift in a wintery metropolitan wasteland?*

"OK," he said.

"Good," Dr. Heidelberg said, flipping through several pages in a manila folder. "Good, good."

The psychiatrist scribbled something onto one of the pages then shut the folder with a smile.

"Is there anything else I can do for you, Mr. Paul?"

§

Stephen hadn't used public transportation frequently in any of the cities in which he'd lived. He always, thankfully, had a vehicle, however shitty it might have been. The freedom of movement associated with having your own means of transportation was what he was dwelling on when the man on the bus ahead of him began violently vomiting into the aisle.

Great, steaming streams of a reddish-brown semi-liquid issued from the scraggly man in mismatched pajamas.

Stephen rose to a half-crouch and moved two seats further back on the bus. He sat down and watched the thick mucus-like substance jiggle with the bus's movement.

The driver looked back in the mirror and Stephen saw the eyes narrow and the brows turn down. He thought he heard a "goddamn" and a "motherfuck" but he couldn't be absolutely sure it had come from the driver. Everyone on the bus cussed.

As the bus pulled over to the curb, Stephen watched the puke pile settle.

An island in the sun. Somebody's most perfect creation, albeit mangled and stinking, gleaming under the fidgety lights of a city bus. The best of someone. The worst of another. What's the difference? What are palm trees but corn kernels in the turd?

"You have to get off," the driver told the man, still heaving and slanted in his seat. "Now."

Stephen looked out the window at the darkening sky between two boarded-up buildings; the graffiti present splattered with little regard to artistic ethos, just names etched, slanted and nearly illegible.

Spawn.

Rider.

Drag.

Jokerman.

Jokerman, Stephen thought. *Now there's a name for the most perfect being.* A man, painted face and all, sunglasses firmly in place, drink topped with a little purple umbrella in hand sweating pleasantly down onto the feet half-buried in silky soft sand, on his most perfect island in the sun basking in the glory of His creation and all of it a joke. The smile, Stephen saw firmly in his mind, was curled and guileless. You should know this is a joke, it said. You should know because what isn't?

§

Stephen sat in the waiting room of the community mental health center for the second time that week. He let his leg bounce a frantic rhythm as he watched two sets of children, black and white and Middle Eastern, fight over magazines. *Sports Illustrated* seemed to be the most coveted and, therefore, the most frayed and ripped as a result of the ensuing war of possession. He heard name calling, mild and childish at first, escalate into bigotry and burgeoning hatred.

"It's mine."

"No it's not."

"It belongs to the building. Duh."

Mothers, in various forms of agitation, spoke in hushed, frenzied whispers for quiet and adherence to their domination but the children were not easily contained. The receptionist calling the names and numbers, depending on reason for presence, was the only thing that quieted them.

Stephen, too, was finally called back for the second of his twice-weekly therapy sessions with Dr. Childers and her clinical-ese.

He had one hope for this meeting: to secure another notebook and writing utensil.

He'd scribbled Bob Barker's bendy prison pencil down to a macaroni noodle stub. He hadn't thought it possible, but he'd grown to prefer the bendy pencil, the anti-shank mark-maker marketed predominately to prisons and jails and those on suicide watch. As he took a seat on the comfortable loveseat in Dr. Childers' office, he was thinking about a way to ask if she had any of those pencils that he could have.

He couldn't figure out a way to ask for one that didn't include outwardly expressing his affinity for them that wouldn't put him back in the hospital in a straitjacket on self-harm protocol.

"Dr. Childers, is there any way I can have a notebook and a pen or pencil?" he asked.

She nodded, put down her own notebook and pen, and walked over to her desk. She opened a drawer near the floor and out came a yellow legal pad. In another drawer she found a black, push-button ballpoint. She handed them to him then sat back down.

"Thank you," Stephen said, testing the pen's bendability.

It gave but only slightly. The brittle black plastic whitened where he bent it, so he immediately stopped.

"You're welcome."

"I filled up the notebook I got at the corner store near my apartment."

"That's great, Stephen," Dr. Childers said. "Did you bring it with you?"

Stephen retrieved the notebook from a jacket his social worker had provided.

"May I?"

Stephen passed the notebook to his therapist.

They sat in silence for some time. Five minutes. Ten. Dr. Childers, at first, flipped through the pages like a child's flipbook, animated cats and dogs chasing each other around the yard, then she turned back to the beginning and skimmed.

After several pages, Dr. Childers looked up at Stephen then quickly to the clock on the wall, cleverly positioned behind the loveseat just to the left of Stephen's head.

"Oh dear," Dr. Childers said. "This is quite good. May I borrow it and read it later? I don't want to use up all of our time reading while you sit there with things to say and situations to discuss."

Stephen felt his body tense and reddened at the childishness of it. He forced himself to smile and nod in acquiescence.

It's not like she's going to steal it, he thought. *She's my therapist for Christ's sake.*

"Thank you," Dr. Childers said. "Now, let's talk—"

§

There he was. Standing stark and black, dripping with the fresh ink of a new pen's creation, against the dull late-summer yellow of the new, unruffled pages of the legal pad. A hero from old, not asking for it but pulled from the great swarths of surrounding void anyway, to stand under that goddamn streetlight and face the overriding nothingness of it all. To face it under the small, fickle glow of an illumination that can't last forever—what really does? The only one around. To make do with what's there—what isn't, even. Just to make, do, make do.

The pages came slower. There was a process now. Introductions that needed to be made. The rhythm was there but it had to be led up to, guided towards, made acquainted with. A new strophic form where the coda, so sweet, sweeping, low and so beautifully cold, wouldn't make sense unless you heard that first refrain. That first wail of complaint and love and desire and the world, exposed for the fraud it was, the gaudiness of it all blaringly evident, and perhaps, for the first time, crashing down all around.

Stephen wrote but, in his mind, he thought of it as singing. Singing for the first time. Sure, he'd spent a lifetime humming. Humming along with the bawdy songs of others. Humming along on autopilot.

This is different, he thought. *This is clearing my throat for the first time.*

He opened his mouth, settled back in the chair, and let his song spill out.

There was something isolating in it, yes, but there was a greater aspect. This was learning the language for the first time and offering up the first thought, the first truth to come to mind, the initial understanding that *I can sing. This is the song of my being. This is what I am right now. Hello.*

§

The days ebbed and flowed piano-like in their dip and swell. Stephen felt light-footed, floating above the page. Soaring in mind and heart and reveling in his forgetfulness, his shedding of preconceived connections, the thought-processes sheared off like cumbersome clothing. The hand connected to the pen, the pen to the page, the page to the words, the words to the world—the real one, stunningly void of meaning in its stark emptiness—the world to the nothingness that really is existence, the nothingness a blanket of comfort and despair, the flicker of the flame to the tenebrific expanse—exposing it for the first time to his flinching but open eyes.

Stephen saw.

He sang.

There is a darkness more blue than black.

§

"I think you need to start compiling all of these," Dr. Childers said.

She was holding up the third filled legal pad Stephen had allowed her to read.

"I mean, this is good. Like, good."

The change of diction, the lack of clinical terminology and precision was not lost on Stephen. He watched her skim the newest pad, in which he'd just given her. He watched her eyes and the soft intonation of her face, the cellist's fingers mapping out great sweeps and gentle dives as the eyes, riveted now with the flash of understanding, read through the wild-eyed composer's experimental take on the nocturne for the first time, knowing that she heard the music already. Knew it at sight and was already in tune. All blues and blacks and purples lighting the night sky a special kind of midnight. That period where time, night slipping and sliding away finally slows. That honey-coated time of sweet sluggishness, sweeping syrupy lifts. A stillness serene. A love supreme.

"I will," Stephen said. "I will after it's done."

The fingers traced the chords for the first time and marveled.

"What?" Dr. Childers said, pulling her eyes up from the crinkled pages with effort.

§

There's a pleasantness to certain fevers. A sweetness on the sweep of the bitter that sometimes rises above all else. A settling in of parched tongues and burning eyes to ride the tide of the fever in a peace filled to the brim and nearing but not quite spilling over into bliss. An acceptance of the situation, knowing it will pass, and coming to terms with the general fleetingness of everything in that same, sacrosanct instant.

Stephen slept and dreamed and woke and wrote and considered the two infinitely related, coupled like cranes in a snow-crusted canebrake at the break of a brilliant, cloudless December day.

To know you're dreaming of a song more blue than black.

The words silent but screaming. Knowing it's the same to laugh as it is to cry and moving on accordingly. The gathering of grief like a coat for the cold. The smiles for the aisles of blue that must be walked through in the great gauze-like haze, a curtain composed of tiny truths interlaced, woven of strands of burgeoning understandings, of the maze of being.

As he neared the conclusion, the coda shone hot, brighter than any flashbulb's strike, yet a shimmer for all of it, dazzling in its sparkle, the luster, both at odds and not with the darkness, somehow more lasting not just for the time but for the sweep of the song and the way it stayed in your mouth like an aftertaste, bitter and sweet and soured and already changing in its memory of what it was that you tasted. A synthesis forever in-progress. A completeness apparent in its consistency for adaptable, fluid formed solidification.

Stephen sang. He let his voice lift to the final chorus, the hallelujah of hallelujahs, letting the last note hang until the heart was choked, so full of life and death and beauty that the tears punctuated the ending. The tears and the trill of laughter.

§

He wrote the last sentence. It ended with a period, which sat like a tombstone reminder of a life lived. A being had sprung, triumphantly alive, from the overwhelming emptiness and grew, and the time allotted

A.S. COOMER

cycled on.

Stephen flipped the legal pad back to the beginning and set the pen down on top of it. He looked over to the small, scuffed bar in his apartment and saw the nub of what remained of Bob Barker's bendy prison pencil. He found he couldn't throw it away. In its uselessness, it had transmuted into something larger and more durable than itself.

A talisman, he thought.

It felt like it was glowing, radiating a warmth and goodwill that Stephen knew only he could feel and absorb.

Some things exist solely for yourself.

The sun was sinking behind him, coming through the broken slits in the battered blinds. Red and full and dipping off behind a factory, coated in various graffiti—not all bad but mostly—windows shattered or boarded over with the cheapest of particleboard, that used to make glass for automobiles.

Stephen turned to face it as it sank.

He crossed one leg over the other. He settled himself into a more comfortable position and found his mind blissfully blank. A sheerness and velocity to the emptiness like open windows on the highway. Stuffed with motion, filled with movement while sitting completely still.

I'm going to be OK.

The thought issued from some unconscious part of Stephen's mind. Some cauldron's constant cooking. Everything that went in, made the rounds, stirred and swirled and simmered. It bubbled to the surface and Stephen believed it. He accepted it outright, immediately. He had no time to build pretense and worry. Anxiety slipped from the room like the unwanted guest it was.

There will be trouble. There will be pain and loss, but you will be OK, Stephen told himself.

The last sliver of sun slipped off and Stephen, smiling but with eyes filled with tears, looked for the moon.

Full Moon

"I have good news, Mr. Paul," Corey Streeter said.

Stephen adjusted his grip on his therapist's desktop phone and waited.

"You can go back to teaching with the summer session."

"That's great," Stephen said. "Thank you."

"Yeah. That Head of the English Department tried to put up a fight, but he had no legs to stand on, legally speaking. He brought up the complaints, both of them, that the Student Grievance Counsel was scheduled to hear, as well as the Academic Affairs issue, but I read him word-for-word of what your contract states on the matter of grievances as well as the judge's ruling that states—"

Stephen waited for the pauses in the attorney's speech and made appropriate replies, but he stopped listening after hearing he could go back to teaching.

He handed the phone to Dr. Childers, who set it back on the receiver.

"Sounds like good news?"

Stephen nodded.

"I get to go back to teaching in the summer."

"That's fantastic."

"Yes."

Stephen knew he should feel elated. With the return of his adjunct's salary, minimal as it was, it would allow him to move out of the HUD housing complex. He knew he should feel something, but he didn't. It was just something else to put off for another day. He couldn't teach right now, and he didn't have the money to move out of the subsidized apartment, so he filed the news under: Delayed Gratification.

Stephen answered his therapist's questions. He gave her the final notebook. He told her the first draft was complete. They talked revision process. She seemed genuinely interested.

Stephen's mind was blank, more than that, it was filled with a fuzzy nothing that was both a comfort and a pill, large and oddly-shaped, that he just couldn't quite seem to get down. He came at the blankness from every angle he could think of but couldn't find a way in or out. It was consuming in its vastness. Empty of handholds and shelter. No shade from the burning blackness of the sun unseen.

The silence brought him out of his stupor.

"Stephen, are you all right?" Dr. Childers asked.

He nodded slowly. The arrangement of his thoughts a pattern askew, a misguided attempt at quilting by an unsteady hand but it a blanket, nonetheless.

"Yes," he said. "I think so."

§

He didn't take the bus home. He walked past the bench, several other people from the waiting room perched and shivering, along the cracked, uneven sidewalk. The smear of the day a stain on the canvas. The light of the sky an oil streaked correctly.

I think so, he told himself.

His brain felt wrapped in gauze. Something both medicinal and recreational, coated and tingling. He felt a prickling from every side.

I think I'm alive for the first time. This must be what it feels like.

He stepped over a half-crushed Busch can. It caught a glint of the sun and shimmered in the tears in his eyes. It was dazzling in its brilliance.

The weight of being. The weight of being. The weight of being.

His thoughts ricocheted off the silver and blue can, and he kept walking. A rusted 'No Trespassing' sign, black and white and red, hung slanted on a collapsing chain-link fence, a divide of unimportance. It made a high-pitched scratching noise as it swung slowly back and forth.

The song of motion. The song of stillness. *These songs are the same song. These songs are the song of being.* The weight of it like a snowflake on the tongue. The stone flung to water. The lily in the sun. The child born and the life lived. The hum of strings. The flapping of wings.

I think so.

Stephen walked the four miles to his apartment, unlocked the door with the single key from his pocket, and slept without dreaming.

§

He went to the library each morning and typed up the pages from the legal pads. He did this in the order in which he wrote them. Page after page of his handwriting and not a word he didn't recall writing. Not a moment he didn't remember the feel of Bob Barker's bendy prison pencil or the pen Dr. Childers had given him in his hand and the flowing river that opened up as he moved it along the blue lines. The yellow of the paper a canvas; he was learning how to paint. Feeling the slick motion of the brush trace the outline of the picture he saw when he closed his eyes; the portrait to be, the landscape in progress.

Stephen edited only what absolutely needed editing. He saved everything in a cloud account Archie had helped him create so many months ago. He printed nothing and carried only the legal pads with him when he walked, the corners of the pages dogeared now from the flipping rolled in on themselves like the exposed tubes of an ant farm.

Insectile the drive. Insectile the bind.

Stephen felt absolutely compelled. He felt entranced, under the spell of making, of doing, of creating, and freed completely by the act, aloof from other torturous desires. He ate when his stomach growled but cared not for what he filled himself with. Creation was filling enough. He was sure he could almost subsist entirely on it.

He walked down to Little J's Corner Spot Carryout and bought another composition notebook.

"This all for you?"

"Yessir."

"All right then."

Stephen carried the notebook back to the apartment in both hands, the child and the prize won, the victory and the spoils. He wrote and wrote and knew, even if he slowed, he would never stop. There was too much of nothing, too much of everything, and the current was swift and carrying and he let himself go, abandoned preconceived notions of the right way or the wrong way and let himself be carried.

§

Stephen finished typing the last sentence of the last legal pad then clicked Save. He watched the icon, a small pixelated thing spin then change color, and he knew it had saved. He read the title softly to himself in the noisy library computer lab: *Memorabilia or How to Beat Back the Sadness.*

It felt like an echo from the void; the last line of the final chorus caught and held, finally released like a crackling whisper from a busted stereo.

Stephen logged off the computer, leaving the library with the legal pad under his arms. The weather was beginning to change. A gentle thawing occurring almost at the peripheries of nature's vision, nearly invisible if you weren't watching. The faintest of greening happening at some level nearly imperceptible.

Stephen saw it. He felt he saw everything now.

§

He researched publishers and agents, decided that he'd submit *Memorabilia* to both. He spent mornings and most afternoons in the library crafting query letters and partials, undaunted by the anxiety of rejection, many of which were quick in coming.

"Confused prose."

"Unfollowable."

"What?"

"Too surreal."

"Best of luck placing elsewhere."

He read them and felt not the slightest concern. The story was new. It was old. It was a memoir unlike anything he'd ever read or known of. He thought it might be unlike anything that had ever existed, and yet, it was always there. It was the song of the void. The call and response from the nothing, a gentle sweep and crushing fall from everything.

It would find a home. Stephen was sure of it.

§

Spring came in great torrents of cold rain and melting snow. The entire city seemed awash in mud and soggy cigarette butts. The runoff was tinged with oil swirls, kaleidoscopic in their rainbow of colors, greens and yellows and blues, reds and purples, hundreds of intermingling droplets.

He got a job working at Little J's Corner Spot Carryout. He'd bought three more notebooks over the course of three weeks and Roger Jameson, Little J, asked if he'd like to earn "a little cash under the table."

Stephen sat behind the register and read library book after library book. He rotated the burnt chicken under the heat lamps, made sandwiches for the elderly men that didn't seem to have any place better to go, thinking they looked like rain dogs, sniffing at the lost memories of home, knowing the rain washed away the last remaining traces of the way but hoping against hope that they'd stumble back upon it someday anyway.

Stephen wrote and waited for the summer.

§

Corey Streeter set up an appointment with Dr. Hagan. Stephen attended, attired in clothes he picked out for himself at the Goodwill with the cash he earned from Little J, and was delighted in Hagan's change of attitude towards him.

"Mr. Paul, we're delighted that you'll be coming back aboard next week," Dr. Hagan said. "We've got you lined up to teach three classes, Intro Creative Writing, Am. Lit. Heritage, & Fiction I, all the paperwork has been processed and approved."

Stephen felt dumbstruck.

"That's great," Streeter said. "I'm assuming that includes all the payroll and insurance documentation for my client has been completed as well?"

Dr. Hagan nodded, the smile seemingly genuine on his face.

"We're all really excited to have you back, Stephen."

Stephen.

The meeting ended, and Stephen followed Streeter out of the English Department and into the bustling halls, students and faculty and the sound of academia in progress.

"What changed?" Stephen asked the attorney.

Streeter smiled. It was a wolf's grin.

"Seems word is out that your manuscript is making the rounds and garnering quite some attention," he said. "What department head wouldn't want a rising star, a genuine hard luck success story, on the payroll?"

Stephen couldn't help but return the smile.

He'd been getting some positive responses about the manuscript. Several offers of publication that he was working through, sending the contracts to Streeter to look over and advise.

He hadn't known Streeter had been in contact with Hagan. Stephen felt he should be annoyed at the lawyer's overstepping, but, on the other hand, he'd gotten the teaching position secured.

"Thank you," he said.

Streeter smiled and opened the passenger side door of his BMW for Stephen.

§

He settled on a publisher and went back to teaching. He felt comfortable and surefooted, both in the classroom and with the pen. He stopped writing on the computer altogether, despite the overwhelming sensation that he couldn't get everything down as quickly as it came. He decided this, too, was important to face. He would write only what was important. It was a form of self-editing in real-time. Processing the import of the material as it flowed. The sieve separating the weevils from the grain.

Stephen wrote. He taught. He worked with the publisher on the manuscript until it was out of his hands.

§

He approved galley prints. He looked over covers. He read blurbs from writers he'd seen on magazine covers and on television; everyone with something exquisitely nice to say about *Memorabilia*.

They'd cut *or How to Beat Back the Sadness* from the title. Stephen had voiced his complaints, but not that loudly. He knew it was a convoluted title, but what wasn't confusing? He figured the refrain was in there, hidden like a blessing or a curse. The few who read the thing would hear it, hum along. That was enough.

Stephen was given a publication date and several events to attend.

§

Splendid work, Stephen! The
reviews are glowing!

- Hagan

§

Stephen was interviewed by the local television station. Then the local NPR affiliate. Then *Memorabilia* was reviewed by half a dozen major
publications and he found himself on a first-class flight to New York for
Good Morning, America.

He felt only slightly annoyed with these distractions. Mostly he'd
come to appreciate his schedule, his time in the mornings spent with hot,
black coffee, his composition notebook, and Bob Barker's bendy prison pencils—he'd ordered an entire box online—his afternoons spent in
the classroom and auditorium, and his evenings reading and taking long,
rambling walks.

He stopped writing and gently flexed the pencil in his hand as he
looked out the window. The mountains of West Virginia, green and rolling hills pock-marked by strip mines, swam by below. Stephen watched
a cloud, no bigger than a Dodge pickup from his vantage point, drop a
haze of rain on an empty parking lot.

Stephen thought about himself, the immeasurably small speck of matter
that didn't matter in the grand scheme of things—because nothing matters
in the grand scheme of things—and was thankful for his time here, there,
everywhere, nowhere. He was thankful to be holding the long, thin tube of
pliable writing material—he brought along three unused bendy pencils for
the trip—and to be looking down on the earth so far below.

He felt thankful in a specific way, the way the stars shine, the way
the water flows downhill, the way certain notes form minor chords. The
way the sun rises and sets, the way sugar dissolves in hot, black coffee.

The way understanding comes from nothing, really means nothing, but is something nonetheless.

Stephen went back to writing and didn't stop until the plane landed. He watched the horizon shrink away, the bend of the Earth no longer visible. The ground swelled, shapes of buildings towering, cars, taxis, people like ants, smoke like the cradled shapeless hands of ghosts, the runway the line of a vein entered. He felt the force of gravity and the slowing of the plane, then the bounce of landing and the roar of the engine fighting back the speed.

Stephen watched the motion, the work of all the people, the carts scuttling around the tarmac, the men in neon jumpers, the faceless people watching from behind the glass of the airport terminals and felt small but secure. He was aware and smiling. He closed his notebook and stored it, along with Bob Barker's bendy prison pencil, in his carryon and waited patiently to exit the plane.

§

The backstage area could've been anywhere. The walls were nondescript, bland even, except for the photographs, all signed in blacks and blues and reds and silvers and golds, of the celebrities that had been featured on the show.

Stephen was shown to a small dressing room in the back and helped himself to a croissant and a cup of black coffee. He sat eating, flakes of the pastry peppering his lips and chin, listening to the flurry of activity raging outside the door. He was alone. He didn't have an agent, though offers had been made, and hadn't thought about bringing anybody with him.

Who would I bring? he thought. *My therapist?*

He didn't socialize. He went to the departmental mixers because it was something he had to do. He spoke when spoken to and offered opinions when he felt inclined to do so, which was rarely. It wasn't that he was antisocial, per se, he just had a natural reticence that he hadn't found worth remedying.

Besides, there was work to do. Stephen thought about writing when he wasn't writing. Vast currents, blocks of understanding bobbing about like ice floes or flood debris, had to be explored, crossed, measured, fished, tasted.

There was a succession of raps on the door, then it swung open.

"We're just about ready for you, Mr. Paul."

Stephen barely had time to register the small mousy man with the headset that met him at the hotel that morning before he'd ducked back into the hallway, the door closing softly behind him.

Stephen finished the last of the croissant, washing it down with a swig from the coffee. *Dr. Hagan probably would've loved to be here*, Stephen thought. *Beaming like a proud parent. Look what I created!*

Magnanimous and glowing was how he pictured Dr. Hagan with makeup in the camera lens. Rows of thick white teeth gleaming in the lights. Eyes shining with a recognition he felt owed.

Since *Memorabilia*'s publication, Dr. Hagan had made it a point to stop by Stephen's office each day and try to chat. He'd knock, not wait for an answer, enter and sit in one of the chairs and just smile at Stephen.

He'd bring up whatever review had just come out or rehash portions of the book that he found particularly engaging.

Stephen rarely spoke at these, usually midmorning, chats. He nodded, smiled, and waited patiently for Dr. Hagan to leave, all the while working on the writing in his head, envisioning the type, the layout, the syntax, word choice. The rhythm of the words highlighting the image of the prose. The blending of poetry and narrative through selected images, impressions, the careful hint of explanation, the work, tireless and sheening, shared between reader and writer.

Stephen rose and crossed to the mirror. He studied himself, brushed off some pastry crust from his shirt and chin. He leaned his head slightly backwards, checking for bats in the cave, as he used to call it when he was younger. And wasn't that what he was doing now? Speaking things in idiom? Universally emoted, a life described in a new way of speaking? Something to pick up along the way and use? Wasn't that how all new things became old things? Born shining, worn down until the luster was frayed, swayed, and waylaid on down the road to cliché?

The door opened, and Stephen was summoned. He followed the mousy man in the headset. Walls with smiling famous people. Stars and comets and blackholes, a pantheon of rapid success and creeping failure. Teeth and eyes and tits and muscle and flab and ego and hair, so much hair, great tidal waves and oil slicks of hair.

Then bright white heat, lights shining, watchful, smiling, beautiful people waiting. A seat hard but not overly so and a settling down punctuated by welcomes and more smiles.

Stephen found it difficult to concentrate. He smiled and took deep breaths, doing his best to smile and nod and answer questions accordingly, but something felt off. There was something about the place he couldn't quite place that had him on edge.

Not the cameras. Not the lights. Not the faces he'd seen on television a thousand times and the realization of their actual in-person size. Was it a smell?

What is it?

"Tell us a little bit about *Memorabilia?*" the hulking ex-athlete said, carefully reading the title off the teleprompter.

"Yeah, you went through a lot to write that book, didn't you?" the journalist asked.

There were concerned and concentrated nonverbal agreements from the other anchors.

It's shit, Stephen realized.

That was what was off. In this glowing, made-for-television set, somewhere hidden probably, maybe on the bottom of one of their shoes, was a steaming pile of shit.

Stephen shifted himself in the chair, crossed one leg over the other, then the other, trying to check the bottoms of his loafers for the offending smell on the sly.

"I know it must be difficult for you to talk about," one of the anchors said.

Stephen offered a smile and nodded.

It's not mine, he thought.

He'd gotten a cursory glance at each foot.

Where's it coming from?

He looked up at the anchors, carefully manicured heads all alight and beaming, all smiles and watchful eyes, all turned to him. Stephen swallowed.

"It was a difficult thing to write, yes," Stephen said.

Head nods. Strands of dyed blond hair fell and had to be artfully pinned back behind powdered ears. The careful ticking of a pen on the desk. The trembling of a hand. The sound of New York City just outside the windows. Someone behind the lights and the camera coughed softly into muting hands.

"You ended up nearly losing your professorship when you had your— when you were hospitalized."

A careful smile. A helping hand, verbally, extended. A man drowning in exposure. Lights and watchful eyes and smiles and the shifting of expensively clothed asses in expensive, showy furniture.

"Yes, that's right," Stephen said. "I'm not entirely sure what happened still. It's hard to describe a complete break with reality once you've come back."

"I bet."

"Sure."

"I can only imagine."

Stephen sat back and did his best to speak clearly and enunciate his words. He talked about the writing process, saw the glazed over look of most of the hosts faces but knew this was what he was most comfortable discussing. He spoke style and form and flow.

They asked about visions and doctors and white rooms.

He talked about narrative as paint, as melody, as intent.

"We've got a special surprise for you, Mr. Paul."

Stephen turned to see which of the hosts had spoken but followed each of their faces towards a humongous television that was wheeled up to the desk and chairs.

"We're going live with one of the memorable, real-life characters from Professor Stephen Paul's book, *Memorabilia*. We tracked him down, which took some doing, I might add, and I'm pleased to introduce to America, and reintroduce to you, Mr. Paul, Mr. Ryan Nowak."

The television brandished a moving logo, bright primary colors and glittering letters, that dissipated into the face of Stephen's cellmate. It took him less than five seconds to recognize the man; he'd been cleaned up for his time on television. His hair had been styled and he was clad in new, sharp blazer, button up shirt, and tie. The horrendous scabs and pocks on the man's face had been carefully concealed by a layer of thick but evenly smoothed makeup.

"There's that writer," Ryan Nowak said, smiling. "The writerman."

The cameraman moved closer, zoomed in on Stephen's face.

"Hi there," Stephen said.

"You two haven't seen each other since sharing that cell in downtown Toledo, have you?"

Stephen shook his head.

"No, ma'am," Nowak said. "Not for lack of trying though. I've sent you a few letters, writerman."

The smile on the man's face was cocked, a sidewise thing that was joyous and devious at the same time.

"Oh yeah?" Stephen said. "What for?"

"To thank you."

"Thank me? For what?"

"For writing about me the way you did."

Stephen didn't know what to say. He stared dumbfounded at the man in the monitor, so different in setting and appearance but the same sly, amused demeanor.

"Yessir," Nowak said. "You wrote about me and when I finally got out, everybody around town knew you was talking about me. That Streeter, he he he, got me off the hook for some BS the police tried to lay on me too."

"Corey Streeter is a prominent attorney in the Toledo, Ohio area, said one the hosts"

"He assisted Professor Paul with the legal issues surrounding his mental health crisis."

"That's fantastic."

"I'm glad there's good-hearted people out there in the heartland, you know?"

"Good Midwestern stock."

"Yeah, he sure is something," Nowak smiled. "They fixed me up with a place of my own and got my check all sorted out. VA finally came through. Disability, all of it. All thanks to you, writerman."

A barrage of smiling faces all turned to Stephen.

"They even said they want to send somebody down here to help me write a little book of my own, writerman."

"That's fantastic."

"Oh, really?"

"I'm sure it'll be a huge success."

"Just like Stephen Paul's latest."

"Speaking of which, I urge everybody to go out to their favorite book-store—"

"Or online, doesn't everybody read on their Kindles and Nooks and phones now?"

"Or online, OK—"

"I love my Kindle, just love it."

"I'm more of a Nook person, myself."

"What about you, Stephen?"

Stephen shrugged distractedly.

Somebody was laughing. Completely unrelated to the banter on the stage. A slow, twanging laughter.

"OK, OK, digital or print, paperback or hardcover, however you get in your reading, I urge each of you," the camera zoomed in on the man's smiling face. Stephen watched it on the monitors above and behind the lights. "To get your hands and eyes and ears on *Memorabilia* by our won-derful guest this morning, Professor Stephen Paul."

"Thanks for coming on the show."

Ha ha ha.

"Wonderful to talk to you."

Ha ha ha.

"My book club is reading it next month."

Ha ha ha.

"We'll be right back after this commercial."

Stephen felt cold. Shivered. A slick wave of nausea swept over him. He felt sweat trickle down his forehead and the back of his neck.

No. Please.

The lights dimmed. Stephen blinked.

Ha ha ha.

"You did great," the mousy man was saying, pulling Stephen by the arm, pulling him to his feet and leading him away from the set.

Stephen turned back and saw the anchors getting touched up by make-up, eyes turned down to phone screens, business moving ahead, the last guest already forgotten.

"Who was laughing?" Stephen asked.

The man looked puzzled, but his motion did not cease. Stephen doubted it ever did.

"No one was laughing at you, Mr. Paul," he said. "You did great. Let's get you back to the dressing room and on your way. I'm sure you're a busy man. Things to do, people to see."

Stephen let himself be ushered down the hall.

§

He tried to do some sightseeing; he had time to kill. He let the hotel concierge book him a ticket to the Statue of Liberty, fisted a pamphlet about the Twin Towers memorial and museum, and slipped back behind the closed door of his hotel room. He paced the length of it, thirty-six steps if you counted the half-step up to the window, the faceless towering giants lurking outside, his room but an unseeing eye in another.

He pressed his forehead against the cold window pane, vertigo and needles prickling across his body at the view. He pushed himself off, spinning slowly on his heels and made the thirty-six steps back to the door before spinning around back to the window again.

Thirty-six steps, Stephen thought. *Thirty-six.*

The sun slipped, the lights of the giants becoming more apparent.

There was a knocking at the door, but Stephen couldn't answer it. He kept up his line, burning it straight across the plush carpet on shaky knees, feet bare in the sweet creamy folds.

He looked at his watch, noting it was fifteen minutes after the meetup time for his trip to see Lady Liberty.

The phone rang but Stephen did not answer it. It sounded loud and abrasive for five tact rings then stopped abruptly in the middle of the sixth.

A weight seemed to settle on Stephen's shoulders. A darkening of the peripheries. Something lurking just outside what he could see. Stephen caught himself turning his head to catch it until he spun around in a complete circle. He stopped pacing in front of the mirror and tried to laugh at himself, jolly folly in the city, but was arrested by eyes he could barely recognize.

There was a swirling in the eyes. It looked gentle until you really looked. A violent, spinning maelstrom, some raging superstorm, in the blue and grey. Something seen from on high, a specter's angle, an angel's view. A darkness more blue than black. He found himself waiting on the lightning strikes.

His cellphone chirped and vibrated, lifting the paralysis. Seven steps to the desk and the illuminated screen of his cellphone. A confirmation email that he'd missed the ferry, the ticket nonrefundable, and would he like to reschedule for another time tomorrow.

Stephen returned the phone to the desk and set about the thirty-six steps.

§

They gave him something they called a Prep Sheet. It was four pages of bulleted points, each with a possible question the host of the show might ask. He was advised to study each bulleted avenue and prepare interesting anecdotes or quirky responses. He was repeatedly asked who and where his "Handler" was. He caught the fleeting uncertainty as to his place in the grand scheme of things when he said he didn't have one.

Who the fuck does this guy think he is?

Who the fuck is this guy?

Why's this guy here?

All in the blink of an eye. A system of snap judgements that reminded Stephen of a viper's bite. A rattleless strike, venom squirts and tensile teeth, some stinging, poisonous fist on a spring, before you even knew you were in danger. The sidelong sighs and cocking of single brows, left Stephen withered and wilting further on the loveseat of another green-room. There was a television, muted with yellow subtitles streaming, hung to the right of the room-length mirror. Stephen watched the parade of images but saw nothing definite, a smear of high-definition colors and lines. The curve of a sagging lower lip. The upturned smoothness of a woman's bulging chest. The immaculate whiteness of a coffee cup that's only held water, or vodka. The desk shielding whatever the hand was doing back there.

Disconnection ringing like a cracked bell in his ears, Stephen tried to read over the bulleted list. He knew he needed answers, good answers, reasons for this, justification for portraying the legal system in the manner he did, reasons for that, the stylistic juxtaposition of the internal dialogue like a schematic diagram of a mind lost, found, recovered, set adrift once more, reasons for everything.

Why'd you write this book?

What compelled you to pull through despite all the trials and tribulations?

What kept you going?

Who was paramount in bringing this book into fruition?

Is there a movie deal? Who would you cast to play yourself?

Plans for a follow-up or sequel to the book?

A buzzing drone filled his ears, a mixture of an already rapid pulse rising and a blanket of dripping dread. He couldn't find the text, couldn't make sense of the little black characters.

Stephen let the stapled sheets flit and flutter to the floor, a weathered white flag finding bloodied ground. He found his eyes in the room-length mirror and saw the storm still raging, little swirls of confusion and fear. The eye of the storm a pupil more blue than black.

Stephen didn't hear the knock. He didn't hear the woman standing in the doorframe with the clipboard and the mouth moving a thousand miles a second. He felt a movement and turned and saw her there. He felt covered in honey, sluggish and slow, some sweetness about the disorientation. She was telling him something she knew he wasn't hearing, last minute advice, instruction, heedless and unanswered, a present unopened days after Christmas for the guest that never arrived. She stepped into the room, eyes narrowed, brow knitted, and pulled him away from the mirror by the sleeve of his shirt.

The hall was dark and long. Stephen thought of catacombs and saw skulls where celebrity faces smiled out from their glossy prints, Sharpie scribbles like a painter's signature, a skeleton's grim smile, naked and gleaming.

The floor was hard, the carpet beaten to the faintest shred of thread on a bed of hardened concrete. With each step, toe-to-heel, slap, Stephen felt it all riding on his back and shoulders, toe-to-heel, slap, and neck. Found the pulse of something beyond just the blood in his veins, toe-to-heel, slap, beating a weighted blackness in his temples, toe-to-heel, slap, tainting the water, a drop of black in the white, covering up the sun, toe-to-heel, slap, returning all to black.

Stephen counted the steps to thirty-six, felt the weight redound and drug his heels. He checked his fly. His hands moving of their own accord. It was fastened. He checked his teeth, though he hadn't eaten since the croissant that morning, he knew something was in there. He checked his pocket for his cellphone, made sure it was switched off.

The woman's grip of his sleeve transferred to his arm. She pulled and pulled and pulled. Her mouth moving, a whisper Stephen could just pick up in a growing din he couldn't place, but he couldn't decipher a single word of what she told him.

I've forgotten something, Stephen thought. *I don't know what it is, but I've forgotten it. I'm not ready. I shouldn't be here.*

The flit and flutter of a handout unexamined. Surrendering the flag of surrender. Stapled white pages on threadbare floor. The cover of a book he couldn't remember anything about.

His head felt caught in a vise, the turning of the gleaming metallic peg and the stifling of conscious will or thought. Sluggard. Captured. Caught.

The woman stopped, cupped her hands behind Stephen's back and nudged him out into a dazzlingly bright light and a rush of air.

§

The camera saw an aged egret, a sickly crane, something arcane and out of place step, cautiously and blinking and of shoulders stooped, out before a host of feasting eyes and glittering white teeth. The clapping of hands. The crash of symbols. A horn's strident heralding. The camera, wide-angled at first, zoomed in and washed itself in the lank and stupor of Stephen Paul.

The host rose and greeted him, the cameras jostling for position and import, the jerk and sway of handshake and gesturing direction, the offering of a chair next to a desk polished to a high gleam. A mug, the disembodied head of the host in caricature, of something mild and nearly tasteless, given.

Stephen lowered himself into the chair slowly, careful not to miss his mark in the white, hot candor. He picked up the mug and brought it to his lips for something to do. He felt examined, studied scrupulously by eyes near and far. The red lights above the cameras' lenses the gleaming reflections of the partially seen watcher.

The house band finished, flourishes and crashes and wails and snare raps, overwrought vibrato syncopations echoing into stillness, and the applause died down.

"All righty," the host said.

Stephen could just make out the line of makeup near the man's ear as he faced the camera. It was thin but distinct, a pale light slipping through the crack.

"Our next guest this evening is," the host told the red, watching eyes, "the author of a truly moving, wonderful and heartbreaking memoir called *Memorabilia*. Professor Stephen Paul, ladies and gentlemen."

A.S. COOMER

Another round of applause. Stephen turned away from the pale crack in time to see the house lights come on above the studio audience. Rows of tightly packed heads and clapping hands. A clashing of colors, hair and skin and eyes and teeth. A momentum of concentration and attention the cameras swiveled to catch and cull.

"Professor Paul," the host said, "or Stephen? Can I call you Stephen, Stephen?"

A spattering of comfortable laughter.

Stephen nodded his head.

"Of course."

"Good. Stephen," the host clasped both of his hands together, a slow and deliberate act that Stephen could almost hear the cameras' tightening of gyres and cogs and glass to document, and set them on the desk, "tell me a little bit about your book, *Memorabilia*."

Stephen opened his mouth to answer.

"It's a tough-read, hard to stomach some of the realities of life with mental health issues," the host said, "but you do just that with such—"

Stephen saw the pale crack as the man looked up and around for the word he was searching for but already had on the tip of tongue. The action was forged, feigned, and Stephen hated the inauthenticity of it.

"Profundity," he smiled, the skin stretching, more space to hide the crack, "and tact and poignancy. It's a real whirlwind of a read that leaves the reader shell-shocked, devastated, but *hopeful.*"

There was the shift. The host turned slightly in his chair. The cameras pivoted and zoomed in and Stephen knew it was his time to speak.

He smiled, a pale thing itself, weak and unsure, and took a sip from the mug.

Cucumber, he realized. *There's a cucumber in this water.*

He looked up from the cup and saw the faint hint of impatience on the host's powdered face.

"I wrote it in composition notebooks and legal pads," Stephen said.

Idiot. No one cares what you wrote it in, he thought.

But he couldn't stop.

"The vast majority of it, I wrote with Bob Barker's bendy prison pencil."

The host looked dumbfounded for a split-second but composed himself with machinelike rapidity.

"Did it have a handy reminder to 'Spay or Neuter Your Pet' on it?"

Laughter. Applause. The temporary redirection of the red-eyed cameras.

"That's all you could write with in the hospital," Stephen said. "I got kind of attached to them."

The host nodding his head, a smile that didn't touch his eyes.

"They have this give to them," Stephen said, setting the cup on the corner of the desk. "You can work them between your fingers between sentences and it's almost like self-hypnosis or meditation or something of that nature."

"I see," the host said. "How long did it take you to write the entire book out longhand? That's kind of old-fashioned, isn't it? Writing an entire book out by hand. That's, like, Dickensian or something. A throwback to an older era, pre-computers and word-processors and internet and all that. Are they really made by Bob Barker? I was wondering what he'd been up to since punching out Adam Sandler."

"They're not made by that Bob Barker, apparently," Stephen said.

"That's a shame," the host said. "I can picture his white-haired mug just below the eraser. Those glittering eyes and gleaming teeth smiling, a little retro microphone just below his chin."

More laughter. Incremental adjustments to direction and attention.

"They use them because they can't be fashioned into weapons."

A pause. Tick. A tock.

Stephen felt he could almost see the host weighing the pros and cons of making an insanity joke. Debating the political correctness of a prison shank bit.

"I see," he said, smiling. "But you found a way to fashion it into a weapon, didn't you? You used it to cut into the bestseller list."

More laughter sprinkled with handclapping.

"And it's been up there in the top ten just slashing away ever since," the host said. "That must feel good, doesn't it? To have this thing, this heavy, personal, *very personal,* thing to be ranked up there and appreciated by so many people, influential people, people who take note, critics and the general reader alike. Everybody seems to be in agreeance that this—"

The host picked up a hardcover copy of *Memorabilia* that Stephen hadn't noticed was standing on the corner of the desk and held it up for the greedy red eyes of the cameras.

"Is the book that everybody should be reading and talking about," the host said.

Stephen shifted his weight in the seat. He felt uncomfortable, some extra weight about his carriage. He took another sip of the cucumber water and waited.

"I mean, you went through some serious trauma to write this," the host gestured the book towards Stephen before standing it back up on the corner of the desk.

Stephen nodded.

"Hospitalized for what we used to call 'a mental breakdown' back in the day," the host used quotey fingers for the term. "Months and months in a psychiatric facility. Nearly losing your job. I mean, Trials and Tribulations with capital T's, Stephen."

"Yes."

"Where do you think it came from?" the host asked. "Is mental illness something that runs in your family? Did you have some sort of traumatic experience that set it into motion? I know you dedicated the book to your friend and fellow writer, the late, Robert Wilkins, who committed suicide. I mean, help us understand this, Stephen."

Stephen smelled it. Despite the lights, the watching room, the dark, shadowlands left like eddy pools, the waiting host behind his island desk, the odd taste of watered-down cucumber, it screamed out to the forefront of all his senses, a beacon of worry, a flashing of portent.

Shit.

Manure. Not fresh but pungent. The central essence of the thing there but muted, made more palatable by the decay. The kind farmers used to fertilize their fields.

To know your dreaming…

Stephen went cold.

while still in the dream…

A deeper concentration. A narrower field of observation. The room of lights and camera and audience drifted into the background.

is to be the spider caught in another's web.

The farmer was there. Stephen could feel his gaze now. Somewhere in the crowd maybe. Sitting along with the rest of them, spikelet of wheat slowly being worked over in his mouth. The bib overalls a stain in the New York chic. In the shadowlands, the space where the darkness pooled, perhaps.

Stephen searched.

Behind the glowing red eyes of the cameras, maybe?

He waited for the laughter he knew was coming.

"Stephen?"

The stripping of the skin down to the bone.

"Are you all right, Stephen? Professor Paul?"

The flaying of rational thought; the first trickle, droplets of understanding, slipping through the blossoming hole in the bottom of awareness. The complete convergence of thought and emotion, twin streams swollen and muddied at the confluence, spilling over their banks into each other before emptying out into the expansive, panoramic sweep of panic, at the rolling of a solitary tongue, a made-up thing, a chuckle imagined.

Stephen rose from the chair on unsteady legs. He made to steady himself on the corner of the host's desk and knocked over the mug of cucumber water. He used his right hand as a visor to shield the lights from his eyes. He searched.

"Mr. Paul? What are you doing? Are you OK?"

There. Standing at the end of an aisle, sticking out like the sorest of thumbs, unnoticed by the crowd around, was the farmer. The bibs hung loose, and Stephen could make out the nubs of ribs around the stained denim. The hat was cocked way back on the man's head; the spikelet of wheat seemed to glow like the ember of a joint.

Oh.

"Mr. Paul?"

No.

The farmer smiled and made his way down the steps, taking them leisurely, his worn-out boots treading easy and sure. His voice, the tinkling of soft laughter, the suck and pull, the blossom of a mushroom cloud, the emptying out of all but itself.

The farmer emerged from the darkness behind the cameras, stepped out into light and cast no shadow. Stephen searched for it frantically.

He's not here, Stephen told himself. *He's not real. Keep it together.*

"Howdy, Stephen," the farmer said.

"You're not real."

"'course not."

"What do you want?"

"Mr. Paul?"

"We all like to plant, you know?"

"What are you talking about?"

"We're going to take a quick commercial break, folks."

"Just a seed, slipped silently into the waiting soil, dampened by rain and incubated by sun."

"Wha—"

"We'll be right back."

The farmer, hands sunk deep in the pockets of his bibs, stepped up to Stephen, just as the red blinked out of the cameras and a different set of lights, these high and softer, blanketed the room with a gentle yellow luster.

"Most seeds grow into something, you know."

Stephen saw and shrank. The weathered face, smirking and patient, attached to a body that cast no shadow, a person nobody else could see or smell, was that of his friend, Robert Wilkins. It was the haunted hollow of cheeks. The lines around the eyes. The mouth constantly working. It was also the face of Rivers Stanton. The bags purpled and drooping. The waiting and searching etched and worn like a hand-hewn headstone. A character comprised and pried loose by the dripping of tear-soaked eyes, stalagmites of attrition and desperation. It was the face he couldn't recognize in the mirror. The need and needling of a life's winter kindling, something to make it through. It was the face of all the trinkets of creativity, the castings of molds, the trestle of sentences, the lattice of imagery, both real and fiction, the truth in all things, that bit of darkness

A.S. COOMER

more blue than black, the rope of the damned and the ghosts that dance and prance like pagan deities or snowflakes mistaken for ash after the blast. The understanding that to laugh and to cry might just be the same thing, different sides of the same coin, a coppery thing that leaves your grubby hands sweat slick and sickly green, the absurdity that holds the thing together.

A spotlight shined, expertly aimed directly into his eyes, but he ignored it.

Stephen stared into the face of the person he conjured and did not blink.

Author photo by Adrian Lime

———— ABOUT THE AUTHOR ————

A.S. Coomer is a writer, musician, Kentucky Colonel, and taco fanatic. Books include The Fetishists, Shining the Light, The Devil's Gospel, Flirting with Disaster & Other Poems, The Flock Unseen, Memorabilia, and Misdeeds. He runs Lost, Long Gone, Forgotten Records and coedits Cocklebur Press.

Author website: www.ascoomer.com

11:11 Press is an American independent literary publisher based in Minneapolis, MN. Founded in 2018, 11:11 publishes innovative literature of all forms and varieties. We believe in the right to freedom of artistic expression, the realization of creative potential, and the transcendental power of stories.

CPSIA information can be obtained
at www.ICGtesting.com
Printed in the USA
FFHW022219081119
56013279-61902FF